*"I think for the good of everyone concerned, you'll forget I'm a woman."*

Impossible, Clay decided. She filled out the officer's uniform to sweet perfection. His gaze moved deliberately back up to her face, back to those blue eyes that blazed with—what? Hurt? No, that couldn't be. This woman was as tough as they came. She was from the Trayhern military dynasty. Her famous relatives had racked up a two-hundred-year record of Congressional Medal-winning service. Until 1970.

Clay rubbed his neck, continuing to size her up in the thickening silence. Sweet angel face and the heart of a pit bull, he thought.

"If you could try to judge me on my own merits instead of my family name, it would help both of us," Alyssa said, her voice strained.

Clay went cold with fury. "As far as I'm concerned, you're Morgan Trayhern's sister. Your gender and name have nothing to do with anything. "He stabbed a finger at her. "You're the sister of a murderer and traitor."

\* \* \* \* \*

*No Surrender*—the gripping second volume of **LOVE AND GLORY**. Each book stands alone—together they're as thrilling as the American Dream....

**MONROE COUNTY LIBRARY**
**FORSYTH, GEORGIA**

Dear Reader,

Once again, six Silhouette **Special Edition** authors present six dramatic new titles aimed at offering you moving, memorable romantic reading. Lindsay McKenna adds another piece to the puzzling, heart-tugging portrait of the noble Trayherns; Joan Hohl revives a classic couple; Linda Shaw weaves a thread of intrigue into a continental affair; Anne Lacey leads us into the "forest primeval"; and Nikki Benjamin probes one man's tortured conscience. Last, but certainly not least, award-winning Karen Keast blends agony and ecstasy into *A Tender Silence*.

What do their books have in common? Each presents men and women you can care about, root for, befriend for life. As Karen Keast puts it:

"What instantly comes to mind when someone mentions *Gone with the Wind*? Rhett and Scarlett. Characterization is the heart of any story; it's what makes you *care* what's happening. In *A Tender Silence*, I strived to portray two people struggling to survive in an imperfect world, a world that doesn't present convenient black-and-white choices. For a writer, the ultimate challenge is to create complex, unique, subtly structured individuals who are, at one and the same time, universally representative."

At Silhouette **Special Edition**, we believe that *people* are at the heart of every satisfying romantic novel, and we hope they find their way into *your* heart. Why not write and let us know?

Best wishes,

Leslie Kazanjian, Senior Editor
Silhouette Books
300 East 42nd Street
New York, N.Y. 10017

# LINDSAY McKENNA
# No Surrender

*Silhouette Special Edition*

Published by Silhouette Books New York

**America's Publisher of Contemporary Romance**

To Midge Wagner—
a special and dear friend.

SILHOUETTE BOOKS
300 East 42nd St., New York, N.Y. 10017

ISBN: 0-373-09535-X

First Silhouette Books printing July 1989

Printed in the U.S.A.

**Books by Lindsay McKenna**

Silhouette Special Edition

*Captive of Fate* #82
*\*Heart of the Eagle* #338
*\*A Measure of Love* #377
*\*Solitaire* #397
*Heart of the Tiger* #434
*†A Question of Honor* #529
*†No Surrender* #535

*\*Kincaid trilogy*
*†LOVE AND GLORY series*

Silhouette Intimate Moments

*Love Me Before Dawn* #44

Silhouette Desire

*Chase the Clouds* #75
*Wilderness Passion* #134
*Too Near the Fire* #165
*Texas Wildcat* #184
*Red Tail* #298

*Awards:*

1984 Journalism Award for fiction books from the Aviation/Space Writers
    Association for *Love Me Before Dawn*, Silhouette Intimate Moments
    #44

1985 Journalism Award for fiction books from the Aviation/Space Writers
    Association for *Red Tail*, Silhouette Desire #298

1987 *Romantic Times* Best Continuing Series Author Award for the Kincaid
    trilogy, Silhouette Special Edition (#338, #377, #397)

Waldenbooks Romance Bestseller:

1985 *Texas Wildcat*, Silhouette Desire

## LINDSAY McKENNA

spent three years serving her country as a meteorologist
in the U.S. Navy, so much of her knowledge about the
military people and practices featured in her novels comes
from direct experience. In addition, she spends a great
deal of time researching each book, whether it be at the
Pentagon or at military bases, extensively interviewing
key personnel. She views the military as her second family and hopes that her novels will help dispel the "un-
feeling-machine" image that haunts it, allowing readers
glimpses of the flesh-and-blood people who comprise the
services.

Lindsay is also a pilot. She and her husband of fifteen
years, both avid "rock hounds" and hikers, live in Ohio.

# LOVE AND GLORY: BOOK TWO

## The Trayherns

**Chase "Wolf" Trayhern**
U.S. Air Force
General, retired

m.

**Rachel McKenzie**
U.S. Army Nurse Corps
First lieutenant, retired

**Morgan Trayhern**
U.S. Marine Corps
Captain and company commander
Missing in Action, Vietnam

**Noah Trayhern**
U.S. Coast Guard
Lieutenant

m.

**Kit Anderson**
Miami Police Department
Former narcotics agent

**Alyssa Trayhern**
U.S. Navy
Second lieutenant
and pilot

m.

**Clay Cantrell**
U.S. Navy
First lieutenant
and pilot

**Melody Sue Trayhern**

## Chapter One

*January 1976*

What now?'' Clay Cantrell growled under his breath. He swung through the huge open bay doors of an old blimp hangar. Exhaustion from an arduous twelve hours as pilot on the United States Navy P3 Lockheed Orion was making his mind fuzzy. Clay didn't want to look too closely at his emotions. This past mission had been a bitch. They'd busted an oil line in one of the four turboprop engines.

Staying to the left of the yellow safety line, he glanced toward the center of the busy complex. Several P3s were in for maintenance checks, mechanics crawling all over them. Clay took off his garrison cap and ran his long fingers through his military-short black hair. Those who knew him well could recognize that particular gesture as a sign of frustration. Just what the hell did Commander Joe Horner want? Clay knew he'd been walking a dangerous line for the past year, ever since—

He brutally rejected the memory. Rejected the rush of violent emotions that came with it. He swallowed against a forming lump, his gray eyes growing cold and distant, *Screw the past. You've got to forget it. What counts is now, Cantrell.*

With a muttered oath, Clay opened the door that would take him into the outer office of VP 46's commanding officer. Chief Yeoman Jo Ann Prater looked up. She was a woman in her late forties with red hair tucked neatly into a bun at the base of her neck. Women with red hair always intrigued Clay. It was as if the gold and copper highlights woven into the auburn strands promised complexity of character. And he liked complex women. Women—not situations. But right now, judging from the suddenly concerned look in Prater's hazel eyes, he was about to step into one.

"Good afternoon, Lieutenant Cantrell," she greeted him briskly, rising. "Have a seat." She pointed toward the leather couch to the left of her desk. "I'll let Commander Horner know that you've arrived."

"Thank you," Clay said, taking off his garrison cap and tucking it into a pocket of his dark green flight suit. He sat as gingerly as if he were sitting on a carton of eggs. He noticed that his hands were sweaty as he clasped them. Often, they shook—but so did any carrier pilot's hands. Clay reminded himself that he was no longer an F-14 fighter pilot. He'd been relegated to the slow, matronly P3s. It was a safe transfer—safe and out of the way. His old squadron commander aboard the *Enterprise* had said it was best under the circumstances.

Running a hand wearily over his face, Clay tried to ignore a burgeoning headache. What was up? His mind raced with possibilities—all of them making him uneasy. For the past year, he'd been unable to think in positives, only negatives. Funny how one plane crash could change his entire outlook on life. Well, that was the past. What did Horner want? Clay had made a lousy landing three days ago after a rough twelve-hour mission out over the Pacific Ocean, and the bird would have to have extensive maintenance on the port landing gear assembly, as a result. Could that be it? Or was it something worse?

Their antisubmarine warfare squadron base, at the tip of San Francisco Bay, was shorthanded. All pilots were working more missions than was advisable. The squadron commanding officer was trying to remedy the situation by bringing new pilots on board, but it had been a slow process. Navy pilots, the cream of the crop of aviators, didn't just grow on trees. They had to wait for the next group of pilots to graduate from Pensacola, the U.S. Navy flight school. Too many missions and not enough time off was everyone's problem right now.

Since coming to U.S. Naval Air Station Moffett Field, Clay had felt abandoned. Not even San Francisco's magic spell could lift his depression. Maybe that was it. Clay admitted he wasn't the pleasantest person to be around right now. Could it be that his crew was complaining about his constant snarling and the sharp, angry orders?

Running his hand through his hair, Clay realized that he'd lost the prankster side of himself at the time of the crash. He never smiled or joked anymore. He didn't see much to laugh about. Yeah, the CO was probably going to chew him out about his attitude problem. *Damn.*

"Lieutenant Cantrell? The CO will see you now."

Clay rose, forcing a smile in Prater's direction. "Thanks." *Here it comes.* Clay knew no way to brace himself emotionally, because he had nothing left with which to defend his vulnerable feelings. Prater's eyes gave her away. She looked almost sad for him as he walked by her desk.

Joe Horner was standing when Clay entered the inner office. Snapping to attention, Clay announced himself. Horner, a man in his early forties with graying hair, nodded.

"At ease, Lieutenant." He pointed brusquely to a leather chair in front of his huge maple desk. "Have a seat."

"Yes, sir."

Horner sat down, his blue eyes never leaving Clay's tense features. "I've got some good news and bad news, Clay."

*Great.* Clay nodded. "Sir?"

"As you know, we've been flying shorthanded around here for the past quarter. Transfers and a computer screwup in D.C. have left us holding the bag."

Relaxing slightly, Clay tried to ferret out Horner's strategy. What was this preamble leading up to? "Yes, sir, it's been tough on everyone," he said cautiously.

Horner's narrow face thawed slightly. "Well, D.C. is finally starting to remedy the situation. They've given us two of the top graduates from Pensacola."

"That's good news, sir." Even a rookie pilot out of Pensacola was better than nothing. They could be taught cockpit procedure here. Clay brightened. Maybe he was getting a new copilot!

"Very good news." Horner sat down and tendered two files sitting in front of him on the desk, holding his gaze on Clay's suddenly hopeful expression. "I'm assigning one of the pilots to you."

"Great!"

"Perhaps," Horner hedged. His thin mouth tightened. "Second Lieutenant Alyssa Trayhern is being assigned to you, Clay. And yes, she's the sister of Morgan Trayhern, the traitor who cost an entire Marine company their lives." Horner sat up, folding his hands and leaning forward. "I know your brother Stephen was the assistant company commander for the company that was wiped out, and that he was killed along with everyone else." Joe pushed the orders toward Clay, continuing to watch him closely.

Clay sat, stunned. First rage, then numbness hit him. He stared at Horner, his mouth falling open. Snapping it shut, he rose. "No," he rasped hoarsely. *"No!"*

"I'm afraid so, Clay." Horner gestured toward the orders. "Read them yourself: direct from D.C. You're to train her."

Reeling with shock, Clay stood, breathing in sharp gasps. His chest hurt, his heart ached. Tears wedged unexpectedly into his eyes, but the instant it happened, he jerked himself back to the present. Fight-

ing for control, he uttered harshly, "I won't take her!
*Sir.* There's no way in hell I'm working with the sister
of the traitor who murdered my brother. Not now. Not
ever!" He spun, dazed, to leave the office.

"Lieutenant!" Horner's voice rolled through the
office like a shot being fired.

Clay froze, his hand inches from the brass doorknob. *Grab it!* his subconscious shouted. *Grab it, twist
it and jerk it open. Get out! Escape!* This was a nightmare. He had to be dreaming. Clay's hand shook
perceptibly, his fingers still reaching out.

"Get a hold on yourself," Horner ordered coldly,
"and get back here."

Hatred poured through Clay as he slowly pulled his
hand back. He gulped for air without success, and he
could no longer jam his shredded emotions deep inside where he'd always kept them prisoner. Bitterness
coated his mouth as he stood stiffly, his back still to his
CO.

"Look, I had nothing to do with this pairing, Clay.
These are orders from Washington." Horner's voice
grew soothing. "Come on, have a seat. There's nothing either of us can do about the situation. It's just one
of those things. I'm sorry."

*Sorry?* Clay turned slowly, his eyes narrowing with
anguish and burning rage. What little pride he had left
intact after the crash, he used to salvage himself in
front of his commander. With a monumental effort,
he straightened, throwing his shoulders back as if rid-
ding himself of some invisible load.

"Have a seat," Horner invited one more time. "I
know this comes as a shock, Clay. I know how you feel
about your brother dying in such a useless tragedy."

"No, sir, you don't." The words were ground out—a dog crushing a bone between his massive jaws. That was how Clay felt about this new assignment. He wanted to savage Trayhern. He wanted to hurt this brat of a woman who thought she could be a Navy pilot.

Horner's face grew closed. Insistent. "Sit, Lieutenant. Histrionics isn't going to change one damn thing about this assignment for you or me."

The CO's cold analysis was like ice hitting Clay. He sat, his knees suddenly shaky. He gripped the arm of the chair, his knuckles whitening. "This can't be real, sir. Someone's got it in for me back at the Pentagon." Were they trying to drum him out of the service? Get him to retire after his first six years? Clay had wanted to make the Navy his career. He had only a year to go before fulfilling the mandatory six-year enlistment, but he intended to reenlist—providing he was recommended for it. Ever since the crash, though, Clay had wondered if they might politely railroad him out of the service. There were many ways to accomplish it, and this was one of them: make the environment so miserable that he wouldn't think of reenlisting.

"Let's not overreact," Horner was saying. He paced the length of his small office. Outside, they could hear the whistling whine of a P3's turboprop engines revving up to trundle down the ramp toward takeoff.

"Then give me one reason why Trayhern was assigned to me," Clay demanded. His voice cracked, and he felt a warm flush crawling up his neck into his face.

With a shrug of his thin shoulders, Horner said, "I can't give you one."

"Sir, with all due respect, I can't handle this assignment. She's the sister to the man who killed my brother. My God—"

"Look, I know this is tough." Horner pointed to a board hanging on the wall, showing the names of pilots to fly the missions. There were many more flights than pilots. "You can see I'm strapped. I don't have many pilots with more than a year's experience in P3s, and I can't put a green pilot and a copilot together. We'd be asking for disaster."

"But—" Clay grasped at straws, any straw "—why can't I have the other graduate? Couldn't we make a trade?"

Tapping the file with Trayhern's name on it, Horner said heavily, "Orders are orders."

Helpless rage entwined with real panic deep within Clay. "Then make a phone call. Surely this is a mistake. Whoever paired us didn't realize Stephen was my brother."

Compassion showed in Horner's taut face. "I've already made a call, Clay. And I *did* explain the situation."

"And?"

"No go. The pairing stays as is."

*Somebody's got it in for me.* Clay almost said it out loud, but bit down hard on his lower lip to stop himself from blurting out the words. The handwriting was on the wall. They wanted him out. He was a washed-up F-14 driver. In some head honcho's eyes back in D.C., he was no longer a valuable commodity to the Navy. They didn't want him to reenlist.

Horner's voice cut through Clay's spinning revelations. "...Trayhern got top grades. She finished at the head of her class both at the Naval Academy in Annapolis and later at Pensacola. I think she's a credit to the U.S. Navy, regardless of what her brother did five years ago. You should let the past remain there, Clay. Don't confront her on the issue. Let it stay buried."

Buried. The word haunted Clay. Trying to maintain a poker face, which he was usually good at doing, he straightened in his seat. His stomach was knotted so tight, it hurt. Horner was asking for a miracle from him. Stephen had been murdered by Morgan Trayhern's cowardly act, and their mother had died two days after receiving the news, as surely as if Trayhern had left her, too, on that hill. Clay had never known his father, so in two days he had lost his entire family. Morgan Trayhern had ripped the heart out of him by snuffing out the lives of the two people he loved most in the world.

"Do you hear me, Lieutenant? Leave the past alone. You deal with lieutenant Trayhern as you would any green copilot trainee coming out of Pensacola."

Clay fought his anger, his utter anguish over this unexpected trial. He didn't know how he was going to overcome the palpable hatred he felt. "Yes, sir," he choked out. He wondered obliquely if Alyssa Trayhern knew she was being assigned to him. How would she react to the news? As he looked out the window, he saw a storm gathering in the west. Any moment now, it would begin to rain at the station. Was there *ever* a storm coming....

* * *

"I hate rain," Aly said to no one in particular as she drove her red Toyota MR2 sports car down the freeway. It was eight in the morning, and traffic speeding into the city of San Francisco was at its peak. She slanted a quick glance at the passenger seat where Rogue sat. The black and white Border collie whined, as if in answer.

"The landlord of our new apartment said they call this the Bloody Bayshore. He mentioned it has more bloody accidents than any other highway system leading into the city. What do you think about that, Rogue?"

The collie tilted his head and wagged his tail in a friendly fashion.

Aly chuckled. "God, Rogue, I'm really beginning to feel free. Sometimes, I think this is all a dream after the past five years." She narrowed her eyes in memory as she stayed alert on the rain-slick freeway. Were her trials really over? she wondered. Were the taunting, the insults hissed in her direction calling her a traitor, really over? Her hands tightened momentarily on the wheel. Aly knew she didn't dare allow all her hurt and anger to surface. Like a true Trayhern, she had kept her head high and her shoulders squared, pretending to be impervious to the slings and arrows hurled at her because of Morgan.

The Marine Corps had never officially listed her brother as missing in action or dead. His body had never been found after the 1970 slaughter on Hill 206 at the close of the Vietnam war. The only survivor, a private, had said that he saw Morgan escape into the arms of the North Vietnamese, a traitor. But Aly violently rejected that scenario. No way was Morgan a traitor! He'd *never* leave 180 men—his men—on a hill to be decimated by their enemy. He'd have died with them.

So what had happened? Aly's head spun with questions, and with obvious answers that she instantly denied. She knew her brother. He was a good man, a strong person with a streak of undying loyalty toward those he was responsible for, bred into him just as it was bred into the very bones of Aly and her other brother, Noah. Morgan would never have left that embattled hill just before the dawn attack, taking with him the only working radio in the company. That radio could have put them in contact with air protection and kept the company from being overrun. The press had repeatedly accused Morgan of turning coward and surrendering himself to the enemy in order to live, instead of dying with his men, but there were so many unanswered riddles and dead ends to Morgan's disappearance.

Agony sliced through Aly, tears surfacing unexpectedly in her eyes. More than two hundred years of Trayhern military service were permanently stained. And so were the lives of Noah, of herself and of her parents.

Wiping away the errant tears with the back of her hand, she muttered, "We're supposed to be happy, Rogue. We just leased an apartment. Today we shop for groceries, and tomorrow I sign on board at Moffett Field. This is the start of my career. Mom and Dad are so happy and proud of me." She looked over at her Border collie, feeling not triumphant but only tired and drained. "We've made it, Rogue. This generation of Trayherns is on its way—hopefully—to bril-

liant military service. Maybe Noah and I can erase
some of the black mark put on our name by the Defense Department and the press. We've made it—''

The rest of her words were torn from her as a large
white car slewed sideways in front of her as it tried to
change lanes too quickly.

Everything slowed down to single frames in front of
Aly's widening eyes. The white car's brakes screamed,
water spraying in high sheets. The water slammed
against the windshield of her Toyota, temporarily
blinding her. Cars were braking and swerving ahead
and around her, as if the six lanes in front of her had
become nothing more than a bumper car track.

Aly's reflexes were fast and skilled. Acting only on
instinct, Aly wrenched the wheel to the right, moving
quickly into the lane closest to the shoulder of the
freeway. A blue car suddenly loomed ahead, skidding
sideways, coming directly toward her. Sucking in a
breath, Aly slammed on the brakes, putting her car
into a spin. The red sports car spun once, twice. The
screech of tires, the odor of burning rubber entered
Aly's brain. In seconds she found herself and the
sports car off the road on a wet grassy slope, safe.

Sudden silence overtook her. She blinked once in
amazement. All the cars involved in the crisis had
straightened out. No one had been hit! It was a miracle. Her heart pounding in her chest, Aly leaned back
and closed her eyes.

She took long slow breaths, trying to calm her racing pulse. At the sound of a sudden decisive knock on
the window of her car, Aly opened her eyes and looked
up in surprise.

The concerned face of a man in his late twenties stared back at her. It was still raining lightly, and she could see the darkened splotches appearing on his well-worn leather jacket. It was his eyes that mesmerized Aly. They were large and gray, with huge black pupils, and fringed with thick lashes. Somehow they seemed to penetrate her deepest, most secret self. Strangely she wasn't put on the defensive by the intensity of his stare. Instead, Aly felt a powerful wave of concern for her emanating from the stranger.

Shakily, she rolled down the window. He crouched, hand on the door.

"Are you okay?" he asked.

His voice was husky, a balm to her jittery nerves. Aly nodded dumbly. "I—yes, I am."

Clay pulled a handkerchief from his back pocket. "I'm not so sure. You've cut yourself," he said as he reached in and pressed the cloth to the woman's bloodied hairline. "That was a fine piece of driving you pulled off. I thought for sure you'd bought the farm." He smiled slightly as she raised her hand, pressing her cool fingertips to where he held the handkerchief in position on her temple. God, but she was pretty. Red hair, too. And then Clay laughed to himself, feeling lighter and happier than he could recall in a long time.

"I got lucky," the woman admitted hoarsely.

"Red sports car, red hair. It all fits," he told her, withdrawing his hand from hers. She was pale and shaken. But who wouldn't be? Hell, her tiny little car had stood every chance of getting smashed between a couple of those careening behemoths. Clay liked her wide, vulnerable blue eyes, and her nose was aristocratic with small, finely flared nostrils. But it was her mouth that he couldn't drag his gaze away from. Her lips weren't full, but they weren't thin, either. It was the delicate shape, maybe, that entranced him. There was utter sensuality about them, and it sent a sheet of heat flowing through him.

She lifted the handkerchief away, staring at the red blood on it. "I don't even remember hitting my head," she said softly.

"Probably hit it against the window when you deliberately threw that car of yours into a spin to miss that blue Buick sliding at you. You'd make Parnelli Jones look like a rookie with the moves you put on this girl." He patted the door fondly, as if to reward the car for its part in the effort.

With a sigh, Aly leaned back, closing her eyes. She kept the cloth pressed firmly against the wound. Head injuries were notorious for bleeding heavily even if this one was a mere scratch. And that was all it was—a little cut on her left temple. The adrenaline was making her weak and shaky in its wake. She needed at least another fifteen minutes to recover. Rogue whined, nosing her gently. Patting him reassuringly, Aly returned her attention to her rescuer.

An unfamiliar warmth surrounded Aly's pounding heart as she lifted her lashes, drowning in the care exuding from his dove-gray eyes. He had a square face, a stubborn chin, a flexible, intriguing mouth and a nose that had obviously taken some punishment earlier in life. Aly liked his hard, intelligent eyes. He wasn't a huge man—moderate build and about six-two in height. There was a nice balance to him, she decided. More than anything, she liked his long, expressive, large-knuckled fingers. Hands capable of molding and shaping.

"I—I owe you so much for stopping to see how I was."

He grinned. "My pleasure. If I'd known it was a beautiful redheaded lady in front of me, I'd have put my Corvette between you and those bruisers that wanted to play bumper cars on the Bayshore."

A hesitant smile pulled at Aly's mouth. There was so much warmth radiating from him. She noticed no ring on his left hand. For the first time in five years, Aly felt herself responding to a man on a strictly feminine level. It felt good—right. "I just moved here," she explained. "My landlord warned me that they call this the Bloody Bayshore." She shivered, sitting up slightly. "I almost became a part of its legend, didn't I?"

Out of instinct, maybe need, Clay placed his hand on the woman's small shoulder. She was getting paler, if that was possible. "Close, but no cigar. Hell of a welcome to this area, wouldn't you say?" He gently kneaded her left shoulder and neck, feeling her visibly relax beneath his ministration.

"Y-yes, a hell of a welcome," she agreed faintly. She took the handkerchief away from her head. The bleeding had stopped. "I think I'm going to live, now. Thanks." She handed the cloth back to him. "You'd better get that home and into some cold water or the stain will never come out."

Clay folded the handkerchief and placed it in the pocket of his jacket. "I'll do that. You said you just moved here?" Clay wanted to drown in her dark blue eyes. Her face was porcelain, with freckles sprinkled across her nose and cheeks. Her red hair was shaped into a flattering pixie style that barely brushed the bottom of her delicate earlobes and emphasized the oval contour of her face. Small pearl earrings and a single pearl resting against her throat simply multiplied her femininity.

"Yes, just a week ago," Aly said, "from Florida." She turned, realizing suddenly that Rogue must have been tossed around, since he couldn't wear a seat belt as she did. The Border collie sat, panting, enjoying the sudden attention as Aly ran her hands carefully over him just to make sure he hadn't broken any bones.

"Your dog okay?"

Aly liked his concern. She liked people who liked animals. It said something good about them as far as she was concerned. Giving Rogue an affectionate pat, Aly returned her attention to the man. "He seems fine. Probably got a few bruises we'll never know about."

Clay glanced at the traffic zooming by them. The rain had stopped, leaving only a pall of gray clouds hovering about a thousand feet above them. Typical January weather for the Bay Area. He noted the color creeping back into her face. Her pupils weren't as dilated. "Looks like you're feeling a bit better."

"I am, thank you." Aly met and held the gray gaze that seemed to silently caress her. Her heart wouldn't settle down, and she realized that it was *him* affecting her so strongly, not the reaction to the near accident. "I don't even know your name. My friends call me Aly." She offered her hand through the open window.

"Clay. Clay Cantrell." Clay took her hand, surprised at the firmness of her grip. Grinning, he said, "You've never been to California before, eh?"

"I'm brand-new. No, I've never been to the state, much less to the fabled city of San Francisco. Rogue and I were going to go shopping for our groceries this morning and stock the shelves of the apartment I just rented."

Reluctantly, Clay released her fingers. Her flesh was soft and inviting, like the rest of her. She lured powerful emotional responses from him, and it puzzled Clay. No woman had ever affected him like this. Was it the shimmering red hair entwined with gold strands that enticed him? Or those huge blue eyes filled with every feeling she was experiencing? And then he groaned internally, his gaze falling to her parted lips. Lips that were begging to be pleasured and seduced. To his chagrin, he felt himself growing hot and turgid. If he kept up this line of thought, she'd soon know just how she affected him, too. Heat crept into his cheeks.

"Look, I know this is a lousy introduction to the Bay Area, and you're new. If you haven't got too many irons in the fire, how about if I give you the grand tour of our city this coming Saturday? I'll even treat you to the best pizza in the world, afterward. We could have dessert at Ghirardelli Square."

Aly laughed, delighted by Clay's candor. His eyes crinkled, a smile burning in their depths that stole her heart. His mouth curved deliciously upward, and molten fire stirred deep within her. "As long as we're both free, I'll accept your invitation."

Laughing, Clay dug out notepaper and a pen from the breast pocket of his light blue shirt. "Free, eligible, good-looking and one hell of a good deal."

Aly couldn't stop the laughter from bubbling up within her. My God, how *great* it felt to laugh again! Her world had consisted of nothing but darkness and pressure for so long that she had forgotten that light moments could exist. Clay was like sunlight.

"Here's my phone number, Aly. Give me a call Friday, after five. Get settled into your new home, and we'll set up that tour tomorrow evening." Never had Clay so much wanted any woman to say yes.

Aly liked his style and his easygoing confidence. Clay reminded her strongly of the instructor pilots back at Pensacola. They were cocky veterans, brazenly confident of themselves on every conceivable level. Clay had that same virile bearing—that mark of the lone eagle flying the blue sky in triumph. She liked his lack of pressure about a possible date. "Aren't you even going to ask me for my address and phone number?"

Giving her a wink, Clay slipped the paper into her waiting fingers. "No, ma'am. I learned a long time ago through the school of hard knocks not to pressure a lady."

"Sure this isn't some new line?" Aly teased, meeting his confident smile. He *knew* she'd call him!

Clay patted the door of the sports car. "I don't think so. But I'll let you be the judge of that." He sobered slightly. "You sure you feel up to getting back into traffic?"

"Yes, thank you." She held up her hands. "See, they're not shaking anymore."

Clay wondered what it would be like to have those long, delicate fingers moving across his body. The thought was startling, intense. Normally, he didn't think of a woman on such a sensual level, but Aly was incredibly heady stuff. He was happy, he suddenly discovered. Her smile was a rainbow to his dark existence.

Finding his voice, Clay said, "I'll look forward to your call."

Aly tucked his phone number into her small black leather purse. "You'll be hearing from me, Clay." And then her voice lowered with feeling. "Thank you for stopping. It means a lot to me. . . ."

Clay rose to his feet and threw her a salute. "I'll see you later, pretty lady. You go ahead and climb back up on the Bayshore and I'll follow you a ways to make sure you're doing okay."

He had to be a military pilot! That stance, that carelessly thrown salute and confident grin smacked of his unknown career. Aly almost called Clay back to ask him if he was a Navy pilot. Of course, he could be Air Force, too. Travis Air Force Base was just north of San Francisco. Shaking her head at the sudden turn of events, she rolled up the car window.

As she maneuvered her Toyota back into the morning rush-hour traffic, Aly told Rogue, "Well, this is quite an interesting start to our life here at Moffett Field. And tomorrow morning I sign on board at the station. I wonder what kind of adventures that will bring?"

## Chapter Two

"Welcome on board, Lieutenant Trayhern." Lieutenant Jack Donnelly stretched his hand across the desk toward her.

Aly took his hand, shaking it. "Thank you, Mr. Donnelly." All morning she'd filled out forms, signed them, and then filled out some more at the base personnel office. Her hands were sweaty, and she realized that Donnelly had noticed. The sandy-haired officer obviously didn't like her much. As usual, her Trayhern name had preceded her.

"Take a seat." Donnelly reached for a file on his desk. "In a minute I'll have our driver take you over to your new home, VP 46. The CO, Commander Horner, is aware that you're here, and he wants a few minutes of your time. Induction and all—you'll get your squadron assignment through him."

"Sounds good," Aly said.

There was a savage twist to Donnelly's smile as he ended the monologue. She glanced around the small office, photos of the graceful P3 Lockheed in a picture frame behind his desk. Moffett was primarily a sub-hunting base, little else. On another wall was a photo of the powerful F-14 Tomcat, the fighter utilized aboard all naval carriers.

"I understand we have an F-14 squadron here," Aly said.

"Huh?" Donnelly looked up. "Oh, yes. The past five years Moffett's had a training squadron based here. Normally, F-14s are on a carrier, but because we're close to the Pacific Ocean and near a deep-water port, the base is utilized as a training site for graduates out of Pensacola before they begin flying those babies onto carriers for the first time."

"They practice their landings here," Aly guessed.

"That's correct. We've got some instructor pilots on board who work with the greenhorns. One of them, Lieutenant Jeff Starbuck, is a pretty amusing character."

Aly managed a small smile. What fighter jock wasn't colorful?

F-14s made her blood race. If she had been a man, with her top grade-point average at Pensacola, she would have been given the plum assignment of becoming a fighter pilot upon graduation. Instead, because women weren't allowed to fly combat aircraft, she was appointed to fly the land-based P3. She curbed her disappointment. The chance to fly *any-thing* was enough for her. It was her life's ambition.

"Just sign this last set of papers, Lieutenant Trayhern, and you're free of us."

Aly leaned forward and dutifully placed her signature one last time. Finally! Now, she'd get to tour the station, her new home.

The men's and women's barracks, the chow hall and Operations, which consisted of meteorology and the control tower, were located on one side of the base. On the other side were three huge blimp hangars that had been modified to serve as the home of Anti-Submarine Warfare Squadron, VP 46. Only the three long, massive airstrips separated the outdated hangars from the more modern side of Moffett. Aly got her first look at the NASA installation on board the station, sitting right across the street from the WAVE barracks. The driver told her that NASA had one of the world's largest wind tunnels at the state-of-the-art facility. A silly smile curved Aly's lips. How could the enlisted women sleep when that wind tunnel was revved up right across the street from them? The entire station must shudder when it was activated.

Aly's eyes widened as they drove around the end of the main runways and toward the gaping mouths of the blimp hangars. The graceful P3s, gray on top and white beneath, had long booms that looked like dangerous needles, extending ten feet from the tail assembly, much like the stinger on a hornet. In the tail boom, she knew, was highly responsive radar equipment. It was sensitive enough to locate and track Soviet submarines far beneath the surface of the ocean. The P3s looked like such graceful steeds. She itched to sit at the controls and feel what it was like to fly one.

"We're here," the driver announced, braking the vehicle to a halt. He'd pulled up at the side entrance to Hangar One, the largest of the three. "Just follow that yellow safety line, Lieutenant. About halfway down on the left is Commander Horner's office. You can't miss it."

"Thanks." Aly climbed out. She was in her black wool uniform, with a white blouse and black tie. Placing the garrison cap on her head, she pulled the black leather purse over her left shoulder. The right hand had to be free to salute with. Shutting the door, Aly took a deep breath, trying to stabilize her wildly fluctuating emotions.

As she walked down the concrete expanse toward her destination, her black heels clicking sharply, Aly absorbed the spectacle to her right. At least four P3s were in for maintenance. In the 1930s, the driver had told her, Moffett had been the largest blimp station on the West Coast. With the advent of propeller-driven planes, the blimps had met a slow and eventual death. The hangars were now used for the more advanced aircraft that succeeded them.

Horner's office was easy to find. His chief yeoman looked up when Aly entered. She felt instant camaraderie with the woman because she had red hair, too. Trying not to appear nervous, Aly offered her a small smile.

"Hi. I'm—"

The yeoman broke into a genuine smile. "Don't say it, I know." She pointed toward the gold aviator wings that rested over the top of Aly's left breast pocket. "You're Lieutenant Trayhern. I'm Chief Yoeman Jo Ann Prater. Welcome aboard."

Relief flowed through Aly. This woman was the first person at the base to smile and sound as if she was honestly glad to see her. Was Prater unaware of the blackened Trayhern history? Probably. Anyone who carried the memory never treated her with such unabashed cordiality. In the military mind and heart, the worst thing one could be was a traitor to his country.

"Thanks, Chief." Aly took her hand, shaking it.

"Commander Horner is expecting you. Go on in."

Swallowing hard, Aly nodded and walked past the desk and through another opened door. This was her new boss. *Dear God, don't let him hate me. Let him judge me on my own merits, not the past. Not—*

"Lieutenant Trayhern, come on in." Horner rose, extending his hand.

A weight formed in Aly's stomach as she appraised Horner's narrow face. A cry started deep within her as she saw barely veiled animosity in the CO's narrowed eyes. He hated her. For the past? For the fact that she was a woman in his male world? Probably both, she decided with disappointment, shaking his hand. "Commander Horner," she said, her voice firm and unruffled-sounding. A far cry from all the violent emotions clamoring deep within her.

"Have a seat, Miss Trayhern." And then Horner cocked his head in her direction, pulling out a pipe and beginning to fill it after he sat down. "Or, do you prefer Ms.?"

It was game time again. As always. How many times had her male instructors at Pensacola jabbed her with the same question? Aly looked Horner straight in the eye. In the military, they respected an adversary's strength, not his weakness. "Either is acceptable to me, Commander."

Horner lit a match, holding it close to the pipe, puffing on it. Bluish-white smoke rose in a cloud around his head. "I see." He sat down, flipping the match into a glass ashtray nearby. "Well, welcome to VP 46."

"Thank you, sir."

Picking up her file, Horner said, "Your record at Annapolis and Pensacola is outstanding. I'm glad to have someone of your caliber on board."

*Liar.* Her heart was beginning a slow beat of dread. There was coldness in Horner's eyes. He was saying the right things, but there was no enthusiasm or sincerity in his voice. "I'm planning on at least thirty years in the Navy, sir," Aly responded. "This is my home, my way of life. I tried to get off on the right foot with good grades."

"You certainly did that." Horner puffed a few more times before continuing. "Now, as to your assignment. Because we're shorthanded, I'm going to be putting you into intensive Link cockpit training immediately." He saw the surprise on her face. "You've been assigned to one of our best pilots, who is also the Link instructor for our squadron. I have every belief that between his education of you in the cockpit and the ground training, you'll qualify for copilot status in record time so that we can put your flying skills to work in the P3. I need every able-bodied pilot behind the yoke as soon as possible."

Aly blinked once. Usually a new pilot spent at least three months in a ground trainer, flying under the hood with various difficult situations that might be encountered with that particular aircraft in the air.

After her brother Noah had graduated from the Coast Guard Academy, he'd had two terrible years under a commander who wanted to railroad him out of the service because his name was Trayhern. She slowly closed her right hand into a fist, realizing that Horner was possibly gunning for her, too. There was no way he should be putting a green copilot in a plane in such a short period of time, no matter what the personnel problem with the squadron.

"Sir, while I respect the fact that VP 46 is short on pilots, don't you think this is rather—"

"Lieutenant," Horner droned, "the manpower situation with VP 46 is critical. Ordinarily, I wouldn't throw a green pilot into a P3 this soon. But—" he got up, scowling "—in the past quarter we've had more Soviet sub activity down in the Baja region of Mexico, and we've been pressed to fly twice the missions anticipated. Something's up." He turned and buttonholed her with a dark look. "The other new pilot coming on board tomorrow will get the same treatment. I'm not singling you out."

Aly had the good grace to blush. Horner wasn't one to beat around the bush. "I see, sir."

"Believe me, you've been paired with our best man. He's a capable pilot, a damn good instructor, and he's been in on most of the hunts this past year."

Her hopes rising, thinking that perhaps she was wrong about Horner's intention to sandbag her career, Aly said, "I appreciate you putting me with someone like that, sir."

"Don't worry, Clay will help you make up for any deficiencies of learning about this bird of ours in Pensacola. I've also assigned him as your liaison officer. He'll be in charge of helping you get situated on and off station. He'll show you around, get you set up for Link training and, in general, make your transition here to Moffett as easy as possible."

"Clay?" The name rang a definite bell with Aly. He couldn't possibly mean the Clay she'd met yesterday on the Bayshore, could he?

Horner came around the desk and faced her. He methodically tapped the pipe against the ashtray. "Lieutenant, there's one more thing you need to know," he began heavily. His scowl deepened as he met and held her gaze. "You aren't going to like this. I don't, either, but it's out of my hands."

Immediately, Aly went on guard. Her fist tightened until her short nails dug into the palm of her hand. "Sir?"

"Before I tell you more about your assigned liaison, and your instructor pilot in the cockpit, I'm going to need your understanding."

Just what the hell was he going after? Aly wondered bleakly. By the set of Horner's jaw and the funeral sound of his voice, he was acting as if someone had just died. "Go on, sir."

Horner folded his arms against his chest. "I've got a situation on my hands, Lieutenant Trayhern. And you can either make it easier or tougher on me, on yourself and on the crew you'll be flying with—depending on how you handle it."

"What's going on, Commander?" she demanded huskily.

"Washington, D.C., sent specific orders to pair you with this pilot."

Frustration ate at her. "So?"

"So I want you to realize from the outset that this was out of our hands. I've already tried to change the orders or in some ways rectify the situation, but it's a no-go situation."

Aly's eyes narrowed. What could possibly be such bad news? "Sir, why don't you just tell me the gist of these orders?"

Horner smiled briefly. "You've got that shoot-from-the-hip Trayhern trait, don't you?"

"It's a family tradition, sir. We've served two hundred years with honors in the various military services. My father passed on his endurance and candor to me."

"Obviously." Horner sighed. "Well, you're going to need both, Lieutenant. Your mentor is a pilot by the name of First Lieutenant Clay Cantrell." He drilled a look into her widening eyes. "His brother was Stephen Cantrell. One of the men who died on Hill 206 five years ago."

Aly started to rise. And then she fell back into the chair, a gasp escaping her. Clay Cantrell! His brother was Stephen! *Oh, my God!* She sat for frozen seconds, assimilating the news. The man she'd met on the Bayshore *was* the same man. She'd been so drawn to him. For those precious minutes, he'd eased the coldness that had inhabited her for so many years.

The sting of reality replaced that wistful memory. Judging by Horner's reaction, Clay Cantrell was going to make it very tough on her. How could he not dislike her? Morgan had supposedly gotten his brother killed on that infamous hill. She bit down so hard on her lower lip that she tasted blood. And Clay was her IP in the Link trainer. And once she qualified as co-pilot, she'd be flying with him on every mission. She'd be spending hours at a time every day with him. . . .

"Oh, God," Aly whispered, pressing her fingers against her brow.

"Get hold of yourself, Lieutenant."

Her head snapped up, her eyes narrowing. "My reaction is warranted, *sir*. And don't worry, I'm not going to faint or get hysterical."

Horner nodded and slowly made his way around the desk to sit down. "Glad to hear it, Miss Trayhern."

*Swallow it, Aly. Swallow everything. Just like you did before.* Real anguish flowed through her as she realized that there was never going to be a time or place in her career where she could afford to be her real self or show her true feelings. Horner was watching her closely. She had to shore up and wear that impervious military facade. Internally, Aly girded herself, playing the game, denying so much of herself.

"Does Lieutenant Cantrell know about this assignment, sir?" Her voice was husky again, but in charge. Emotionless.

"He does."

"His reaction?"

"Negative."

Aly wanted to cry. She wanted to scream out at the unfairness of the situation. She came from a military family that knew the military way of life. It hadn't escaped her that someone in D.C., probably some admiral, wanted to wash her out of the Navy because she was Morgan's sister. There was no room for a traitor's family in the service. God, how many times had she heard that?

"Can he separate his personal emotions from his duty toward me?" she demanded tightly.

Horner shrugged. "I told him he'd better."

*Great.* "And if he can't, sir?"

"Come and see me. But," Horner growled, "I'm expecting both of you to behave maturely about this. After getting cockpit qualified, you've got a P3 and a crew of ten other men on board. *That's* your focus, your responsibility. I won't tolerate any bickering, sniping or back-stabbing coming from either one of you. Is that clear, Lieutenant Trayhern?"

Aly rose unsteadily. She locked her knees, coming to attention. "Yes, sir, it is. Permission to leave, sir? The sooner I meet with Mr. Cantrell and clear the air, the better."

Again, Horner gave her an amused smile that didn't quite reach his eyes. "Bulldog tough. That's what they said about your father, Chase Trayhern—he was one tough son of a bitch in a fight. I wish you luck, Lieutenant."

"Thank you, sir. Where can I find Mr. Cantrell?"

"He's in the Link Trainer office across the way. When he's not flying, his duties include scheduling continued Link trainer education for all pilots of VP 46." Glancing at his watch, he said, "It's 1130. Usually, Clay heads to the chow hall about noon. You'll probably catch him before he leaves." Horner got up, extending his hand. "Good luck and welcome aboard, Lieutenant."

Aly gripped his hand, her fingers icy cold. She said nothing, coming to attention and making an about-face. Blindly heading out the door, focusing on the worst confrontation she'd ever come up against, she didn't even say goodbye to the friendly red-headed Chief Prater.

The day was cloudy, but patches of blue sky could be seen between the fleecy gray and white stratus overhead. Bits of sunlight slanted through, striking the revetment area where the squadron of P3s stood like gallant, silent chargers waiting to be called into battle. But Aly couldn't enjoy any of it. Her heart hurt, her head ached. Somehow, she had to gird herself for the collision with Clay.

As she walked around the perimeter of the hangar, Aly wrestled with a gamut of feelings. Clay had been friendly and likable yesterday. Thank God, she'd seen his good side, because it might be the last time. No matter what happened, she would keep reminding herself that he had stopped to help her when no one else had. There was integrity and humanity in his soul and heart. She liked the warm gray smile in his eyes, and that mobile mouth that drew into such a careless, little-boy grin. But yesterday he hadn't realized that she was Morgan's sister.

Taking a deep breath, Aly entered a door that had a sign posted: Link Trainer Officer. The door led to a narrow passageway lined by at least ten offices up and down the east side of the hangar. Straight ahead, through the glass-paned window, she saw Clay sitting at his desk, buried in paperwork. Glancing around, Aly saw no one in the passageway. She took the few seconds of reprieve to put a tight clamp on her feelings. Her father had always counseled her never to allow her emotions to enter the field of any battle. Keeping a clear head was the only way to win, he'd told her time and again. For five years Aly had used his wisdom with success. But could she now?

Taking a look at Clay, her heart unraveled, heedless of her father's stern warning. He appeared tired, one hand resting against his head as he scribbled something on a yellow legal pad in front of him. His short black hair shone with blue highlights in the lamplight from overhead. The desk was cluttered, and Aly wondered if the responsibility as Link Trainer Officer combined with his many flights was wearing him down. His mouth was pursed, almost as if he were in pain. And today his skin appeared washed-out, darkness shadowing beneath his eyes.

Aly released a shaky breath, knowing she couldn't hate this man—not even remotely. But instinctively she knew he'd hate her. It was just a question of on what level and how much. There was something else, something gossamer and fleeting that had touched Aly's aching heart. The vulnerability in Clay Cantrell held her captive. She had no explanation, no proof of that; it was simply something she *knew*. And because of that, she was going to be exposed to him emotionally. That meant he could get to her, hurt her.

*Give me the courage, give me whatever it takes to handle this. Please...* And Aly placed her hand with determination on the doorknob.

Clay heard the door open and close. He looked up. A rush of breath was expelled from his lips as he stared up... up into that angelic face once again. It was her! The woman he'd stopped to help on the Bayshore! The pen dropped from his hand. His eyes narrowed as he took in the uniform she wore. Shock rocketed through Clay. His gaze flew to the gold name tag over her right breast pocket: A. Trayhern. *No!* The words were almost ripped from him. My God, what kind of fate was stalking him? She couldn't be Alyssa Trayhern! She just couldn't be! He sat for almost a minute, wrestling with his violent emotions.

*"You!"* The word exploded from him. He rose ominously to his feet, his hands resting in fists against the surface of his desk. *No!* his heart shouted. Fury tunneled through him like molten lava flowing up from a fissure deep in the earth. She was so damned pretty, her blue eyes wide and pleading. That irresistible mouth was parted, looking incredibly sensual. But it was her name that screamed at him. How could someone so damned fragile-looking be the sister of the man who'd killed Stephen? There had to be a mistake. Some kind of sick, twisted mistake!

Clay drew himself up, watching her stand before him. Part of him admired her. The other part hated her. "Just what the hell is this?" he snarled.

Aly wanted to die. She saw the shock, the anguish and then the fury in his burning pewter-gray eyes. That wonderful vulnerability that had drawn her effortlessly to Clay was buried in the mire of old memories and old hate dredged up by the guttural tone of his voice. Her stomach turned with nausea. "I'm sorry," she began, her voice unsteady. "I didn't know who you were. I mean, yesterday..."

Words jammed in Clay's throat. He glared at her. "You're sorry?" he whispered hoarsely. "No, I'm the one who's sorry. Sorry that you got assigned to me.

Sorry that your traitor of a brother got Stephen killed.
Sorry that—''

"Now you wait just one damn minute!" Aly walked
up to the desk, breathing hard, her voice trembling.
"Morgan *was not* a traitor! I know my brother! He'd
*never* leave a company of men exposed!"

Real hatred raged through Clay. He wanted to wrap
his hands around her slender neck and choke the life
out of her—just as Stephen's life had been choked
from him. "Your brother—" he breathed harshly,
leaning forward, not more than six inches from her
face "—was a goddamned traitor! He allowed nearly
two hundred men to die that morning on that miserable hill in Vietnam. Your bastard of a brother left with
the only radio that could have gotten his men safely
out of that situation and disappeared into the jungle.
He left Stephen and his Marine company wide open to
NVA attack. The only survivor, in case you don't
happen to remember, *saw* your brother hightail it to
the other side." He punched a finger toward her. "So
don't you come waltzing in here telling me Morgan
Trayhern wasn't a traitor. I know different! The whole
damn country does!"

Agony warred with Aly's anger. She felt herself unraveling before him. Each word, spit forth with such
virulent loathing, plunged through her undefended
heart. "My brother is *not* a traitor, Lieutenant," she
rattled. "And I won't stand here and be insulted by
you."

"Oh, yes, you will. Because your brother killed my
brother." Clay smiled savagely. "Do you know how
many years I've lived with the nightmares? I have
dreams about going to your family's home in Florida

and knocking on the door. Your father answers and I'm screaming at him, wanting to kill him the way Morgan killed Stephen.'' He leaned forward, his voice flat with disgust. ''Five years, Trayhern.''

*Get hold of yourself, Aly. He's losing it. You've got to keep your cool.* Aly slowly straightened, deliberately placing her hands at her sides. ''All right, Lieutenant Cantrell, now's your chance.''

Startled by her sudden composure and the throaty coolness of her voice, he scowled. ''What the hell are you talking about?'' he grated out.

As much as it hurt, Aly held his blazing gray gaze. ''If you've still got that much hatred from that many years, it needs to be released. I'm my father's daughter. You can't punch him out, but you can me. Go on, take a swing at me if it will help.''

Her voice was utterly devoid of emotion. Clay was shocked at the change in her. Yesterday... He closed his eyes, remembering her wide, trusting blue eyes and the smile that could steal the heart of the most hardened men. He trained his gaze back on her. Now she was pale, calm and almost detached. Almost. He saw the pain in her eyes.

''I was taught never to strike a woman,'' he whispered.

Her voice hardened. ''Make an exception, Cantrell, because I'm not going to put up with your anger from here on out.''

He saw her set her jaw, as if braced for a possible blow. The whole thing would have been ridiculous under any other circumstances. Her spine was ramrod straight, her blue eyes challenging, her voice no longer soft. This was the Annapolis graduate. Clay had come up the hard way: through college and then flight school at Pensacola. But Aly was a ring knocker, an Annapolis graduate—one of those elite few who had the "right stuff" to make it through four of the toughest years ever thrown at an individual.

Her courage tempered his hatred of her just enough. A lazy smile pulled at the hard line of Clay's mouth. "Lucky for you that you're in a woman's body. Otherwise, I would invite you out back."

The tension in the room was frantic. Aly was thrown off guard by his amused smile. And when he straightened, throwing back his shoulders, she grew afraid. Really afraid. Her ploy to meet him head-on had defused some of his anger. But not all of it. She saw a flicker in his eyes of some emotion she couldn't name. But it sent a chill of apprehension through her, knotting her stomach.

"I think for the good of everyone concerned you'll forget I'm a woman."

Clay threw his hands on his hips, studying her, sizing her up. Impossible, he decided. She filled out the black officer's uniform to sweet perfection. Alyssa Trayhern was a looker, there was no doubt about it. And he liked the tousled pixie haircut that gave her a girlish quality. She was small breasted and waisted, her hips boyishly slim, but most of all, Clay liked her long, slender thoroughbred legs. His gaze moved deliberately back up to her face, back to those blue eyes that blazed with—what? Hurt? No, that couldn't be. This woman was as tough as they came. She was from the Trayhern military dynasty, there was no doubt. Her famous relatives had fought in America's struggle for independence, blazing a two-hundred-year record of prestigious and Congressional Medal-winning service. Until 1970. Sweet angel face and the heart of a pit bull, he thought, seeing the strength in her compressed lips, in her tense stance. Even her hands were wrapped into fists.

Some of the tension flowed out of his shoulders and the back of his neck. Clay rubbed his neck, studying her ruefully in the thickening silence.

"If you could try and judge me on my own merits, not my family name, it would help both of us," Aly whispered in a strained tone.

"As far as I'm concerned, you're Morgan Trayhern's sister. That's all. Your gender or first name has nothing to do with anything." He stabbed a finger at her again. "You're the sister of a murderer and traitor."

Blood sang through Aly, heated and furious. She stared at him. God, but he could be one cold bastard when he chose to be! She tried desperately to remember their first meeting, remember his warmth and openness. "I won't respond any longer to your name-calling, Cantrell." Aly leaned forward, only the desk separating them. "Whatever ax you have to grind with me will be done in private. I won't tolerate this kind of behavior in front of our crew or the enlisted people. I don't like this situation any more than you do, but let's try to make the best of it."

Clay smiled lethally. "You can bet your sweet face that I'm not having my fitness report screwed up because of you. Don't worry, Trayhern, our private war will stay private. I have one of the best crews in VP 46, and they aren't going to know how I really feel about you."

Aly nodded. "Fine, I can cope with that." But could she cope with his continued nearness? Dear God, Clay affected her powerfully. She was hurting. Aly wanted to see that carefree smile, to watch his gray eyes glimmer with sunlight. She was so tired of fighting...of defending Morgan and her family name. "Look," she uttered, "all I want to do is get along, Lieutenant. I don't expect any favors. I've worked hard all my life for everything I've ever gotten. I'll do my best to weave into the situation here at the squadron. You give me orders and I'll die trying to follow them."

The sudden exhaustion in Aly's voice caught Clay off balance. He saw the bleakness in her blue eyes and heard the raw pleading in her husky voice. For a split second, Clay felt guilt. But just as quickly as it came, he smashed it. "As I said—I'm not screwing up my career because of *you*."

"Likewise."

Clay almost smiled. What a little hellcat she was. For her size and weight, which couldn't be more than 120 pounds, she was a fighter. He allowed himself to admire her for that. "Okay," he muttered, looking around his desk, "let's get this miserable show on the road."

The puncturing of the tension nearly unstrung her. Aly sat down, her knees shaking. She hoped Clay hadn't seen it, because he'd probably wonder if she was up to the task of flying as his copilot on the multimillion-dollar aircraft.

Tossing a file folder across the desk, Clay said, "I've been ordered to set up your Link training for the next quarter. You'll start tomorrow. Aviation Engineer Chief Random is assigned to start running the computer programs for you. I'll be 'flying' as your IP and take you through an introductory phase on the P3." His eyes grew dark. "And I hope for your sake you're a fast learner, Trayhern."

Aly opened the folder, quickly scanning the first page. Link training would take place every day, five days a week, for at least two to three hours at a time. She began to sweat as she had before every flight at Pensacola. It was a fear sweat. "Isn't this schedule a little demanding?"

"Yes, it is. But so is the position the squadron's in. VP 46 flies from the Bering Strait of Alaska down to the tip of Baja, Mexico. We protect the entire West Coast from Soviet subs that ply off our twelve-mile limit. I'm sure Commander Horner told you that there's been a lot of unusual activity in the Baja California area lately. More Soviet subs are in that region. Civilian shipping is frantic because the Reds are ghosting their movements. There have been some close calls."

"In what way?" Aly was relieved to get on a neutral topic. But it in no way lessened the hatred she saw burning in his eyes every time he glanced over at her.

Clay moved to a wall map of the West Coast and Pacific Ocean. He circled an area with his index finger. "We've got Soviet freighters plying their trade to the Central American countries here. The Soviet subs dogged the heels of friendly U.S. freighters in that area. One Red sub took a torpedo shot at an American-registered ship last week."

Aly's eyes widened. "And they got away with it?"

With a slight, triumphant grin Cantrell said, "No. We dropped a depth charge from the P3 I was flying, right in front of the bastard's nose, to let him know we weren't going to allow him the privilege of a second shot. The ship wasn't in any real danger. It was only harassment by the Soviets. But we're there to make sure they know we'll interdict any game they want to play with U.S. shipping."

Excitement thrummed through her. "Then what happened?"

"The sub dived and hightailed it back out to sea."

"Does this kind of thing happen often?"

Clay tried to ignore the sudden enthusiasm in Aly's voice, the shine in her azure eyes. What would it be like to see that same warm glow in them after he'd made love with her?

Where the *hell* did *that* thought come from? He gave himself an internal shake. Alyssa Trayhern was doing things to him he had no control over, and that shook him. No woman had held that kind of power over him. Ever! Angry at the train of his thought, he snapped at her.

"It happens a lot. And for your sake, Lieutenant, you'd better be up to the demands of it. Flying a P3 at fifty feet over a raging ocean and knowing that any second a down-draft could suck you and your entire crew into a watery grave isn't for weaklings. Or women," he added viciously.

## Chapter Three

Clay's words haunted Aly. It was a barely veiled threat that if she screwed up, he'd be the first to point out her error and log the mistake into her fitness report. And blots on her fitness report, issued twice a year on every officer, could hurt, even destroy, her budding career. No, Clay held the sword of Damocles above her head and they both knew it. Aly hefted the three large manuals he'd given her just before she left the training office. They were manuals that covered cockpit procedures, emergency procedures and defense measures for the beautiful, graceful P3.

It was noon, but Aly had lost her appetite. If she studied nonstop over the weekend, she *might* gain an edge on cockpit procedure for Monday morning so that she'd impress Clay. The plan was a lot better than the opposite possibility—disappointing him.

As Aly hurried down the safety walk toward the side entrance, she heard a long, loud wolf whistle. She ignored it. Probably some enlisted man, she thought, irritated. But again came another long whistle.

Slowly, Aly turned and saw a pilot in a green flight suit, his garrison cap at a cocky angle on his head, following close behind her. He was smiling, his brown eyes sparkling. His walk was jaunty, self-assured. Aly saw a patch on his olive-green flight suit that identified him as an F-14 Tomcat pilot. And then she saw the inspector pilot's patch on the other side of his chest. She frowned as he ambled up to her and threw his hands on his hips.

"Hi, there. The name's Starbuck. Jeff Starbuck. Scuttlebutt was flying around the hangar this morning that a good-looking lady was on the premises." His grin deepened as he met and held her defiant gaze. "I said, 'Nah . . .' And they said, 'Yeah!' So the chief of maintenance said he saw her go into that lucky bastard, Cantrell's office. I decided to scope it out for myself."

Starbuck drew himself up and snapped off an impressive salute. "You've got to be Alyssa Trayhern," he said and offered his hand. "Damned glad to have you on board."

Aly refused to take his hand. "Lieutenant Starbuck, your manners are not impressive."

Starbuck looked crestfallen, his oval face losing some of its joviality. "What?"

"I'm sure you've been in the Navy long enough to realize that whistling at an enlisted woman or a woman officer is considered sexual harassment."

His mouth tightened. "Well, gosh, I meant it as a compliment, Miss Trayhern." He cocked his head to one side, deliberately checking out her legs. "I mean, what a set of legs!"

He was irrepressible, Aly decided, and she relented. Starbuck's demeanor was typical of fighter jocks. Typically male chauvinistic, egotistical and self-serving. Despite that, Starbuck was a bright spot in her gray day. His brown hair was neatly cut, and he had large, hawklike eyes. The devil-may-care smile on his full mouth enhanced the youthful appearance of his face, although he had to be in his late twenties. There were crow's-feet crinkling at the corners of his eyes and deep grooves around his mouth, indicating that he smiled and laughed a great deal.

"Okay, Mr. Starbuck, thank you for the compliment."

"But?" His smile deepened.

"Look, I just spent four years at Annapolis and a year with you guys at Pensacola."

He rubbed his chin. "Hmm, sounds like something serious. Betcha you're going to tell me I'm just like all the rest, eh?"

"Roger that."

"But," he said dramatically, "I'm the best-*looking* F-14 driver at Moffett." He jerked a thumb over his shoulder. "The trash haulers who fly the P3 are a pittance compared to me. I got the looks, the time and—" he held up his left hand for her to observe "—I'm free."

"And I'm not. Sorry, Starbuck, I've got things to do. If you'll excuse me?" Not waiting for his response, Aly turned and walked toward the mouth of the hangar.

"Hey! Wait up!" Starbuck trotted up alongside and grabbed the manuals she was carrying. "At least let me help the lady with her books."

Aly groaned, wavering between stopping to wrest the books from him and giving in. Starbuck wasn't going to be easy to get rid of. "If I didn't know you had ulterior motives, Lieutenant, I might be impressed with your thoughtfulness, but I'm not."

"Can I at least carry these to your car—ulterior motives or not?"

He was an engaging character, Aly decided. "Oh, all right." And she took off at a fast walk. Her red Toyota was parked halfway down the other side of the hangar, a long walk to endure with the fighter jock.

"Beautiful day, isn't it?" Starbuck asked, gesturing to the sky. "Man, I just got done flying up there. Air's smooth as a woman's—" He flushed. "Sorry, I'm used to talking to male pilots, not female ones."

Aly gave him a flat look of disapproval. "I can tell, Lieutenant."

He grinned self-consciously, color heating his neck and cheeks. "Sorry, Alyssa. Do you mind if I call you by your first name?"

"No, I don't care," she answered. Her mind, and if she was honest with herself, her heart were dwelling on the confrontation with Clay Cantrell. They were at a terrible impasse with each other. How could she overcome the barriers he'd thrown up and get him to wave a white flag of truce so that they could survive their time together?

"Well," Starbuck said, noticing she was ignoring him, "as I was saying, it was great flying up there this morning. We've been hearing about a woman pilot being assigned to Moffett for the past two weeks. I was really excited about the opportunity."

"I'll bet you were," Aly answered dryly. Probably thought he was going to be the first to bed her down, and then go around strutting and bragging about his latest conquest to every man on the station who would listen.

"Ahh, there you go again, Alyssa. You don't trust my intentions, do you?"

"Not in the least, Lieutenant."

"You can call me Jeff if you want. My buddies call me Iron Eagle."

"In or out of bed?" Aly flinched inwardly. Now she was trading tit for tat. Offense was the only defense against someone like this arrogant jock.

Laughing heartily, he said, "Good sense of humor, too. I like that in a woman."

"I'm not keeping score, and neither should you."

"You must have met that sour bastard, Cantrell," Starbuck said, glancing at the stack of manuals under his arm. "And it looks like he's thrown the homework at you."

He was right on that account, Aly acknowledged silently. "Lieutenant Cantrell is my mentor for my training-in period."

"Yeah, I heard you got stuck with him."

An ocean-scented wind blew in off the bay, and Aly inhaled the fragrance. She could see the salt marshes that grew right at the end of the airstrip. A lot of sea gulls were wafting on the unseen currents over the

station. Right now, all she wanted to do was fly. Fly
and forget. Let the sky take her into its arms and hold
her for a while.

"I don't know what you're talking about," she re-
torted sharply.

Chuckling indulgently, Starbuck watched a sea gull
sail overhead. "Well, sooner or later you're going to
hear about the infamous Cantrell."

"From you, no doubt, whether I want to or not.
Isn't that correct, Lieutenant?"

He curbed his smile, seemingly struggling to remain serious. "What I'm going to say isn't gossip,
Alyssa. These are things you should know. I mean,
after all, you've been assigned to fly with him, right?"

"Yes." She shot Starbuck a warning look. "I don't
like gossip, mister. Especially the malicious variety. If
that's what you've got on Lieutenant Cantrell, you can
stow it."

He nodded, growing somber. "Fair enough. I
imagine you've had plenty of gossip about yourself, so
you're a little sensitive in that area."

Aly was stunned by his sudden insight. "Well—
yes," she stammered.

"See, we aren't all the insensitive jocks stuck on our
egos that you thought," he teased, smiling again.

Aly smiled unwillingly. "You're a big tease and I
know it."

"But a harmless one," he pleaded. "Really."

"Sure."

"You know how we fighter jocks talk. I mean, we're
bred to have confidence. You gotta have a healthy ego
in order to lift a fifteen-million-dollar aircraft off a
pitching carrier deck in the middle of an ocean."

"That's the truth," Aly agreed. She pointed toward the Toyota. "That's my car."

Starbuck drew to a halt while she fished around in her purse for the keys. "Look, I meant what I said about Cantrell. There are some things you need to know. It might save that nice-looking rear of yours, someday."

Aly ignored the remark and jammed the key into the lock. "I don't want to discuss it."

Starbuck handed her the manuals, which she stowed in the rear of the sports car. "Give me just five minutes, okay?" He held up his hands in a sign of truce. "I promise you, everything I'm going to tell you is true."

Sighing, Aly muttered, "Five minutes, Starbuck, and that's it."

"A year and a half ago, Cantrell was an F-14 driver like me. We flew off the *Enterprise* together. He was one of the hottest pilots in our squadron, and we were both vying for the top-gun slot at Miramar. Then he screwed up on a deck landing. Cantrell ended up crashing the bird he was flying into the deck. He ejected, but his radar officer bought it." Starbuck's voice dropped with feeling. "Cantrell ended up in the hospital for a while, and the flight surgeon grounded him. He'd lost his nerve. Every time he tried to requalify as a carrier pilot, he failed. The Navy finally rerouted him to a land-based aircraft. He's been here at Moffett for a year." Starbuck pointed to the P3 parked closest to them. "That's his bird. It's been downed. Three days ago he made a rookie pilot's landing and did some major damage to the port landing gear. The whole strut is going to be replaced later today.''

Instead of being worried about Clay's past, Aly felt her heart ache for him. She'd heard of fighter pilots losing their nerve out on the carrier. They flew under the toughest, most demanding of flight conditions possible. "Look, Starbuck," she said coolly, "his past is no concern of mine."

"It is if you're sitting in that cockpit with him," he challenged, his eyes flashing with irritation. "Look, you've worked hard to get this far. I'd hate to see your career screwed up because that guy's in the process of losing his touch."

"You don't know that—you don't fly with him!" What the hell was she *defending* Clay for? Aly didn't have time to analyze her response.

Starbuck lifted the garrison cap off his head and settled it back on with feeling. "His *crew* knows it. His copilot, Randy Hart, just transferred out of here to his next assignment. Hart is a damn fine pilot. Every once in a while we'd have a beer or two over at the Officers Club after a mission, and he'd tell me what it was like to fly with Cantrell."

Aly threw her purse into the passenger seat. "That's enough, Lieutenant. I told you: I won't listen to gossip."

"This isn't gossip! Cantrell's hands shake so bad after a mission that his entire crew thinks he's close to the edge. All he does is bitch at them. He doesn't have a kind word for anyone."

"I suppose next you're going to tell me that he's a heavy drinker, slopping them down at the O Club after every mission?"

With a groan, Starbuck held up his long, expressive hands. "Whoa, sweet thing. I'm just trying to prepare you for what you're up against." He grinned slightly, his eyes taking on a familiar twinkle. "I just found you. I don't want you run off by a sourpuss like Cantrell."

Aly couldn't decide what Starbuck's motives were. He'd flown with Cantrell in the same squadron, and Aly knew that competitiveness was the chief gestalt between fighter pilots vying for top-gun selection. Starbuck might hate Clay because Clay was a better pilot than Starbuck before the crash. She didn't know, and at this point, didn't care.

"Lieutenant, do you know who I am?" she challenged.

"Yeah, you're Alyssa Trayhern."

"I'm the sister of Morgan Trayhern. Does that name ring a bell with you?"

With a shrug, Starbuck answered, "Of course it does. Look, I don't bear grudges. It was your brother that gave your family a black mark, not you."

Aly eyed him in silence, evaluating. His face was free of tension, his eyes lacking guile. "And you know that Lieutenant Cantrell's brother was in the same company with my brother?"

"I heard about that. Scuttlebutt has been thick and heavy ever since we found out you were assigned." He rubbed his chin, studying her frankly. "That's another reason I wanted to warn you about Cantrell. He's not the type to forgive and forget. He bears a grudge for a long time. I know from experience, because I beat him out for top gun and went on to win the honor for our squadron."

*No kidding about Clay holding grudges,* Aly almost blurted out. But Starbuck was a dangerous person to confide in, she decided. As badly as she wanted to break down and tell someone about her trials with Clay, she knew it wouldn't be Starbuck. No, she sensed a vicious streak in him, despite that disarming smile and teasing manner.

"Look, I appreciate your two cents worth on Cantrell. But if you don't mind, I don't want to hear any more war stories. Now, if you'll excuse me—"

"Hey! What about a pizza tonight? There's a terrific little parlor over in Mountain View. Mama Cara's has the best Italian food in the Bay Area. How about if I pick you up, say, around 1900, and we'll get better acquainted over some great pizza and good wine?"

A little pain stabbed through Aly's heart. She winced outwardly. Was it the same pizza place that Clay had referred to yesterday? She had been looking forward to that date with him. "Thanks, but no," she said and climbed into her sports car.

Crestfallen, but not giving up, Starbuck shut the door for her.

"Probably shouldn't, with all those training manuals to study this weekend." He smiled. "Get your beauty sleep tonight. I'll be seeing you around, Alyssa," and he threw her a salute.

*Don't count on it.* Aly nodded and backed the car out of the parking spot, anxious to escape the cloying attention of Jeff Starbuck. Right now, all she wanted to do was go home, have a good cry, get herself back together again and call her parents. They had been her stanchion of strength, of wisdom. And right now, she needed both. Desperately.

\* \* \*

"Hello, Dad."

"Punkin! Well, how was your first day at your very first station?"

Aly shut her eyes, gripping the phone hard. It was nearly six o'clock. She had come home earlier, cried, taken Rogue out for a five-mile jog around their new neighborhood, gotten a hot shower and unpacked more boxes. Needing to talk to someone, Aly had finally picked up the phone and dialed.

"Its been terrible, Dad." She explained the entire sequence of events. Just talking about it to an understanding ear helped. Afterward, Aly rubbed her face tiredly.

"What do you think, Dad? Does someone back in D.C. have it in for me?"

"Let me make a few phone calls and feel this out," Chase muttered. His voice was deep with concern. "It does sound as if some admiral has it in for you. That's why those orders were cut that way."

Aly knew her father had powerful and influential ties to all the services. He had retired a brigadier general in the Air Force just before Morgan's tragedy. Generals were power brokers, and her father knew how to infight politically with the best of them. But since Morgan's terrible tragedy, her father's awesome political clout had been brutally undermined. Despite his forty years of service, few of his friends remained such after Morgan was declared a traitor. Aly knew her father's access to the Pentagon to investigate her problem would be severely hampered, if not hamstrung from the beginning.

"Can you do it without stirring up problems, Dad?" Aly didn't want whoever was trying to kill her career to get wind of his delicate inquiry.

"I'll be careful, Punkin, you can count on it. For now, how are you going to handle this? Is Cantrell someone you can reason with?"

"No," she said miserably, propping an elbow on the table and resting her head in her hand. "He's filled with hatred, Dad. I hurt for him. I think Clay's back-logged with emotions from five years ago, that he never released his grief over his brother's death."

Chase's deep voice softened. "You hurt for him, honey?"

Aly laughed weakly. "Oh, Dad, you don't know the other half of it," she explained, and she told him about their meeting on the Bayshore.

"I see," he murmured. "So you're attracted to him despite the situation, Aly?"

"Yes. This is the first time I've ever been knocked off my feet, Dad. He just took my breath away. No man has ever done that before."

"Sounds serious."

Aly's depression lifted. "I love you, Dad. You always know when to tease me and get me out of the hole I've dug for myself."

Chase's voice grew tender. "Listen, Punkin, you're our only daughter. Your mother and I are terribly proud of you. The past five years have been utter hell on you, too."

Closing her eyes, Aly nodded. The rest, what her father didn't say, was: because of what happened to Morgan. No one in the family believed Morgan was a traitor. They all knew something had happened that

Morgan had been caught in the middle of. Chase felt his older son had been made a scapegoat. But for what? They didn't even know if Morgan was alive or dead. And her father had been thwarted from all angles in trying to investigate his son's disappearance off the face of the earth. She sighed tiredly. "I thought my hell was over, Dad. I had so many hopes and dreams about Moffett. I finally felt as if all the shadows from the past were dead and buried...."

"Take this one day at a time, Punkin. Perhaps your liking Cantrell might make it easier in one way."

"Oh?"

"You're not defensive with him. You understand where his pain is coming from, and you won't go for his jugular each time he attacks you. It might give you the patience to outdistance his hate. Sooner or later, he'll run out of hate. That's what you've got to count on."

"But by liking him I'm leaving myself wide open, Dad. Everything he said to me, I've heard thousands of times before, and it never cut me like it did coming from him."

"I know, honey," Chase soothed. "I wish I could protect your heart where he's concerned. But I can't. No one can. You have a choice: put up walls to protect your heart, or go ahead and feel your way through the situations and take the hurt that goes with the territory and the decision."

"Which would you do, Dad?" Tears stung her eyes, her voice wobbling dangerously.

Chase sighed. "A better question is: what do you want to do about it?"

Aly sniffed, wiping her nose. "Mom always counseled us to feel our emotions, don't run away from them."

"That's true. And she also taught you to listen to your gut instincts. What are they telling you?"

Aly's heart hurt, and she rubbed the area unconsciously. "Th-that Clay's like a hurt animal, biting anyone who comes remotely near him, whether they created his pain or not."

"Okay, and what do you do with an injured animal?"

"Care for it as carefully as you can, remain objective and don't try to pet it."

"That's right. A hurt animal doesn't equate a stroke on his head with comfort. He just sees it as a hand attacking him and will strike out at it."

Managing a choked laugh, Aly said, "Dad, do you ever think I'll get wise about people and their emotions the way you and Mom did?"

Chase chuckled. "I think, Punkin, that at twenty-five, you're way ahead of most women your age. You have savvy, intelligence and a world of traveling and experience behind you. My money's on you to win out in this situation with Cantrell. Just be patient. And don't get your hand close enough for him to bite."

It was drizzling rain again on Sunday. Aly felt as depressed as the low-hanging gray clouds that embraced the Bay Area. She hefted the cockpit manual under her left arm and climbed out of her car. Moffett Field was almost deserted on Sunday, except for those who had to stand the duty. Dressed in jeans, a pink turtleneck sweater and a warm beige jacket, Aly ran to the closest entrance of Hangar One.

Inside, she went to the duty chief's office. An aviation engineer first class was standing the duty office, busy with paperwork when she entered.

"Hi, I'm Lieutenant Alyssa Trayhern."

The tall string bean of a man, dressed in a light blue chambray shirt and dark blue serge trousers, straightened in the chair. His red hair was close cropped, his skin sprinkled with copper freckles. "Oh..." And then he grinned sheepishly and rose, sticking out his hand. "Miss Trayhern, I'm your engineer on board our aircraft. The name's Dan Ballard. I'm happy to finally get to meet you."

Aly flushed at his softened words. The man meant what he said, his hazel eyes alight with unabashed enthusiasm as he pumped her hand long and eagerly.

Reclaiming her hand, she rewarded him with a shy smile of her own. "What a wonderful welcome. I hope the rest of the crew's as happy about me as you are."

Ballard nodded. "To tell the truth," he said in a conspiratorial tone, "since we found out about this two weeks ago, I've been telling the crew that it's the best thing that could happen to us."

Placing the manual on the desk, Aly dried her hands by wiping them across her jeans. "Oh, why's that?"

Scratching his head, Ballard blushed a dull red. He avoided her gaze. "Well...you know... My wife, Sandy, is a real feminist." He held up his hand, assuming Aly would take his comment the wrong way. "We've been married some twelve years now, with four kids between us, and I've seen a woman's strength compared to a man's. She was saying the same thing I was: that you're going to add some dimensions to the crew that we didn't have before. Good things, I think, that will help...." He stumbled, groping for the right words.

Starbuck's conversation came back to her. Maybe he hadn't exaggerated the situation with Cantrell's crew. Ballard reminded her of an eager puppy just dying for a warm pat on the head. She liked him. He was open and honest. "Help what, Dan?" she probed gently, hoping to get an answer.

"Ahh, don't mind me, Miss Trayhern. I just get carried away and all. Just know that the crew is going to welcome you with open arms. We need a lady's sensitivity and her gentle way of handling us. You know what I mean...."

Aly nodded and pretended to know. "Well, look, Dan, if you don't mind, since you're duty chief, I'd like to have your permission to climb on board number 7 and sit in the cockpit to familiarize myself a little. Is that possible?" The P3 was still in the hangar, and Aly could see that the old landing gear had been replaced with new on the port side of the aircraft.

"Sure. Of course. I'm sure Mr. Cantrell won't mind." He came around the desk and opened the door for her. "Would you like some help? I'm the guy who sits right behind your seats working the four throttles while you're flying. I'm also certified to taxi the gal, and qualified on engine start-up and shutdown procedures."

She warmed to his generosity. "Maybe later? Right now, I just want to sit and acquaint myself with her."

Dan opened the door, nodding. "Sure, Miss Trayhern. Want me to drop by in about an hour? The only thing I gotta do is be here in the hangar. We've only got one P3 out on track, and that bird isn't scheduled back from the mission for six hours."

"Kinda bored?" Aly guessed, smiling.

"Yes, ma'am."

"Give me an hour, Dan, and then you can quiz me on procedures, okay?"

"You got it, Miss Trayhern." He beamed.

Aly's step was lighter as she walked across the concrete floor in her sensible brown shoes. Every sound was amplified, echoing off the walls. It was ghostlike, the pall of rain and gray clouds hanging silently outside the opened bay doors of the hangar, increasing her sense of loneliness. Still, Aly felt her first real ray of hope with Dan Ballard, who was obviously delighted in her arrival.

The fuselage door was open on the port side of number 7, a ladder placed up against the hatch. As Aly approached the ladder, she reached up, running her hand across the smooth, cool skin of the P3.

"Hi there, Gray Lady," she whispered. Her eyes darkened. "Let's you and me be friends. We're both women in a man's world." The gray aluminum skin warmed beneath her palm. Aly could swear the aircraft was alive, possessing a unique personality. She'd always named her planes, her animals, her car and anything else that would stand still long enough to be given a name.

"Gray Lady, be my ally. Help me," she pleaded to the strong, silent aircraft. It was time to go on board. She'd never stepped inside a sub-hunting aircraft. Slowly Aly entered the plane. Inside, the port and starboard fuselage were a complex array of radar screens. A desk ran down both sides. So much electronic equipment was squeezed into the small working space that there seemed barely enough room for the eight crewmen at the consoles. Looking aft, past a small entrance without a door, she saw two more seats and a collapsible bunk that fitted tightly up against the fuselage wall. One seat was for the radioman, the other for a meteorological observer.

The aircraft was flawless, Aly decided with admiration. Everything was stowed neatly and efficiently. She located the sonobuoys that could detect a Soviet sub beneath the oceans if they were dropped out the rear hatch of the P3. The depth charges weren't on board, so she assumed they must be loaded on the aircraft for the mission and then taken off when the plane returned to the station.

Aly's heart beat a little harder as she moved forward into the cockpit. She saw the four throttles that Dan Ballard would kneel before and monitor. Her hands grew damp as she halted, glanced around the small instrument panel in front and overhead. Her fear dissolved as she began to look at the individual gauges. This was Gray Lady's circulatory system. The P3's heart consisted of four powerful turboprop engines. Some of the many dials would tell Aly how the fuel was getting pumped and distributed to her heart. Triumph soared through her as she sat down for the first time in the copilot seat, her position for at least the next two years of her life.

A sense of belonging swept through Aly. She laid the manual open across the throttle case. Running her hand gently across the copilot's yoke, new excitement thrummed through her. One of these days, she'd be

allowed to fly Gray Lady. What she'd give to feel the
plane come alive under her careful, supervised skill!
Would the P3 give over her power to her? Or would
she fight every step of the way like some prop and jet
trainers Aly had flown at Pensacola?

"Enough daydreaming," she muttered, giving the
aircraft a quick, friendly pat. "Down to work!"

Clay shielded his eyes from the downpour. Having
parked near the entrance to Hangar One, he dived inside. He shook the excess water from his well-worn
leather jacket and headed straight for his P3. Looking around, he realized the hangar was all but deserted. The other men had families to go home to, they
had wives...children....

His family was the Navy, his woman that gleaming
P3 that stood like an elegant queen before him. Eyes
narrowing, he bent and moved beneath the plane's
graceful undercarriage. The damage sustained in that
landing had been repaired. Clay carefully checked the
mechanics' work. He trusted them, but he had to be
sure. Any pilot concerned with his plane's performance would do the same. Besides, as usual, there was
little to do on the weekend when he didn't have the
duty. Clay felt better just being on the station. This
was his life.

Satisfied, he ran his hand down the steel strut. On
the last mission there had been a malfunction with the
low-altitude altimeter or LAA. He wanted to go on
board and see if it had been repaired and checked off
the maintenance sheet by the ground crew. He and his
crew would be flying this girl Tuesday, and he wanted
her in tip-top condition.

As Clay climbed the ladder, he could have sworn he heard a woman's voice. A husky voice. Impossible. Frowning, he halted at the lip of the P3. Confusion turned to disbelief as he looked toward the cockpit area. Although the light was dim, he could see a mop of unruly red hair glinting dully in the cockpit.

*Aly!* And then Clay sternly chastised himself. *No, her name isn't Aly!* He'd sworn he'd never call her by her first name again. But he couldn't help himself, and he stood mesmerized as she leaned over the manual, muttering out the names of the dials and gauges.

Closing his eyes, Clay hoped that she would disappear. She didn't. He was intensely aware of her red hair, clean profile and those parted lips. As he inhaled, he could faintly smell the fragrance she wore—something spicy, like herself. And when she placed her finger against her lower lip, studying the manual with undivided intent, he felt himself begin to tighten with desire.

Disgusted with his reaction to her, Clay moved silently up the passageway toward her, letting his anger at himself mask his real feelings. There was savage pleasure in realizing she was so focused on the manual that she didn't hear him coming until it was too late. Clay told himself he was going to enjoy this.

"Just what the hell do you think you're doing here, Lieutenant Trayhern?"

Aly jumped, her head snapping up, her eyes wide. Clay Cantrell's dark, shadowed features loomed above her. The anger in his eyes consumed and struck her viciously. She could only stare, stripped of any defense, because he was the last person she'd expected to run into today. Despite the fact that he was wearing a civilian light blue shirt, that same old leather jacket and a pair of brown trousers, he still held an invisible power over her.

Swallowing, Aly choked out, "I—I study better if I've got the real thing in front of me."

Placing his hands on his hips, Clay glared down into her frightened eyes. Blue eyes he could fall into and seek warmth from in his freezing, empty world. His voice came out in a low snarl. "I don't give a damn what your excuse is, Lieutenant. I'm your training officer. What I say, goes. I told you to take those manuals home and study them over the weekend. I didn't tell you to come here of your own volition and sit in the right seat of a P3." He saw his words land with the desired effect upon her. Why should he care if they hurt her? Fighting any sympathetic reaction to her flinch, Clay added savagely, "Lady, you may think you're copilot material, but until I sign that piece of paper attesting to it, you don't deserve to sit in that seat. Now get the hell out of here and go home."

Aly sat stunned, incredible pain welling up in her chest. Clay was like an avenging angel, hovering darkly above her in that gray cockpit. She opened her mouth to speak, but nothing would come out. Her throat was suddenly clogged with tears.

She blinked and bowed her head, afraid that Clay would see her tears. She didn't dare let him know how badly he'd wounded her. Fumbling with the manual, she accidentally let it slip from her fingers, banging to the steel deck with a thump.

"Dammit, can't you do anything right?" he snarled, jerking the manual off the deck and tossing it her direction.

"Hour's up, Miss Trayhern," Ballard sang out from the ladder. "I'm ready to help you with start-up and shutdown proced—"

Clay turned, ominously facing his chief engineer, who stood frozen in the middle of the P3. "Just what the hell is going on here, Ballard?"

"Well...uh, Mr. Cantrell, I thought I'd help Miss Trayhern learn the instruments...." The rest of his explanation died in the icy silence of the aircraft. Ballard shrugged, seeing how upset his skipper was. "I was just trying to help her, sir."

Clay's nostrils flared with fury, and he advanced upon the AE. He opened his mouth to deliver a verbal tongue-lashing to his chief, who had no business helping train any copilot unless he gave the order.

"Don't you dare chew him out!"

Clay heard Aly's strident cry. He halted, halfway between both of them. Jerking his head toward her, he saw that she had risen to her feet and climbed out of the cockpit. Her eyes were hauntingly large, pleading.

"This isn't his fault, Mr. Cantrell. I asked Dan to come and help me in about an hour."

"But," Ballard admitted, obviously noting the mounting rage on the officer's face and not wanting Aly hurt further, "it was my idea, skipper."

Clay didn't know whom to bite first. It was obvious Ballard was covering up for her. That made him twice as angry. "You're dismissed, Ballard," he ground out. "I'll deal with you later."

Hesitating, Dan looked toward Aly uncertainly before grudgingly saying, "Yes, sir."

Waiting until Ballard had disappeared, Clay slowly turned back toward Aly. She was still frozen at the entrance to the cockpit, her face shadowed and tense in the dim light. His smile was withering. "You've already wrapped Ballard around your finger," he began silkily. "But it won't do you any good. This is my plane and my crew. You try pitting any of them against me, and you'll pay, Trayhern. And in ways you never thought possible. Do you understand what I mean?" His eyes bored into hers.

A quiver ran through Aly. The sick, injured animal was biting again. It would do no good to fight back, he'd only rip her into more pieces than he had already. She tried to remember her father's words of wisdom, tried to rise above her own pain. Deliberately breaking the sizzling tension strung between them, Aly bent down and retrieved the second manual on the throttle case. She clutched both of them to her breast and slowly walked toward him. When she was within a foot of him, she halted.

"Your engineer had nothing to do with me being in this cockpit. It was my decision and my fault," she said, keeping her voice calm.

Clay stared down at her. Her jaw was set, her lips compressed with very real anxiety. He hated himself in that anguished second. And he could barely meet her shadowed blue eyes, riddled with hurt and confusion. "Ballard gave you permission to come on board because he's the duty chief this weekend. I'm not going to chew him out. Now get the hell out of here. Be at the Link trainer at 0800 sharp, tomorrow morning, Lieutenant."

"Yes, sir," she ground out.

Clay moved aside, not wanting contact with her. But the aisle of the plane was too narrow, and his breath lodged in his chest as she brushed past him. He saw her eyes narrow and heard a small gasp of air escape her. She hated him so much that she was disgusted by minimal contact with him, he thought wearily.

Clay stood, feeling little shocks move through him, long after she'd disappeared. Her arm had barely grazed his chest. But the contact had been electric. He was sure they'd both felt it, whatever it was.

*Such a stupid, trivial thing,* Clay upbraided himself as he turned toward the cockpit. How could a woman's arm merely brushing his chest make him go hard with longing? Running his fingers through his hair, Clay muttered an oath and settled into the pilot's seat. As he sat examining the LAA, he couldn't escape pangs of guilt.

He shut his eyes, rubbing them tiredly. Sleep hadn't come at all the past two nights—only dreams of the past involving his mother and Stephen. Alyssa Trayhern's entrance into his life had stirred up all the buried grief and loss. And yet, as he sat, leaning heavily against the seat, he knew Aly didn't deserve his hatred and anger. One look into those distraught blue eyes and he knew....

## Chapter Four

*Damn!* He was late for work! Clay rolled out of bed, glaring at the alarm clock. It read 0745. It was Monday, and he wasn't going to be on time to meet Aly at the Link trainer.

As he staggered toward the bathroom, rubbing his eyes, he stubbed his toe on the edge of a rocker he kept in the corner.

"Ouch!" He hobbled the rest of the way, his left toe smarting. Fumbling for the electric razor in the drawer, he finally found it and shoved the plug into the outlet. He had to hurry. He tried to shave without looking in the mirror.

The rest of his Sunday had been spent at his apartment, studying some new training procedure manuals for the P3. Dismayed by his cruelty to Aly, he'd wanted to hide from those feelings of guilt, shifting his mind to technical demands. Last night he'd tossed and turned, unable to erase Aly's hurt features from his mind. Getting up at 0200, he'd downed a shot of Scotch, thinking it would numb the dirty feelings inside himself. It hadn't. Somewhere around 0400 he'd finally dropped off. Vaguely, Clay remembered the radio alarm clock beeping at 0530, his usual time to get up, but he'd hit it, shutting off the alarm.

His hand shook now as he placed the shaver on the tile expanse. Risking a look into the mirror in order to quickly comb his short hair into place, Clay winced. He looked like hell. He felt like hell. What was he going to do about Aly?

"Dammit!" he breathed, throwing the comb down on the counter. It skipped along the tile, falling into the washbasin. He didn't want to think of her as Aly. She was Trayhern—just another pilot. Pilots always called one another by their last names or by the nicknames they'd received at Pensacola, denoting some special feature. When Clay graduated at the top of his class, his squad mates had dubbed him Wolverine, because he was relentless and tenacious in the air.

Placing his palms against the surface, Clay ruthlessly studied himself in the mirror. His eyes were bloodshot and there were puffy bags beneath them. With his mouth pulled into a slash, he looked like a grim reaper, in his estimation. Why couldn't he just refer to her as Trayhern? Why did some miserable part of him automatically call her Aly? Clay turned away, automatically going through the steps of donning the loose-fitting olive-green flight suit.

The sun was already up, and the Bay Area was going to enjoy one of those cool but sunny January days.

Clay drove hell-for-leather, pushing his Corvette along the Bloody Bayshore, weaving expertly in and out of traffic. So, okay, he'd grudgingly call her Aly to himself, but never out loud. If some part of his mind refused to coldly classify her by her last name, he wasn't going to fight it anymore. But she was still the sister of the man who had murdered the two people he loved most in the world. And for that, he could never forgive her.

Rubbing his eyes because they ached, Clay wondered what Aly would think of his being late for their first training session. Would she automatically think he was arriving late on purpose? Another ploy to make her nervous and unsure of herself? His conscience needled him. His hands tightening on the wheel, Clay felt backed into a corner as never before. Ordinarily, he was never cruel. It wasn't his nature. But every time he got around Aly, he was aware of an incredible tension that sizzled like fire between them. He rejected the idea of being drawn to her. She was the sister of a murderer. And so, there was no alternative but to treat her coldly and jam the rest of these new and unexpected feelings down into some deep, dark corner of himself—as he had with his grief for the past five years.

At exactly 0800 Aly arrived at the Link training facility, which was located at the rear of Hangar One. The room was large and spacious. The control booth, which held hundreds of computerized disks, was enclosed with glass. Chief Bill Random, who sat at the large computer terminal, came out and introduced himself. He was about fifty-five, small and brisk. But a smile wreathed his face when he pointed toward the two-seat Link trainer that would serve as her home for the coming months on a daily basis.

"I think somebody's already sweet on you, Lieutenant Trayhern."

"Oh?" Aly saw Random gesture toward the opened canopy on the Link. The trainer sat on a single movable steel pylon. When they climbed in and closed the hood, that pylon would move in any direction, simulating flight.

"Yes, ma'am. Go take a look at what's on the co-pilot's seat."

Mystified, Aly walked over to the trainer. Her eyes widened considerably when she saw a single red rose lying across the seat. There was a small white envelope tied to the stem with a pink ribbon.

"Clay..." she whispered, and reached down, gently cradling the rose in her hands. Having slept poorly last night, Aly had wrestled with a gamut of feelings. She had seen Clay's eyes go from anger to regret once during their explosive confrontation Sunday in the P3. Some part of him didn't want to be the bastard he was to her. Was this his way of apologizing?

Eagerly, Aly opened the envelope. Inside, neatly printed were the words: *I'm sorry*. Her heartbeat quickened, underscoring her unleashed emotions. Turning away so that Chief Random couldn't see her face, she caressed the rose, inhaling its delicate scent. Her fingers trembled as she followed the smooth curve of the large red bud. Maybe there was hope after all. Maybe...

Turning, Aly walked to the control room where Random was setting up the computer tapes that would be played for them during the training session.

"Chief, where's Mr. Cantrell?" she asked, deciding that she wanted to thank him in private.

Random punched in a program and glanced in her direction. "Oh, I'm sure he's around here somewhere. Mr. Cantrell practically lives in this place. He comes in around 0630 every morning. Probably got caught up in some last-minute scheduling problems over at his office." He waved her toward the trainer. "Why don't you climb aboard the trainer, strap in and get comfortable? I'm sure he'll be here any second."

Pressing the rose to her breast, Aly nodded. "Okay, Chief." Much of her nervousness had abated with the knowledge that Clay had chosen such a wonderful and romantic way to apologize for his behavior yesterday.

In the cockpit, Aly began to refamiliarize herself with the instrument panel. Just having an hour in Gray Lady had helped her confidence immensely. From time to time, she glanced down at the rose in her lap. More of her anxiety dissipated as she began to focus on the dials and gauges in front of her. By 0830, Aly had relaxed a great deal in the mock-up of the P3 cockpit.

She heard the door to the training room open and close. Glancing out of the Link, she saw a harried Clay Cantrell come through the door dressed in his flight suit. There was a scowl on his face and his eyes were dark and angry. Automatically, Aly tensed. What was he upset about now?

Not wanting to risk being seen, she ducked back under the hood and waited patiently for Clay to come over to the trainer. She heard him and Chief Random talking in lowered voices. Clay sounded positively irate. What had happened? Her fingers tightened around the stem of the rose, her heartbeat racing.

Clay stalked over to the trainer. He ran his fingers through his hair as he approached the pilot side of the Link. Unable to ignore his unraveling feelings as he arrived at the trainer, he tried to steel himself to work with Aly.

"Good morning," she said cautiously.

Her voice was husky. Warm. Clay looked at her. How had Aly grown more lovely? Her cheeks were flushed pink, her blue eyes seemed soft, and her red hair was copper and gold beneath the bright lights. He tossed a manual into the trainer.

"It's morning," he growled, climbing into the left seat and strapping in. God, it was impossible to ignore her! The scent of her perfume encircled him, and unwillingly Clay inhaled it. She smelled so good, so clean in comparison to how he felt inside.

Nervously, Aly lifted the rose so that Clay could see it. "I—uh, I wanted to thank you for this...."

Clay stared at the rose and then up at her. Shaken by her vulnerability, he growled, "What's this?"

Aly tried to ferret out the confusion in his voice and the sudden shock registering in his dark gray eyes. "The rose," she offered huskily. "It's beautiful...and a beautiful way to apologize for yesterday."

"But—"

A shy smile pulled at the corners of her mouth. "I'm sorry, too, Clay. All I want to do is fit in around here, not fight with you."

Her admission tore a scar off the festering wound in his heart. The rose trembled in her hand as she held it out to him. Her shyness shattered his anger. And when she called him by his first name, a tendril of longing sang through him. Aly had a voice that would tame the fiercest of wild animals.

Clay had no idea who had given her the rose—a fact that irritated him more than he cared to think about. But he wasn't going to let her think he'd given it to her. He opened his mouth to speak.

"Hey!"

Aly tensed at the sound of Starbuck's booming voice. She closed her eyes momentarily. Why did he have to show up just when there was a tentative truce between her and Clay?

Starbuck strode around to the front of the trainer, a triumphant grin on his face. He was dressed in tight-fitting G-suit chaps that hugged his lower body to masculine perfection. His helmet bulged beneath his left arm. A pair of red eagle wings had been painted on either side of it, and the name *Iron Eagle* was visible.

"Just thought I'd drop by, Cantrell, and visit your good-looking student." Jeff winked at Alyssa. "How's my favorite girl doing this morning?"

Clay glared at the fighter pilot. "Lieutenant, this trainer is off-limits to anyone not on the training roster."

The F-14 pilot's smile disappeared, his brown eyes hardening. "Ease off the throttles, Cantrell." He put back his winning smile for Alyssa's benefit, and patted the trainer. "I just wanted to steal a minute and get her reaction to the rose I left her."

"Oh, God," Aly blurted. She glanced over at Clay; his face was thundercloud-black with anger. Heat flamed from her neck into her face, and she wanted to die of mortification.

"A beautiful rose for a beautiful lady," Starbuck said. He turned to Clay. "For once, buddy, you lucked out. After that crash that took your RIO's life, I thought a black cloud was hanging over you. T'ain't so, anymore, is it? You've got this luscious-looking woman who's going to be flying with you. I'm jealous as hell, Cantrell."

Clay gripped the manual. It hurt to breathe. It hurt to feel. Starbuck's malicious attack reared memories of the crash and John's death. "Starbuck, get the hell out of here," he snarled softly.

Aly tensed, hearing the raw anger in Clay's voice. Instinctively, she reached out, her hand resting on his arm, as if to stop him from rising to climb out and hit the fighter pilot. She handed the rose back to Starbuck.

"Lieutenant, I don't approve of your tactics, either. Why don't you go play in the sky with your F-14? Mr. Cantrell and I have some serious work to do. I don't appreciate your barging in."

Starbuck took the rose, his expression suddenly stiff. He smiled, but his eyes were cold upon her. "Sure thing, Alyssa." He lifted the rose and gave them both a mock salute with it. "I'll see you later, boys and girls."

Aly suddenly remembered her grip on Clay's arm. She jerked her fingers away as if burned. The training room was quiet after Starbuck's departure.

"I'm sorry, Mr. Cantrell," Aly whispered, too embarrassed to meet his eyes. "I thought the rose was from you. It was a stupid assumption."

Clay's mouth softened as he watched Aly. He was just as embarrassed. If he was any kind of sensitive human being, he'd apologize to her. But apologies came hard when so much hurt and pain filled the past between them.

"Don't worry about it," he growled, trying to take the harshness out of his tone. He saw her head snap up, her eyes trained on him. Did he see tears in them? Swallowing against a sudden lump, Clay motioned toward the manual that he placed between them. "Starbuck's a pain in the ass sometimes."

"He's insensitive." Breathing with relief that Clay wasn't going to snarl at her, Aly was anxious to move ahead and forget her faux pas. What must Clay think of her now? His face was pale, his gray eyes narrowed and dark. He must be furious with her and it could mean only one thing: more tension and hatred vibrating between them for the duration of this training session. Suddenly, all her hope was destroyed and her exposed nerves jangled.

Clay handed her the copilot's preflight checklist. "Yeah, he's insensitive all right," he ground out.

Aly didn't dare mention Clay's crash. She saw the rawness in his eyes, and the terror from the past. There was no way she was going to wound Clay with that memory. Fumbling with the elastic strap around her leg, she managed to fit the small board on top of her thigh where she could flip through the plastic-coated pages in rapid succession. The silence was stilted and she muttered, "I don't like roses anyway."

"Oh?"

"I love irises. They're my favorite flower...." Aly's voice trailed off into a whisper. What was she saying? Clay didn't care what she liked or didn't like. He had to put up with her. "Never mind, I talk too much," she muttered.

*Irises.* Clay stole a glance over at Aly. Her cheeks were flushed bright red, almost matching her hair. Somehow, he had to help her settle down. Right now she was so damn tautly strung, she was ready to explode. *Get a hold on yourself, Cantrell. For once, don't jump down her throat.*

"Iris would look good with your hair color," he pointed out awkwardly, trying to establish some neutral ground with her.

Blinking once, Aly risked a look in Clay's direction. Had she heard right, or was she making up this conversation? Struck by the fact that all the darkness had disappeared from his gray eyes, Aly was thrown completely off guard. Clay's mouth had softened. There was so much happening so quickly. Aly avoided his penetrating gaze and tried to focus on the checklist. One moment he could be a bastard, the next, his voice was unhinging her, touching her aching heart with soothing reassurance. That same look of warmth lingered in his eyes—just as it had at their first meeting on the Bayshore.

Taking a shaky breath, Aly said, "I'm ready to start preflight procedures if you are, Mr. Cantrell."

Brusque and efficient. Good. Clay released a held breath, thankful to be on familiar territory once again. "Roger. Okay, let's walk through each page of the checklist. I'll do it slowly, and if you have any questions, stop me and we'll discuss them. Okay?" He drilled her with a look that demanded an answer.

Aly nodded. "Yes, sir." And then she cringed. Now she was behaving like a frightened student pilot with an inspector pilot back at Pensacola. She saw a slight grin ease Clay's set mouth.

"You can drop the 'yes, sir.' Call me by my last name."

Aly wanted to die of embarrassment. What must he think of her? That she was a silly, addled-brained woman so flustered that her emotions were getting in the way of the business at hand? Aly had no defense against him. Clay affected her so profoundly on so many new, awakening levels that she completely lost her usual composure every time she got around him. Forcing a slight smile, she nodded. "I'm ready to start, Mr. Cantrell."

Clay brought down the hood, locking it in place. "Okay, let's get this show on the road."

Two hours later, the hood latch was sprung and opened. Aly took a deep breath of fresh air, relieved to be released from the stuffy, smelly Link. She had sweated like a student pilot at Pensacola, the underarms of her flight suit wringing wet. Wrinkling her nose, she was sure Clay couldn't have helped but notice. There was no end to the humiliation she felt around him. First the rose debacle, and now her less than glorious performance under the hood.

Clay sat scribbling a number of notes on the clipboard resting against his thigh. The tension in the Link for the past two hours had been distressing. To both of them. Each time a green pilot trained in the Link, the IP had to assess and grade his or her performance. Aly had been strained, making the same mistakes over and over again. His conscience railed at him. *Let's face it, Cantrell, you weren't a good IP, either. All you did was snap at her for two hours straight.*

Whipped, her legs feeling weak, Aly climbed out of the cockpit. The feathery bangs across her brow were damp, sticking to her flesh. She had performed terribly. And judging from Clay's closed face, he was going to grade her without remorse. This was worse than the awful pressure applied to the fledgling student pilots at Pensacola. She'd had IPs who had screamed in her ear while she was flying the right-hand seat in the trainers. She'd had them badger her, taunt her, and she had stood up to them and graduated, despite their tactics to try to wash her out of the program.

Wiping her sweaty brow, Aly glanced toward the computer room. Chief Random gave her a game smile and a thumbs-up. That rallied her plummeting spirits, if only minimally. The chief would grade her performance, too. Maybe Random would be more understanding and lenient in his grade analysis than Clay would be.

*God, if I keep screwing up like this, I'll never get approved to copilot.* The thought tore deeply through Aly. She had fought for five years to get here. And today she'd been the worst she could ever remember behind the controls.

"Trayhern?"

Aly turned toward Clay, trying to shore up her shredded defenses to face his evaluation. Forcing herself to meet shore up her shredded defenses to face his evaluation. Forcing herself to meet his eyes, she stood, waiting for the guillotine to drop. "Yes?"

Clay leaned across the cockpit, handing her the clipboard so that she could read his comments and grading. He tried to take the harshness out his voice, noting how pale she'd become as she took the board. "If you've got any disagreement with my analysis, let's talk it over now, before I sign it off."

Taking the board in both hands, Aly tried to focus on his almost illegible scribble. What she cared about most were the four areas that she was graded upon. Her heart pounded once to underscore her disbelief. Clay had given her seventy-five percent in all categories! Aly gasped, looking up at him.

"Well?" he goaded. "You got a problem with that, Trayhern?"

Elation leaked through her terror. Aly knew from being graded for a year at Pensacola that Clay was being generous with her. *Very* generous. She should have dragged a sixty percent, which was a failing grade. Instead he'd given her barely passing marks. Trying to read his scrawl and assessment, there was no indication of personal feelings being involved with his analysis of her abilities today.

"I—no, I don't," she whispered unsteadily.

Clay saw the life come back to her sky-blue eyes as she handed him the clipboard. Color had rushed back to her cheeks. She was excruciatingly vulnerable in that moment, and he had to stop himself from reaching out to caress her cheek. There was gratefulness in her luminous eyes. And that made his heart soar with an incredible sense of elation. And then he saw his dead mother's face waver before him, and he smashed all those fragile new emotions. '

Clay glanced down at his watch. "You've been assigned to Commander Winger's office for collateral duty. He's expecting you any moment. You'd better get going."

Aly nodded, holding her manual tightly against her breasts. "I—right." She wanted to thank him for not failing her. But one look into those sharp gray eyes, and Aly swallowed her thanks.

Watching her go over to a chair to pick up her purse and garrison cap, Clay called, "Be here at 0800 tomorrow morning, Trayhern."

"Yes, sir—" Aly halted and gave him an apologetic shrug for slipping back into student-pilot vernacular. "I mean, I'll be here, Mr. Cantrell."

Grimly, Clay watched her leave. He packed up his manual and clipboard and climbed out of the Link. In the control room, Random handed him his grading sheet. The chief had given her seventy-five percent, too.

"Miss Trayhern was a little nervous," Random told him, as if to defend the percentile grade. "Typical of a young pilot just coming out of Pensacola, wouldn't you say?"

"Typical," Clay agreed, signing off both sheets and handing them back to the chief.

"She's sharp, though," Random continued. "I think once she settles down and realizes no one's out to sink her, she'll catch on fast."

Clay grunted, putting his manual into the briefcase he always carried.

"You want the trainer set up for her tomorrow morning, Mr. Cantrell?"

Placing the garrison cap on his head, Clay nodded. "Yes, I do." He walked to the door and opened it. "Oh, one more thing, chief."

"Yes, sir?"

"I want you to schedule Lieutenant Trayhern into an hour of cockpit training in a P3. Choose any one that's on the line that won't be flown that day. Assign AE Ballard to work with her. He's qualified on preflight, start-up and shutdown procedures. This week, starting Tuesday, have Ballard drill preflight procedures with her."

Random nodded. "She one of those people who do better in the real thing?" he guessed. Some pilots never got used to a Link trainer. And yet in the cockpit of the actual aircraft, those same people performed flawlessly.

"I think so. I'll see you at 1400, chief."

Random nodded. The next student, a green lieutenant just out of Pensacola, was scheduled for that afternoon. "Yes, sir."

Where had the week flown? Clay wondered as he moved up the ladder of P3 number 7, where he knew Aly and Ballard were practicing in the cockpit. It was already Friday afternoon. He slowed his step as he entered the sub hunter parked out in the revetment area. Ballard was in the pilot's seat. Aly was in the copilot's seat. He stood listening to their bantering exchanges, watching her hands fly with knowing ease across the instrument panel. She'd flip a switch here, turn a dial there as Ballard called out each step. After a lousy start earlier in the week, Aly was now moving with typical Navy pilot confidence, her voice firm and sure.

Cantrell almost smiled, settling his hands on his hips, watching and listening. With the morning Link sessions and Ballard working with her every afternoon, Aly was becoming well acquainted with the P3. His heart blossomed with powerful feelings of pride toward her. And just as quickly, Clay tried to push them back down inside himself. Aly invited familiarity. He found himself longing to see her smile. Once, midweek, he'd heard in his office her beautiful laughter pealing down the hallway. It had sent a shaft of hot need through him. Would she ever laugh or smile like that for him?

He doubted it. Clay shoved his hands into his pockets, continuing to watch Ballard and Aly. There was excellent camaraderie between them. They kidded each other between maneuvers. Her laughter was breathy and light, lifting the darkness that haunted Clay. She was sunlight, he decided morosely. Sister of a murderer or not, she reminded him of anything but death.

"Not bad, Miss Trayhern," Dan congratulated Aly. "You know preflight blindfolded."

Aly flushed over his compliment and sat back, relaxing. The P3's windows were large and she could see the blue sky outside. The sun was bright, making the cockpit hot. "Thanks, Dan. You've been a wonderful teacher." She tipped her head in his direction, her eyes twinkling. "I couldn't have done it without you. I still haven't thanked you for asking Mr. Cantrell to let you help me every afternoon."

Dan's red eyebrows arched. "I didn't do anything, Miss Trayhern. That was Mr. Cantrell's idea in the first place."

Stunned, Aly sat up. "It was?"

Dan grinned, closing the large manual that sat on the throttle casing. "Yes, ma'am. I think he realized you relax in the real thing. A lot of pilots do poorly in those trainers. There's just something about them...."

Aly sat there, digesting Dan's answer. So Clay had been responsible for this. Mixed emotions threaded through her. He was so damn cold and distant with her in the Link. She would never have thought he had the sensitivity, much less the insight, to know that she trained better here. Again, he hid so much of his real self that Aly could never hope to understand him. Cantrell didn't want anyone to know anything about him.

"You know," Dan said, breaking into her thoughts, "I'll bet next week Mr. Cantrell might let you fly with us. We've got a training mission coming up next Wednesday. Maybe, if we can get you familiar on start-up and shutdown procedures, he'll give you that opportunity."

Aly rallied. "You think so?" Hope rang strong in her voice, and she didn't try to disguise her enthusiasm.

Dan collected the other manuals, leaning back to relax for a minute. "Don't see why not. Ol' number 7 here is ready to fly again."

"Number 7," Aly murmured softly. She reached over, affectionately patting the top of the instrument panel. "How can you call her that? She's so sleek and beautiful."

Scratching his head, Dan said, "Dunno. I guess you're right. Number 7 sounds pretty detached, doesn't it?"

"I've already given her a name," Aly admitted, watching Dan. He was almost like a big brother to her, and she enjoyed spending time with him.

"Yeah? What?"

"Promise you won't breath a word of it to anyone else, Dan?"

With a grin, he nodded. "Won't say a word, ma'am. Now what kind of name have you christened this gal with?"

Reaching over, Aly ran her fingers across the smooth yoke in front of her. "I call her Gray Lady, because she reminds me of an elegant swan ready to take off in flight."

Dan pursed his lips, giving the name some thought. "I like it, Miss Trayhern." And then he grinned, catching and holding her gaze. "See? I told you that having a woman on board would change things for the better."

Embarrassed because she'd divulged a piece of herself to Dan, Aly muttered, "Oh, I don't know about that. I still haven't met the rest of Mr. Cantrell's crew."

"You will shortly, Miss Trayhern."

Aly gasped, whirling around in the seat. Her eyes moved up...up into the shadowed face of Clay, who stood, his hands on his hips. Instead of finding the dark anger that usually hung in his eyes or in the set of his mouth, Aly saw momentary warmth there instead.

"H-how long have you been here?" she blurted.

Clay moved his gaze to Ballard, who nodded a greeting, unaffected by Clay's unexpected appearance. He returned his attention to Aly. She looked so damned enticing every time she blushed.

"Long enough," he answered.

She didn't dare ask what "long enough" meant. Had he heard her name for the P3? He'd probably use it against her in the future, or ruthlessly spread it around the squadron. Gathering her strewn thoughts, Aly got up. "We're done here, Mr. Cantrell. If you'll excuse me, I'll—"

Clay remained in her path so she couldn't move by him. "Have a seat, Miss Trayhern, we're not quite finished yet."

She didn't like the silky tone in his voice. This was something new. Aly gave Dan a quick look, and he appeared just as mystified.

"Dan, how about giving me my seat?"

"Yes, sir!"

*Oh, no!* Aly shut her eyes. Clay was going to quiz her!

When she reopened her eyes, she noticed a ground crew pulling up in a vehicle outside the aircraft. What was going on?

Clay strapped himself in and barely glanced at her. "Miss Trayhern, I suggest you strap yourself back in."

Dan grinned broadly and knelt behind the throttles. "We going for a ride, sir?" There was enthusiasm in his voice.

"I think Miss Trayhern's ready for her first flight, don't you, Dan?"

Happily, he nodded. "She's an ace at preflight check, sir."

Clay glanced over, positioning the board on his knee. "Let's find out. Okay, Miss Trayhern, you ready to preflight this bird?"

They were going to taxi! Joy leaped through Aly. Learning how to fly a plane consisted of start-up, taxi and, finally, a first flight. Just getting the chance to taxi the P3 was more than Aly dared expect so soon in her training. She stared at Clay, disbelief, she was sure, written all over her face.

"Well?" he drawled.

"I—yes . . . oh, yes, I'm ready, Mr. Cantrell."

Ignoring the tremble of happiness in her voice, Clay nodded and briskly returned to the business at hand. Why should he feel light and pleased at her reaction? Her blue eyes literally danced. Getting to see her smile for the first time since their fated meeting made Clay realize just how unhappy Aly had been the past week. And just how much he longed to see that smile again.

Minutes flew by for Aly. Before she knew it, preflight was complete. She'd performed it perfectly. Her heart was pounding as Clay slowly took her through start-up procedure. Given the thumbs-up by the ground crew, he leaned over to start the first turbo-prop engine on the P3.

Aly held her breath as his Nomex-gloved fingers depressed the start button on engine number three. The whirling whine of the prop began. She felt a shiver run through Gray Lady as the engine caught and moved smoothly to life. Clay repeated the procedure, starting engine number two, on her side of the aircraft.

"Okay, you start the last two," he ordered.

Eagerly, Aly repeated his steps. A thrill moved through her as all four of the P3's engines moved in rpm unison. A smile curved her lips, and she looked over at Clay.

"She feels good. Solid."

Clay understood what Aly meant. The P3 was a reliable plane with heart. "Ready to taxi?"

Aly nodded. Her heart was in her throat as Cantrell waved the ground crew off to one side.

"Use throttle two and three in the center there, to taxi her. Bring up power slow, and watch your rpm gauges."

Placing her gloved hand over the two center throttles, Aly looked to her right and then left. "Clear to taxi?"

"Roger, clear," Clay confirmed. He felt Aly's unbridled excitement and it lifted his gloom. Her face was flushed with delight, her eyes shining with life. God, but she was excruciatingly beautiful. He tore his gaze from her profile, keeping his booted feet near the rudders.

Aly gently applied right rudder, inching the throttles forward, increasing rpm just a bit. *Come on, Gray Lady, work with me. Give yourself to me...please....*

The P3 rolled smoothly out of its revetment berth, moving slowly down the concrete ramp, the turboprop engines whining.

"You're doing fine," Clay assured her.

Another thrill went through Aly and she nodded, keeping her attention focused between the ramp and the engine instruments.

As they neared the end of the taxi area, Aly began to ease back on the throttles and apply rudder brakes to slow down the aircraft.

"What are you doing?" Clay asked.

She gave him a confused look. "Well, you just wanted me to taxi it, didn't you?"

"I said we're going to fly."

Her heart leaped. "Fly?"

It was impossible not to smile. Clay placed his hand over hers, easing the throttles a bit more forward. "Let's take Gray Lady to the end of the runway, and I'll walk you through a takeoff. We'll take a few circuits of the flight pattern and some touch and gos. That will be plenty for you today."

Aly wanted to cry with exultation. That one smile, and the thawing of his gray eyes, made her heart somersault with euphoria. His hand was firm, guiding hers, as he taught her how to delicately monitor the engine throttles. And he had heard her call the plane Gray Lady! But he hadn't been disgusted by it. There was, for the first time, a hint of admiration and respect toward her in his voice.

It was a dream, Aly told herself, as they sat at the end of the runway, ready to take the bird aloft. Her hand just barely spanned the four throttles as they sat there, Clay's hand firmly across her own. For once, she was glad he was in physical contact with her. She needed his assurance and support.

"Okay, everything checks out," Clay told her, catching her attention out of the corner of his eye. "I'm going to let you push the rudders and keep her nose down the centerline. You make the actual takeoff. I'll keep my hand over yours to teach you the art of talking to these throttles."

Aly nodded, licking her lower lip. "Roger." Her voice was trembling. But it wasn't out of fear, it was out of anticipation.

"We've got clearance. Let's roll, Miss Trayhern. Rotation speed is 120 miles per hour."

"Roger. Starting to roll . . ."

Aly's world narrowed to awareness of her boots delicately pressed against the rudders to keep the plane's nose on the centerline of the airstrip. Clay's hand guided hers, and he pushed all four throttles slowly forward until they were against the fire wall. The P3's four engines were fairly screaming around them. Gray Lady vibrated, as if she were a thoroughbred trembling to break the gate and race her heart out.

"Releasing rudders," Aly called out.

"Roger, we're rolling." Clay kept his left hand near the yoke, but didn't touch it. He would not interfere in her takeoff unless it became critical. It was important that Aly be able to have a clear victory in her battle to attain copilot status. Clay grinned to himself at the way she played the aircraft. She had it. She had the right stuff.

Gray Lady moved faster and faster down the strip, the huge blades cutting through the invisible air. She lightened as takeoff speed approached. Wind moved powerfully beneath her long, graceful wings. Aly felt the aircraft strain to break contact with the earth. She kept her hand on the yoke, and the nose remained on the ground. The moment the speed gauge hit 120, she gently eased back on the column.

They were airborne! Aly gasped as the P3 launched skyward in one graceful leap, the engine whine deepening as they climbed.

"Good takeoff," Clay told her in his normal IP tone. "Now level off at fifteen hundred feet and make a ninety-degree left turn."

She listened to his steady, calm voice. Gray Lady was incredibly responsive to her every command! So much more sensitive than any other plane she'd ever flown. Wanting to please Clay because he was going beyond the call of duty and giving her extra training, Aly worked hard.

Clay had her lightly hold the yoke, keep her feet on the rudders and her hand on the throttles as he showed her how to land the P3. It was a light, three-point landing, kissing the deck like a lover.

"Lift her off," he ordered Aly the instant the wheels touched the airstrip.

The second time around, Aly got her chance to land the aircraft for the first time. With the long, extended tail boom, the pilot couldn't come in nose high, or the boom would scrape against the airstrip, causing major damage to the aircraft. A three-wheel landing was demanding in comparison to the normal two-wheel landing of other types of planes. Aly worked the rudders, jockeying the P3 into the correct landing angle. Clay's hand covered hers on the throttles, helping her to monitor the incoming speed.

They were down! The P3 bumped, but not hard. Aly didn't have time to do any celebrating, because Clay immediately ordered her to take off again.

After the third landing, Aly had a good sense of positioning with the P3, and the fourth was her best. She grinned.

Clay nodded. "Nice landing, Miss Trayhern. All right, let's taxi Gray Lady back to her berth. She's worked well for us today."

"Nice landing!" Dan Ballard said, giving Aly a slap on the back as they taxied back to the revetment area.

Flushed with victory, she looked at both men after they had parked and the chocks had been placed beneath each wheel by the ground crew. "Thanks," she whispered, meaning it. "Between the two of you, I don't have any choice but to become a good copilot."

Ballard got up from his position behind the throttles. He chuckled and placed his set of earphones to one side. "Miss Trayhern, you aren't going to be just a good copilot, you're going to be a great one."

Stunned by Dan's assessment, Aly blinked. She unstrapped, nervously wondering what Clay thought of her performance.

"Isn't that right, Mr. Cantrell?" Dan asked, standing in the aisle, waiting for them.

Clay tried to ignore the bliss in Aly's eyes. He'd never seen her so joyful. More than anything, he wanted to drown in those azure eyes shining with gold highlights. Each of her breathy laughs he'd absorbed like a starving man. "Yeah, she's going to be a good addition to the crew, Dan," he said, climbing out of the seat and straightening up in the interior of the aircraft.

Nothing could dampen Aly's spirits as she got up and followed the two men out. Once on the concrete, she turned and reached up, patting the P3 with great

affection. *Thanks,* she silently told the stalwart aircraft.

Ballard had gone on to the hangar. But as Aly
turned, she saw Clay standing there, an odd look on
his face. Avoiding his piercing look, she walked over
to him. "I just wanted to thank her for giving us such
a good flight."

"I see." Clay checked his normally long stride so
that she wouldn't have to run to keep up with him.

The wind was blowing off the marshes, lifting
strands of her red hair. Aly brushed several from her
eyes, still breathless over the flight. "I know you
probably think it's strange to name an aircraft or think
of it as a living thing, but I do."

"I never said I disagreed with you."

Aly laughed softly, her step light. "Then you don't
mind if I call her Gray Lady?"

Clay shook his head. Part of him wanted this heady
moment to last forever. The other part of him said it
wasn't right: Aly's brother had cold-bloodedly murdered Stephen. He studied Aly's upturned face. Was
she a traitor, too? Would she cut and run when the
chips were down? How would she handle the nerve-
racking tension of hunting a Soviet sub, flying fifty
feet above the grasping fingers of a fickle ocean?

"I just wonder, Trayhern, if you can stand the heat
in the kitchen. Your brother couldn't." He saw her
eyes narrow with sudden and unexpected pain. "Today, you did okay flying. But what will you do when
things get tight? Will you run? Flip out? Break under
the strain? What?"

Aly hung her head, wrestling with incredible anguish. Her earlier joy shattered like glass beneath a

sledgehammer. She looked back up at Clay, wondering if he honestly felt that way. Or was she just too much a reminder of the past, every new experience bringing out some facet of his old memories? She drew to a halt, holding his bleak gray gaze.

"You think I'm a coward, don't you?" she demanded softly.

"I don't know what to think of you," Clay admitted. "One member of your family ran when the chips were down. How do I know you won't, too?"

Defiantly, Aly placed her hands on her hips, her voice riddled with anger. "I guess we're both going to find out, aren't we, Mr. Cantrell?"

Clay's shoulders slumped in sudden exhaustion. He didn't want to fight with her, but there was no other way with them. "Sooner or later, we will."

Aly's mouth tightened. "Thanks for the ride today, Cantrell. At least you know I won't lose my nerve on a simple takeoff and landing. That ought to make you sleep better at night!" And she stormed off toward the hangar, fighting the hot tears that threatened to fall.

## Chapter Five

"Stuck with the duty on a Friday night, Miss Trayhern?"

Aly looked up from behind the duty officer's desk. It was five o'clock, and Dan Ballard, like nearly everyone else, was ready to go home. She smiled.

"Afraid so, Dan."

"It's a lousy Friday night, anyway. April rains, and all." He scowled. "I suppose you're gonna study that manual in front of you?"

"Right again. You know me too well."

The red-haired engineer grinned. "Four months in Gray Lady with you has helped, ma'am." He opened the door. "Hope it's a quiet watch for you. I'll see you Monday morning."

"Roger that, Dan," Aly agreed. She watched the lanky engineer quietly shut the door. Through the office window, she could see the cavernous inside of Hangar One. A number of P3s, in for general maintenance, stood silently.

Had four months really flown by? Aly had lost track of time, buried in learning the art of flying the P3 and nonstop studying of so many manuals concerned with sub hunting. Just a week ago, she'd been approved for copilot status. Now she'd be flying every mission with Clay and his crew. Happiness simmered in Aly as she leafed through the first pages of the manual on sonobuoys. *I've made it.* Aly savored the thought. Through four months of hell with Clay, she'd made it, despite their impasse over the issue of Morgan.

*Clay...* Closing her eyes, she pictured his face before her. Her dad had been right; Clay had lost most of his virulent anger toward her. By the end of the first month, the worst of the snipes and barbs had ended. The more she'd proved she could fly, and fly well, the less vitriolic he'd become. Still, he would take shots at her from time to time. He didn't trust her to come through in a crisis; it was that simple.

Sighing, Aly stared down at the manual, not seeing the words. For three months Clay had been a fortress of silence. He never traded a smile or a joke with her as he did with the rest of his crew. They worshiped the ground Clay walked on because of his unique abilities to relate easily with each man. In the cockpit, he was cool and emotionless with her, and that hurt.

"Let's face it, Trayhern, you like him and he hates you." Still, she stood in awe of Clay, because in the cockpit, he never allowed his personal feelings to interfere with their demanding teamwork while flying.

Sometimes she could have sworn she saw burning longing in his eyes when she looked up unexpectedly at him. Sometimes it was the softening of his mouth. Little things . . . but each time, it made her heart ache. Dammit, she *liked* Cantrell! There wasn't much not to like about the man, Aly decided glumly. He was a good officer, a fair man, and unlike what Starbuck's malicious gossip had suggested, Clay wasn't losing it behind the yoke. He was one of the finest pilots she'd had the honor of flying with, and he was teaching her to strive for that same level of skill.

Anger simmered through Aly as she thought of Starbuck. From Dan, she'd found out why Gray Lady had sustained landing gear damage. Clay had landed her with one engine on fire in the middle of a rare thunderstorm over the Bay Area. Dan had told her the truth—that without Cantrell's years of experience as a pilot, his extraordinary skill and sheer bravado, they would have crashed. At the last possible second, with an in-flight emergency in progress, there had been a wind shear across the airstrip they were to land on. The P3 dived earthward, and according to Dan's account, Clay had grabbed the yoke, slammed hard left rudder and settled the aircraft in just like a jet landing on a carrier. If it hadn't been for his carrier landing experience, they would have crashed. They'd walked away from that one, all twelve of them, with only a damaged landing strut.

"Hey!"

Aly's head snapped up. Starbuck, in his khaki uniform, had poked his head through the opened door. "What do you want?" she asked unencouragingly.

With a genial smile, Starbuck entered the office and closed the door. He settled the garrison cap at a cocky angle on his head. "Just dropping by to say hello to the prettiest lady at Moffett."

"Stow it, Jeff. I'm wise to you." The words came out with disgust, but Aly didn't care. If she had believed anything the fighter jock had said about Clay, it would have been dangerous to her own flight career. She would have mistrusted Clay at the controls, creating even more strain between them.

"Aw, come on, Alyssa. If I didn't know better, I'd think you're turning into a sourpuss just like your lover boy."

Rage snapped through her, and she raised her lashes, glaring at him. "That's uncalled for, Starbuck. Or is that the latest nasty gossip you're passing around the base?"

Starbuck shrugged. "So you're not denying it?"

"What?"

"You two are lovers?"

"Stop being ridiculous! I fly with Cantrell, I don't sleep with him!"

Jeff rubbed his chin, inspecting her closely. "I don't know, Alyssa . . . you've been on board here for four months and you don't have a boyfriend that any of us can tell. The only dude you spend time with is Cantrell. . . ."

"Starbuck, why don't you toddle on over to the O Club like you do every Friday night, and get drunk? It's what you do best."

His brown eyes danced with amusement. "You're so much fun to bait, Alyssa. Hey! Guess who I saw pulling up over at the O Club earlier?"

She sat back in the chair, her arms crossed over her chest. How someone so handsome could have such a mean streak in him was beyond Aly. Starbuck's winning smile and geniality were a cover for his ruthless, competitive nature. "I have a feeling you're going to tell me, whether I want to know or not."

Opening the door, Jeff said, "Your lover, Cantrell. Didn't you know he hits the bottle every Friday night? Sits in a dark corner and nurses a couple rounds of Scotch, looking moody. He must be pining away for you...."

"Get out of here!" Alyssa said, rising to her feet. "And take your filthy mouth with you. I'm tired of listening to it, Starbuck."

He threw her a salute. "Later, Alyssa." And he disappeared into the passageway, whistling gaily.

"Damn him," Aly ground out, slamming the manual shut. Starbuck was dangerous. He was a gossiper, and it could hurt her career if anyone believed half the garbage he spread around the station. Ever since she'd made it clear she wouldn't go out with him, Starbuck had waged a campaign to get even.

Going into the back room, which had a cot for sleeping purposes, and a coffee maker, Aly poured herself a cup. After she calmed down, her heart and mind zeroed in on the fact that Clay spent Friday nights drinking over at the O Club. He was so damned alone. He wore those walls around himself like a good friend, she thought angrily. What was he running from? And why did that haunted look always hover in his dark gray eyes?

Clay blinked twice before he could read the hands on his watch. The corner where he sat was dark, and the luminous dial wavered in front of him. He had to stare at it a long time before realizing it was 0100. Good, he wasn't feeling any more pain. No, that wasn't it. He wasn't feeling any more longing for Aly.

A silly smile stretched across his face as he leaned the chair onto its back legs. He watched with disinterest as pilots hustled the women who frequented the club, wanting to snag a fighter jock. The bar was crowded—wall-to-wall bodies—and a haze of smoke hung over the place. Tonight, Clay realized in some dim portion of his slowly functioning mind, he'd really drunk far too much. He watched the single women in miniskirts hunting the eligible pilots. It was a game he never wanted to play. And that was all it was: a game.

Aly's face hovered in front of him. Savagely he rubbed his eyes, trying to erase her image. Dammit! As drunk as he was, she *still* haunted him. Frustrated, he tipped his head back and rested it against the walnut paneling behind him.

How the hell could he reconcile that he liked her, wanted her in every way, with the fact that she was the sister of a murderer? Trying to ignore her breathy laughter and the gold highlights in her blue eyes when she was happy was impossible. The past four months had turned into a twisted sort of hell for him. He'd thought it would be easy to hate Aly. Instead, he was drawn so damn powerfully to her. Her easygoing nature had a quiet, calming effect on everyone during tense cockpit situations, and she had an innate ability to get along with the crew. Clay found himself unable to remain immune to her any longer.

Aly was a thoughtful, caring person by nature, Clay sourly admitted. How many times had he been sitting in the left-hand seat and she'd come back on board after the visual inspection of the aircraft? The men at the consoles all had greetings for her when she boarded. Clay watched enviously as Aly bestowed a sunny smile here, a pat on the shoulder there, and shared a joke with someone else. And then he'd watch the joy dissolve from her face as she approached the cockpit. Aly, the *real* Aly, would die before him.

She would take the right-hand seat, her face closed, her voice devoid of feeling, and begin working in tandem with him. And he'd discovered that hate wasn't the comfortable companion he'd thought it would be. It had been his fault: he'd come out firing the first salvos at Aly. God knew, she'd tried a number of times in the first two months to make amends and establish a truce between them.

But Clay hadn't allowed it. And he didn't know why. Every excruciating minute spent with Aly made him feel the sharpened hunger just to have her smile at him. He ached to kiss those beautifully formed lips. Were they as soft as he imagined they were? As soft as her heart? There was so much tenderness in Aly. Clay saw it in little ways, important ways.

Dan Ballard had turned thirty-five a month ago, and Aly had gone to great lengths to hold a surprise birthday party for him. And then when Sam Henderson's wife had a baby, it had been Aly who'd come around gathering money for a gift for the mother and new daughter. Little things counted a lot with her, he was discovering, and Clay liked her for it. She was family-oriented and loyal to family. And the crew was her extended family. All except for him . . .

The pain throbbing in his chest was growing as his thoughts centered on Aly. Surprised that the liquor hadn't dulled his pain as it usually did, Clay pushed himself unceremoniously to his feet. He staggered, falling against the wall to steady himself. Dizziness nearly felled him. He saw the bar manager, Bob Hudson, give him a concerned look, watching from beneath his bushy gray eyebrows. Pressing both hands flat against the unyielding surface, Clay waited until the worst of the vertigo had passed. Then he stumbled out of the corner and raised his hand in farewell to Hudson. The manager nodded a good-night.

The rain had stopped, leaving the air fragrant with newly sprouted grass and leaves. Clay inhaled, weaving drunkenly toward his Corvette in the parking lot. Aly had the duty tonight. . . . He groaned. Where had that thought come from? How many times had he almost driven to Hangar One to talk with her when she had the duty? And how many times had he stopped himself?

Leaning heavily against his black Corvette, Clay fumbled to find the keys in his pocket. The asphalt gleamed beneath the lights. The ground blurred and that same tidal wave of dizziness hit him again. He threw his hands outward, trying to steady himself, but his feet got tangled and he slipped, hitting the pavement hard. Gasping, he lay there several minutes, completely disoriented.

*Stupid,* he thought with disgust as he found himself sprawled across the wet asphalt, flat on his face. God, if anyone saw him like this, he'd never live it down. *Drank too damn much. Got to get out of here....* As he rolled over and propped himself into a sitting position against the sports car, he shut his eyes. Aly! *God, I need to talk with you so much it hurts. I need—*

"Hey, this is a pretty picture!"

Clay dragged his eyes open. There, in the shadowy light, stood Starbuck. "Get the hell out of here," he mumbled.

But Starbuck came and squatted in front of him, grinning lopsidedly. "Well, well, what do you know. You finally drank too much, eh, Cantrell? Trying to drink away your frustration, buddy? Won't Alyssa give you any?"

Anger flared to life in Clay's foggy mind. "I hope like hell you say that when I'm sober, Starbuck."

Grinning and rising to his feet, Starbuck laughed. "You won't even remember our little chat come tomorrow morning, Cantrell." And he ambled back toward the O Club.

The phone rang, waking Aly. She threw off the lightweight wool blanket and blindly reached for the phone next to the cot.

"Duty Office, Lieutenant Trayhern speaking."

"This is Bob Hudson, bar manager of the O Club, Lieutenant."

She groaned, looking at her watch. It was 0130. "Yes?" What could he possibly want with her?

"I just got a report from one of my people that Lieutenant Cantrell is drunk out in the O Club parking lot. He's so intoxicated that he can't walk, much less drive. I know he flies with VP 46, that's why I called. If shore patrol comes by and finds him lying out there, he'll be in a lot of hot water. You'd better get over here and rescue his rear before they do."

"Thanks, Mr. Hudson. I'll get over there right away." Damn! Struggling into her sensible black shoes, Aly stood. She was wearing her black jacket and slacks. Throwing her black tie around the collar of her white blouse, she headed for the front office. She didn't want Clay picked up by the shore patrol, the station's military police. The damned fool! Grabbing the keys to the duty officer vehicle, she left a message with the the officer of the day at the main gate, informing him that she'd be away from the office for about fifteen minutes.

The gray vehicle started right up. The rain had stopped, and Aly spotted a few stars between the clouds as she drove around the end of the runway, heading toward the central portion of Moffett Field.

To her dismay, she found Clay sleeping in a slouched position against his sports car. He looked like a rumpled Raggedy Andy, and her heart went out to him. His khaki uniform had huge water stains across it, indicating where he'd fallen to the asphalt. As Aly got out, her alarm increased. He had skinned his elbow pretty badly, with blood drying on his lower arm and fingers. But he didn't appear to be feeling any pain.

Stooping, Aly placed her hand on his shoulder, giving him a gentle shake. "Clay? Clay, wake up!"

Clay realized he was dreaming. A smile tugged at the corners of his mouth. This was nice: Aly's husky voice so close to his ear. He actually felt the warmth of her hand on his shoulder. God, but she felt good. Inhaling deeply, he smelled that fragrance she always wore.

"Clay! Dammit, wake up! You can't sit out in the middle of the parking lot like this."

Drowsily, he dragged his lashes upward. Aly's shadowed and concerned face danced before him. "Aly?"

She winced. He'd never called her that before. "You're drunker than hell, Cantrell."

"I-is that really you?" And then he grinned, lifting his bloodied hand toward her to find out.

Aly caught his hand, placing it firmly on his thigh. "Yes, it's me, you damn fool. Can you get up? Walk?"

His brain wasn't functioning at all. He scowled, looking up into her face. Her eyes were so large. She was so pretty. "Wh-what's going on?"

"Bob Hudson called me over at the duty office," and she explained the rest of it to him. Grimly, Aly slipped her arm around his back, placing her hand beneath his arm. "If shore patrol finds us, you'll get written up so fast it'll make that head of yours spin faster than it's already going. Come on, push up with your legs, I've got to get you the hell out of here."

Her words ran together in Clay's drugged mind. He barely comprehended one-quarter of what she was saying, but Aly's arm felt good around him, and he tried to follow her angry orders, pushing upward. He rose unsteadily, his weight resting heavily on her. Dizziness assailed him.

"God, Cantrell," Aly groaned, staggering beneath his weight, "you're too damned heavy! Straighten up! I can't carry you!"

Trying, Clay stood on his own two feet, wavering badly. He grinned at her. "See? I made it."

"Don't be so proud of yourself, jet jock. The next task is to get you into the duty vehicle."

Happiness flittered through Clay. This was all a dream. It had to be! Smiling gallantly, he gestured toward the vehicle. "Lead the way, ma'am!"

It was a tussle getting Clay into the passenger seat. He was like limp spaghetti, and Aly had to keep snapping orders at him to get him to react. After placing the seat belt around him, she climbed in. The front of her uniform was smeared with oil, water and dark blood. Angry over Clay's stupid decision to get drunk, she drove back to Hangar One.

"Where we going?" Clay slurred.

"I'm putting you on the duty office cot where you can sleep off your drunk, Cantrell." She glared over at him. "You pulled a stupid stunt. What if Starbuck caught you out in the parking lot. Aren't you concerned that he'll spread it around Moffett?"

Chuckling, Clay shook his head. "He did—I think.... Besides, that bastard wouldn't dare. He knows I'd clean his clock for 'im...."

"Boys," Aly muttered between clenched teeth. "You're all little boys. Clay, I could just strangle you! This is a bad image for you, for all of us. Just what the hell did you think you were doing?"

Her voice was low with fury, but Clay absorbed the huskiness of it. He closed his eyes, fumbling for her hand. Once he found it, he gave it a squeeze. "I was just trying to forget, Aly."

Her heart lurching in her breast, Aly pulled her hand free of his, concentrating on driving. Clay's action startled her. "Forget what?"

With a dramatic sigh, Clay made a wobbly gesture toward her. "You, of course."

Shock replaced her anger. "Me?" Of course, he hated her twenty-four hours a day. It was probably eating him up inside to have to work with her.

"Yeah," he answered thickly, staring over at her profile. "You..."

Real pain wove through Aly. "Look, we're just going to have to put our past behind us, Clay. I know you hate me. You hate my family, but you can't keep resurrecting it like this. If you're drinking every Friday night to escape the fact that you hate me, then—"

"I drink to forget you...."

She traded a quick glance with him. Strands of hair dipped across his brow, and she could see that haunted look back in his eyes once again. "I know," she answered softly. "Hate does terrible things to people, Cantrell. I wish I knew how to get you to turn it off toward me."

"N-no..." He lapsed into unconsciousness, limp against the seat.

"Great!" Aly muttered. She, too, had gone on the occasional bender over the years just to relieve the terrible tension she'd lived under. But she'd quickly learned that drinking was no escape. Judging from

Cantrell's condition, he'd really be in the hurt locker for the rest of this night and well into tomorrow. Well, she had the duty until noon tomorrow. Maybe by then she could get him sober enough to drive back to his own apartment and lie around for the rest of the weekend recovering from his monumental stupidity.

The next time Clay regained consciousness, he found himself sprawled across a cot. The overhead light hurt his eyes and he squinted. "Hey," he called weakly, "what's going on?"

Aly leaned over him, still breathing hard from practically carrying him from the car into the office and to the cot. "Shut up, Cantrell." She jerked his tie open at his neck and undid the top button of his long-sleeved khaki shirt. When she saw his eyes dilate and settle on her, she softened her voice. "You're dead drunk, Clay. Just lie still, okay? You're safe here."

Safe... Aly's words flowed across him. She was leaning over him, her face inches from his as she worked the knot of the tie loose, and then began to unbutton his shirt. "Aly?"

Aly's fingers froze over the second button. Risking a look at him, she felt her heart give way. Clay's face was vulnerable-looking, without any of the previous walls to hide his real feelings, his real emotions. She tried to brace herself for his hatred, his anger. "What is it this time, Clay?"

"D-did I ever tell you how pretty you are?" His voice was thick, the words mumbled badly. He smiled into her shadowed blue eyes. "I know you hate my guts, but I think you're the prettiest lady I've ever run into...."

Aly's fingers trembled, and she couldn't get the second button undone. Her voice faltering, she whispered, "I've never hated you, Clay. Ever."

Clay scowled. As drunk as he was, he felt Aly's fingers trembling against his chest. "You—don't hate me?"

"No. Never did." She nailed him with a dark look. "You hate *me*, remember?"

He lapsed back into semi-consciousness, relief surging through him. "You don't hate me...."

"Cantrell, you're one sick puppy. Just lie there and shut up! I want to get this shirt off you so I can look at the cut on your elbow."

Once his shirt was unbuttoned, Aly moved around the cot and slipped her arm beneath his shoulders. "Sit up, Clay."

He was weak, and grateful for her help. "You're one hell of a person," he told her as she helped him sit up and take off the shirt.

"God, I don't know if I can take all these compliments from you, Cantrell. The past four months you've had nothing but bad things to say about me." She dropped the shirt over a chair and pulled the first-aid kit from a nearby drawer. Her heart wrenched when she sat down, facing Clay. He looked so lost and confused. Without thinking, she brushed errant strands of hair off his perspiring brow.

"I have plenty of compliments for you," he confided softly.

Examining his right elbow, Aly grimaced. "Well, if you do, you've been keeping them all to yourself, Cantrell. Hold still, this is going to hurt," she said, and she gently applied a warm, soapy cloth to the bloody laceration.

A dull pain drifted up his arm, but Clay was barely aware of it. She was so close, so fragrant and warm. "You make my pain go away...."

Aly tried to steel herself against his admission. "That's all we have between us, isn't it, Clay? Pain? Bad memories? I don't see how I make your pain go away. These past four months, you've made me out to be the biggest pain in existence."

He swallowed hard, focusing on her gentle touch, the warmth of her fingers as she held his arm to doctor it up. "That's—my fault. I was looking for a fight."

"I know you were. And you know something, Clay?"

"What?" He longed to reach over and stroke her hair—to find out if it was really as silky as he thought it might be.

Aly brushed some hair from her eyes. Being this close to Clay, knowing how much he affected her, was sheer agony. And now his voice was like balm to her shredded emotions. They were talking, they were close, even if he was drunk. Come morning, Aly was sure he wouldn't remember any of this. He'd wake up just as cold and distant as before. She hungered for what she instinctively knew they could share with each other. But Clay's natural warmth and dark voice were what she craved, and right now he was giving them to her. "I'm tired of fighting you," she admitted quietly.

Reaching out with his other hand, Clay settled it on the crown of her hair, running his fingers through the clean, coppery strands. "I know," he whispered. Her head snapped up, her eyes wide and startled. Giving her a slight smile, Clay admitted, "So am I."

Taking in a shaky breath, Aly closed her eyes. She'd never dared dream of this! Of Clay touching her as if she were some priceless, fragile object to be cared for. Each trembling touch of his fingers across her hair sent a widening ache through her. Her mind screamed at her to stop him. He was drunk, and therefore not in charge of his emotions. But each caress was healing to Aly. She held his injured arm between her hands and bowed her head, unable to speak, only to feel.

"Look," Clay muttered, sliding his fingers across Aly's high cheekbone, feeling the softness of her flesh, "I don't hate you, okay?" He lifted her chin, stunned by the tears that made her eyes luminous. He saw such pain in them that he winced. "It was my fault, Aly...all of it...." He cupped her cheek, holding her wavering stare. "I couldn't help but hate you, hate what your name stood for."

"I—I know. And I never blamed you for it, Clay." His touch was incredibly light, but she felt the warmth of his palm and saw the tenderness burning deep in his eyes.

He shook his head. "I still can't separate you from the past. As much as I want to, I can't. At least...not yet. But I'm trying."

She nodded mutely, her heart tearing open a little more. "I—I understand—" A sob caught in her throat, strangling off the rest of her reply.

Clay watched two tears streak down her pale, freckled cheeks. He groaned, understanding the volume of the pain he'd caused her. "I'm sorry...so sorry...." He leaned forward, drawing her to him.

Aly's breath snagged at Clay's unexpected move. When his mouth, warm and inviting, moved across her parted lips, all of her anguish dissolved. His mouth was tentative, testing her, relishing her softness. Her mind screamed at her to push away from him. Her heart, which had bled so long without any real sustenance, pleaded with her to consummate the kiss.

A groan started deep within Clay as Aly's lips grew pliant and willing beneath his hungry exploration. God, she tasted so sweet! So warm and feminine. Lost in the texture and liquid treasure of her mouth, Clay slid his arm around her shoulders, drawing her against him. This was what he'd dreamed of for so long! That luscious mouth of hers moving in hungry accord with his own, matching, meeting his escalating desire.

Hunger swept through Aly. Real hunger. She drowned in the heated strength of his mouth cajoling hers. All her pain, their pain, disappeared in that one molten moment torn out of time. As his tongue caressed her lower lip, she trembled with the real fire raging within her. His breath was hot and moist against her cheek, and with her fingers, she caressed the thick, black hair at his nape. Oh, God, Clay was so strong and yet tender with her. His kiss seared her soul, brought her into wild, yearning life and shattered every barrier that had ever been erected between them.

"Sweet," he whispered against her wet lips. "You're so sweet and kind, Aly." He kissed each corner of her mouth. "I'd die to see you smile. I die every time I hear your laughter." Clay held her close, kissing her damp lashes, inhaling her own special womanly scent.

"I'm starving for you...I need you, my sweet woman of fire...."

The duty office was quiet once again, all lights extinguished. Only the shadows and dim light from the hangar stabbed weakly through the window. Aly sat at the desk, staring into the darkness, her heart an open, bleeding wound. For the past three hours, she'd sat there alone, thinking...feeling.

Her arms wrapped around herself because she was feeling nakedly vulnerable after Clay's kiss, Aly tried to sort through the emotions he'd unleashed within her. It was impossible, she decided bleakly. Reaching up, she touched her lips gently, remembering Clay's powerful kiss, which had brought her to brightly burning life. His woman of fire... The words haunted her, taunted her, teased her. If only she could be! If only...

But reality told her differently. It was nearly 0500. Soon sunrise would come, and with daylight would come the harsh truth. Clay would wake from his drunken stupor, remembering neither what he'd said to her nor their kiss. He'd go on treating her just as before. Rubbing her aching brow, Aly let the tears fall unhindered. She sniffed, taking another tissue from the box she'd set on the corner of the desk. How much stock could she put in Clay's drunken admission? Did he really not hate her any longer? Was he just as tired of their battle as she was?

Exhausted, Aly raised her tearstained face, staring sightlessly out the window. Worst of all, she had discovered in that sweet moment out of time that she was in love with Clay Cantrell. And that discovery hurt worse than any other. How it had happened, when it had happened, Aly couldn't say. Maybe it had happened on their first meeting. Who knew? Pressing her hand against her eyes, Aly cried softly for herself and for Clay. He would never know of her love. He would never accept her love. Love couldn't turn hatred around. But this one tender, searching kiss had ripped away the truth that lay in her heart: she loved him. Unequivocally. And that was something she'd have to bear the rest of her life alone.

At 0600 Clay regained consciousness and got sick. Aly awakened from her restless slumber, head resting in her arms on the desk. Turning on the light to the bunk room, she found him in the bathroom. All her fears, her apprehension melted when she found him leaning weakly against the basin, pale and shaky.

"Hold on," she whispered, grabbing a cloth and wetting it. Her heart twinged with fear when he lifted his head, his dark eyes upon her.

He said nothing as she gently wiped his nose and mouth as a mother would her child's. She got him a cup of water, and he took it in his shaking hand.

"Slosh it around in your mouth and spit it out," she told him, keeping her arm around him. He was incredibly weak, and she strengthened her grip to steady him as he followed her directions.

"Good," she soothed, taking the cup from his hand. "Come on, you need to get back to bed."

Clay placed his arm around Aly's small shoulders, leaning heavily upon her. His mind spun, and he was totally disoriented. "Where?" he managed to rasp, resting his head against her soft hair.

Aly told him, guiding him back to the cot. His uniform was soaked with sweat, and he was shivering. "You've really tied one on," she muttered.

Collapsing back on the cot, Clay shut his eyes, and the room spun wildly. He threw an arm across them. "I—don't remember coming here...."

Aly tucked him in. "With as much as you drank, I'm surprised you even remember your name."

He was feeling too sick to respond. After she shut off the light, he muttered, "Thanks..." and fell back into a deep sleep.

The next time Clay awoke, clarity was there. The room was quiet, and his gaze moved slowly toward the entrance. The door leading into the duty office was open. His mouth tasted like mothballs, and the pain at his temples was like massive hammers striking blows inside his head. It was agony to move.

Slowly events of the night before trickled through his clogged mind. He lay very still, vividly remembering his conversation with Aly. And their kiss. He groaned softly. Sweet God in heaven, he'd kissed her! The entire sequence of events came back—every feeling, every nuance of emotion shared between them. His chest felt constricted, as if he were going to have a cardiac arrest. But he was stripped of his own armor and defense, and all he could do was feel...feel those powerful emotions sweeping through him as savagely as a dam bursting.

There was no hate toward Aly left in him. Just the opposite, Clay admitted haltingly to himself. The luminous look in her blue eyes last night had told him everything. There was only love between them, not hate. And if he was any judge of their fiery, breathtaking kiss, she wanted him, needed him, as much as he did her.

A ragged sigh escaped him. *What a mess. A miserable mess!* Clay couldn't find it within himself to overcome the last hurdle that stood between them: he could never forget that Aly's brother had murdered Stephen. The fact loomed like a ghost in his mind and heart every time he was with her. She didn't deserve any of this, his heart whispered.

Dragging his arm away from his eyes, Clay stared up at the ceiling. Aly was a casualty of the war, just as he was. She carried ghosts just as he did. But they were on opposite sides. Sides that could never meet and bury the sword. But he loved her, dammit! And Clay knew she cared for him. No one, not even Aly, deserved that kind of sentence.

Clay knew what had to be done. He would protect Aly the only way he knew how, and that was to continue the charade. Let her think that he remembered nothing of the night before, their conversation or the kiss. With time, Aly's affection for him would wither on the vine of their relationship. He loved her enough to free her from the past that would always haunt him. Never again would she suspect his true feelings for her. That way, she would be free to find someone who could truly make her happy. And God knew, she deserved a little happiness after the hell he'd put her through.

## Chapter Six

I hate September weather," Dan griped, settling down behind the throttles.

Aly went through the automatic motions of preflight with Clay. Six months ago, she'd sweated out the procedure. Now it was second nature. "Why, Dan?"

"Typhoon season down south along the Baja where we've been flying one too many missions."

"I see." Aly began engine start-up at Clay's nod. In the nine months she'd been part of his crew, they'd melded into a smoothly functioning team.

"You don't have to sweat it today, Dan," Clay said, snapping off a salute to the chief ground crewman standing outside the port window. "We're just taking Gray Lady out for a spin to test this new engine."

Dan nodded happily. "Okay by me. There's a typhoon raging in Baja right now. I want no part of it."

Aly grinned at the chief engineer. "You're hoping we don't get called out for a mission in the next five days, is that it?" P3s flew in all kinds of weather, and Aly knew from grim experience that flying below fifty feet, skimming the surface of the ocean, was dangerous at all times—good weather or bad.

"Yes, ma'am," he chortled.

"Let's get this show on the road," Clay ordered. "Miss Trayhern, you take the controls. I'm playing copilot today."

Pleased that Clay was allowing her the privilege, she smiled. "Yes, sir."

Flying the P3 was easy in Aly's estimation. She took Gray Lady off the runway, the turboprops singing deeply as the plane moved through the cloudy afternoon sky above San Francisco Bay. Dan took over the throttles, his long, sensitive fingers playing with them until all engines were perfectly synchronized. Aly's gaze swept the instruments. Keeping her hand firmly on the yoke, she guided the responsive aircraft up and out of the heavy traffic patterns that plagued the West Coast. They would be heading far out to sea to begin testing the new engine thoroughly. Aly knew that with a full load of fuel aboard, Clay intended to be out at least four or five hours. A new engine could have quirks, and through a series of prepared tests, they'd find out just how well it was functioning, and whether it needed any adjustment by the mechanics.

That was all right with her. It was Friday, and she had a long, lonely weekend ahead of her. Flying released her from the constant heaviness that resided in her chest. Aly stole a look at Clay. His profile was clean, his mouth set, as usual, into a single line. Only his eyes gave him away—sometimes.

Aly had never forgotten that morning he'd kissed her and made the admission that he didn't hate her. Their relationship had changed subtly since that time. Clay had taken fewer angry shots at her. No, he'd grown only more distant. Never a smile, never a teasing remark like those the rest of the crew traded with her. Just that haunted look she sometimes saw in his gray eyes when he didn't think she was aware of him staring at her.

Sighing, Aly had no answer for how she still felt toward Clay. His praise for her flying ability had grown over the months, and he'd given her more and more flight responsibility on each mission. For that, she was grateful. It meant that he trusted her not only with his life, but with the lives of his ten-man crew. With time, she had thought her feelings toward him would die, but they had not. If anything, those emotions clamored even more strongly to be expressed. But Clay hadn't given her one sign that he really did care for her. Not with the past in their way. With a shake of her head, Aly concentrated on the series of tasks to come. Flying was a balm to her aching heart, but not the cure.

"Salty Dog One, Moffett Control. Over."

That was their call sign. Clay signaled that he'd answer the radio transmission from the station. "Salty Dog One, over."

Aly listened intently. They were flying three hundred feet above the ocean, fifty miles off the coast, near San Diego. They had been in the air only two hours, putting the engine under a number of test stresses and logging the results on a specially prepared engine chart that Clay held. Her heart began to pound when the transmission ended. She saw Clay's features cloud.

"They want us to go down to Baja, on Jester Track, to relieve Salty Dog Three?" she asked in disbelief.

Clay nodded. "Yeah, number 3 has a broken oil line. They can't stay on track with that condition. They're going to have to shut down that engine and start back to the station immediately."

"But," Dan said, "we don't have a full crew, Mr. Cantrell. What do they expect us to do?"

"There's an Israeli frigate by the name of *Titania*, being shadowed by a Soviet sub off the coast of Baja. Operations is afraid that if number 3 leaves the area without another replacement on scene, the sub might try to make an attack on the frigate."

"They wouldn't dare," Aly muttered, scowling.

"Don't count on it," Clay answered heavily. He pulled out a map, looking at the coordinates given to him by Ops. "Put Gray Lady on this heading."

Dan scratched his head. "Sir, we don't have any weapons or radar operators on board. How are we going to discourage this Red sub from dogging the heels of that frigate?"

"Hopefully, just by showing up. The sub will know we're in the area. We'll fly low and make some radio exchanges with the *Titania*, which they can monitor. Moffett's getting the standby crew ready to take number eight. They'll be in the air within the hour. We're to hold Jester Track surveillance until number eight arrives to relieve us." Clay glanced down at his watch. "We'll be on track within forty minutes. It will take the standby crew another hour to get down here. Then we can head home."

"Doesn't sound too bad," Aly agreed. She chewed on her lower lip, coaxing the P3 up into smoother air. "We'll be a decoy. That sub will never know we're not armed and prepared to take action."

Clay nodded to her. "Right."

"What about the weather?" Dan asked, worry in his voice.

"That's the bitch," Clay muttered, busily planning their flight. "That typhoon is full strength, with winds at a hundred miles an hour around the *Titania* and the sub."

"Damn," Aly whispered. "Wave height?" That was critical knowledge, because if the P3 flew fifty feet off the surface, a twenty- or thirty-foot wave could catch a wing and smash the aircraft into the ocean, killing all on board.

"Salty Dog Three will give us an update on oceanographic conditions over the track in a minute."

A cold shiver wound through Aly. It was the first time she'd ever experienced such a sensation. Her stomach knotted with fear. Fear! Where had this reaction come from? She had flown the P3 at fifty feet above the ocean in all kinds of stormy weather. But never in a typhoon. The only safety she felt was the fact that Clay and Dan were there. There wasn't any finer pilot or engineer.

"Looks bad," Clay muttered, signing off the radio with Salty Dog Three half an hour later. "Twenty-foot waves with rogue waves up to forty feet down there, and not a prayer. Damn."

Only the familiar vibration of the P3 soothed Aly's mounting terror. She hated rogue waves. They could crop up out of nowhere, coming from an entirely different direction than the rest. Frequently, they were ten to twenty feet higher than the other waves. They could be the death of a P3 if the copilot wasn't alert enough to see one coming and yell at the pilot in time for him to ascend to a higher altitude and miss it. They were on track, descending through the murky midafternoon soup, rain slashing relentlessly across the cockpit windows. She and Clay were tightly strapped in, with Clay at the controls. Dan had no support, kneeling at the throttle base, jostled with each bump and shudder as the plane fought its way downward through the heavy, buffeting winds.

"Aly, contact that Israeli frigate." Clay silently chastised himself at the slip. Every once in a while, when things got tense, he'd accidentally call her by her first name. But if she'd noticed his mistake, it didn't show in her voice.

"Right." Switching the radio dial to the ship frequency, Aly made contact with the *Titania*. She knew Clay was counting on the Soviet sub to eavesdrop on the plane-to-ship conversation. That would warn the sub that the frigate was still being protected, despite the deteriorating weather situation.

As Cantrell brought the P3 into a standard pattern of flight approximately four miles from the frigate, leveling off at fifteen hundred feet, the buffeting weather got worse.

Aly's job was to keep an eye on the altimeter, and on the plane's elevation in relation to the ocean that frothed like mountains and canyons not far below them. The peninsula of Baja was no more than ten miles away, but nothing could be sighted because of the heavy pall of rain that surrounded them. Flashes of lightning licked from one cloud to another, blinding her for an instant. Her palms became damp.

"Mayday! Mayday!" *Titania*'s captain screamed. "I'm under attack! Repeat, I'm under attack!"

Instantly, Aly was on the radio. "Salty Dog One to *Titania*. What is your status, over?"

"Salty Dog One, a torpedo has just been launched at us! We're trying to turn out of its way, but it's going to be close! Help us! Help us!"

Aly swiveled a glance at Cantrell. His face glistened with perspiration. She could feel sweat trickling beneath her armpits. "Clay?" She hadn't meant to call him by his first name, but it had come out in a plea.

"Radio Ops. Tell them what's going down. Dan, prepare to drop this girl to fifty feet."

"Fifty feet?" Aly gasped after making the call. That was suicide in weather like this. "That water could rip off a wing!"

Clay's mouth tightened. "You heard me. Prepare to descend immediately."

"You're gonna make that Red sub think we're going to drop a depth charge on him, sir?" Dan guessed.

"That's right, Dan. You'd better play those throttles like your life depends on it."

Dan grinned weakly. "Don't worry, sir, I will."

Shaken by the turn of events, Aly shut off her emotions. She had to become a thinking machine. She radioed the *Titania* to let them know that the P3 was going to make an attack run. Below, on the turbulent ocean, they could see the *Titania* turning to starboard, hitting high, powerful waves in order to avoid the torpedo.

"Let's go down."

Cantrell's voice was taut as he gave the order. Aly nodded. Her entire responsibility centered on the low-altitude altimeter, or LAA, that sensitively monitored the plane's height between ten to fifty feet above the ocean's surface. It was a delicate instrument, sometimes given to being inaccurate. As copilot she had to divide her attention between using her eyes to estimate the plane's altitude from the ocean and checking the LAA for possible inaccurate readings. On a number of occasions, Aly's quick observation had saved them from plowing into the ocean when the LAA had messed up.

Sweat formed on her upper lip, and she quickly wiped it away with her gloved hand. "Descending... now," Aly began hoarsely, "five hundred feet... four hundred feet..." The ocean grew closer. Each wave that reared skyward looked a little bigger, a little more ominous. The P3 bucked and quivered. And each time it did, Clay ironed out the craft's reaction with his skillful flying abilities.

"Make the turn to two-five-zero, ten... nine... eight..." Aly used her watch, counting down the seconds. The P3 always made an attack on a sub into the wind.

"Three... two... one!" The *Titania* flashed under them.

Clay brought the P3 into the wind, steadying her out.

"Three hundred feet..."

"Wing lamps!" Clay ordered tightly. Every P3 was equipped with huge, powerful lights at the end of each wingtip, plus one beneath the nose of the aircraft.

Aly reached down, gripping the switch. "Wing lamps on." The bright beams of light surged through the graying light of early evening, stabbing bright patches through the blinding spray and spume thrown up by the murky ocean below them.

"Nose lamp!"

"Nose lamp on." Now three blinding lights emphasized the angry sea's territory, helping Aly to ascertain distance between them and a possible watery grave.

They were going to need all the help they could get, Aly thought disjointedly, her gaze swinging from the instrument panel to the LAA, and back out the window to check their elevation.

In case the sub had picked up their radio frequency, Clay went through the attack sequence as if there was a full crew on board. Aly worked with him, tension mounting in the small cabin.

"Two hundred feet—" Aly's voice broke. The ocean looked so close!

"One hundred feet."

"On attack run, keep her steady," Clay told Dan tensely.

The P3 slipped through the turbulent wind and vicious rain, her wings skimming the surface. Each tiny air pocket, each up or down draft, was a potential crash situation. Clay kept both hands locked on the yoke, sensing and correcting each of the aircraft's reactions almost before it happened.

"Easy," he crooned to the plane.

# ⇥ IT'S A ⇤

## SILHOUETTE HONEYMOON

## A SWEETHEART

## OF A FREE OFFER!

### FOUR NEW SILHOUETTE SPECIAL EDITION® NOVELS—FREE!

Take a "Silhouette Honeymoon" with four exciting romances—yours FREE from Silhouette Special Edition®. Each of these hot-off-the-press novels brings you all the passion and tenderness of today's greatest love stories . . . your free passport to a bright new world of love and adventure! But wait . . . there's even more to this great offer!

### A LOVELY BRACELET WATCH— ABSOLUTELY FREE!

You'll love your elegant bracelet watch—this classic LCD quartz watch is a perfect expression of your style and good taste—and it's yours free as an added thanks for giving our Reader Service a try!

### AN EXCITING MYSTERY BONUS—FREE!

With this offer, you'll also receive a special mystery bonus. You'll be thrilled with this surprise gift. It will be the source of many compliments as well as a useful and attractive addition to your home.

### PLUS

### SPECIAL EXTRAS—FREE!

When you join the Silhouette Reader Service, you'll get your free monthly newsletter, packed with news of your favorite authors and upcoming books.

### MONEY-SAVING HOME DELIVERY!

Send for your Silhouette Special Edition® novels and enjoy the convenience of previewing 6 new books every month, delivered right to your home. If you decide to keep them, pay just $2.74* per book—21¢ less than the cover price with no additional charges for home delivery. And you may cancel at any time, for any reason, just by sending us a note or a shipping statement marked "cancel" or by returning an unopened shipment to us at our expense. Either way the free books and gifts are yours to keep! Great savings plus total convenience add up to a sweetheart of a deal for you!

# **S**ILHOUETTE SPECIAL EDITION®

# FREE OFFER CARD

**4 FREE BOOKS**

**FREE HOME DELIVERY!**

### PLACE HEART STICKER HERE

**FREE BRACELET WATCH**

**FREE FACT-FILLED NEWSLETTER!**

**PLUS AN EXTRA BONUS MYSTERY GIFT!**

**YES!** Please send my 4 SILHOUETTE SPECIAL EDITION® novels, free, along with my free Bracelet Watch and Mystery Gift! Then send me 6 SILHOUETTE SPECIAL EDITION® novels every month and bill me just $2.74* per book—21¢ less than the cover price with no additional charges for shipping and handling. If I'm not completely satisfied I can cancel at any time as outlined on the opposite page. The free books, Bracelet Watch and Mystery Gift remain mine to keep!     235 CIS R1X5

NAME _____

(please print)

ADDRESS _____ APT _____

CITY _____

STATE _____ ZIP _____

*Terms and prices subject to change without notice. Sales taxes applicable in N.Y. and Iowa. Offer limited to one per household and not valid to current Silhouette Special Edition subscribers. All orders subject to approval.          PRINTED IN U.S.A.

**BUSINESS REPLY CARD**

First Class    Permit No. 717    Buffalo, NY

Postage will be paid by addressee

Silhouette Books
901 Fuhrmann Blvd.
P.O. Box 1867
Buffalo, NY  14240-9952

NO POSTAGE
NECESSARY
IF MAILED
IN THE
UNITED STATES

**CLIP AND MAIL THIS POSTPAID CARD TODAY!**

Aly forced a breath, some of her tension dissolving beneath Clay's deep, steadying voice.

"Fifty feet," she croaked.

"Roger, fifty feet. Keep me apprised of our altitude."

"Roger." Sweat ran freely down her temples. Aly kept glancing out the window. Spume from the tops of the twenty-foot waves were flung into the sky, smashing into the P3. She could barely see! The windshield wipers labored heavily on the front windows, unable to keep them clear enough to fly by sight alone. She saw Clay switch to flying by instruments.

"One minute until depth charge drop!" she reported.

"Roger, one minute. Keep her steady, Dan!"

Sweat stood out on the chief engineer's face as he tried to maintain his balance and watch the engine gauges, continually adjusting the throttles for each draft or air pocket. "Yes, sir!"

"Fifty feet maintaining," Aly said, holding on to the handrail position on the starboard fuselage as a gust of wind hit them hard. The P3 shuddered sickeningly. They were skidding! A scream lurched up her throat.

Clay applied left rudder to halt the downward skid. He checked the yoke, bringing it an inch to the left. The P3 steadied.

"Altitude!" he croaked.

"F-forty feet!"

Too low! A hiss of breath came between his clenched teeth as he pulled back fractionally on the column. It was at that moment that the new engine faltered. With the unexpected loss of power, the P3 descended.

"Look out!" Aly screamed. She braced herself as the waves loomed higher.

"Damn!" It was the last expletive heard over the radio. Cantrell reared back on the yoke, asking the P3 to recover from the shallow dive that the engine had placed them in. Ballard feathered the engine, jerking the throttle, stopcocking it. He shoved the other three to the fire wall, asking for all the reserve power they had to give them.

The P3 gallantly tried to respond, the three engines straining. But another powerful gust of wind threw the nose up, creating a stall condition. The aircraft hovered at the angle for what seemed an eternity before sinking, tail first, toward the grasping, greedy fingers of the ocean twenty feet below them. A forty-foot rogue wave caught the P3, slamming into it on the port side, sending the aircraft skimming on its belly across the waves.

Nightmare seconds collided. Aly saw the waves coming up, felt the P3 shudder into a stall. She gripped the handrail, a scream caught in her throat. In those split seconds before they crashed, she felt sorrow, not fear. Sorrow that she and Clay would end their lives enemies, not friends.

The P3 sank downward, the tail boom entering the water first. Ordinarily, because of the Lockheed's construction, the plane would have disintegrated upon impact. But because the tail took the initial contact, it was torn from the fuselage instead. The P3 skipped sideways across the water like a stone skipping across a pond. Froth and spray shot skyward. Tons of water exploded into the air as the plane sliced through wave after wave. A rending tear could be heard for agonizing moments as the left wing separated from the main body of the aircraft. The starboard wingtip dug into the water at a much slower speed, cartwheeling the craft high into the air before it settled drunkenly on the ocean's surface, and that was what saved them.

Aly was thinking clearly. The P3 was still afloat, drifting in a trough between huge, stalking waves. Because of their training in emergency survival, she and Clay quickly unstrapped and were relatively unhurt. It was a different matter for their chief engineer.

Clay stepped over the unconscious man, who lay blocking the aisle. He leaned down. The gurgle of water could be heard entering the plane through the broken tail section. In less than a minute, the P3 would go down, slipping into the ocean's depths.

"Aly!" Clay yelled above the roar of the typhoon, "get to the raft. Get it released!"

Her knees knocking so badly that she fell onto the slippery aisle filling with water, Aly crawled aft in the listing P3. The twelve-man life raft on board was stowed in the rear. In the dimness and poor light, Aly finally reached it. Her breath came in ragged sobs as she fought her way through knee-deep water. Thousands of gallons of water were pouring in from the broken tail section. Leaning upward, she triggered the latch that would enable her to drag the raft forward toward the first hatch.

Cantrell hefted the bleeding and unconscious Ballard across his shoulders. As he turned, he saw to his relief that Aly had reached the life raft. She had thrown open the rear hatch door and put the raft into position for immediate inflation. Staggering under Ballard's weight, and from the fact the P3 was slowly turning on her side, Clay fought his way through the ankle-deep seawater.

Aly flipped the toggle switch, and the life raft began inflation just outside the hatch. Made of a tough, resilient material with a cover over the top, the raft rose in place as the entire rescue assembly took shape. She gripped the nylon line with both her gloved hands, the ocean tugging hard at it, wanting to pull it out of her grasp. As Clay approached, her eyes widened. Dan Ballard was bleeding heavily from the face and head. She met Clay's narrowed gaze.

"Hold that raft steady," he bellowed, positioning Ballard to be dropped forward into it.

"Hurry! We're sinking!" she screamed over the roar.

The P3 groaned, listing more to port as the water burped and belched into the fuselage. Another wave hit the aircraft. Aly was thrown violently forward on her knees. The line sang through her hands, burning them. With a cry, she looped the rope around her elbow to halt the raft's movement. She was jerked forward again, and she twisted around, using her feet to throw her sideways, lodging herself behind the hatch. Her entire shoulder exploded in pain. A cry tore from her. She saw Clay make it into the raft after getting Ballard aboard.

This was Clay's chance to get rid of her, Aly realized, pain making her light-headed. She held the raft steady, using her own body as a wedge against the aircraft to do so. Clay could leave her behind and she'd die.

"Aly! Jump!"

His scream impinged upon her numbed senses. The pain drifting up her shoulder into her neck and head was nearly paralyzing her.

"Aly!" Dammit! Clay moved awkwardly to the rear of the covered raft. Something was wrong! He saw how pale her face was. Her hands were slipping! She was allowing the line to slide through her fingers. What was she doing? Looking up, Cantrell saw the fuselage moving over on top of them. One more wave would bring it smashing down on the raft and they'd all die.

Cursing roundly, Clay made a flailing leap from the raft back to the lip of the wallowing P3. He jerked Aly away from the hatch where she had lodged herself against the interior. In one motion, he literally threw her into the raft and dived headlong into it himself.

Grabbing a paddle, fumbling with it, Clay dug it into the brackish green water. They had to get out from beneath the P3! He looked over at Aly. She lay sprawled on her back, unconscious next to Ballard. This was one time he wasn't going to have their help. He wasn't a man to pray, but he did it then. Digging the plastic paddle in quick, deep strokes, he moved the raft sluggishly forward.

The P3 groaned, the scream of metal against metal shearing above the shriek of wind and the roar of the angry ocean. Clay ducked, digging harder, paddling faster, still praying. The raft floated upward, caught on another huge wave. He chanced a look across his shoulder. Gray Lady was going down! A part of him cried because she'd been such a valiant aircraft under the worst of circumstances. The last scream of metal

against metal rang through the early evening like the
cry of a woman dying.

Ripping pain brought Aly quickly back to consciousness. She was aware of the howling wind whistling through the open flaps, and that she was soaked
to the skin, and freezing. She tried to sit up, but pain
sheared through her left shoulder. With a cry, she fell
back to the floor of the raft, sobbing for breath.

Clay had stopped paddling as soon as they were
clear of the sinking P3. With shaking hands, he had
located the first-aid kit in one of the raft's many side
compartments, and he placed a battle dressing around
Dan's bleeding head. Finding no other evidence of injury, Clay moved him amidships to the center of the
raft. Just as he finished tending Dan, he heard Aly
moan. He crawled over to her on his hands and knees.
The raft moved like a roller coaster, tipping and sliding at the whim of the ocean's quixotic current and the
direction of the wind.

"Lie still," Clay gasped, his breath coming in jerky
sobs. Aly's face was waxen, and she was gripping her
left shoulder, her mouth stretched in a silent scream.
He ran his hand across her life vest, trying to find out
if she'd broken her arm or something. "Where's it
hurt?" he demanded, leaning over her.

"Sh-shoulder. Oh, God, I think I broke it, Clay."
Aly sobbed, biting back a cry.

As quickly as he could, Clay got her turned on her
side, facing him, so that she leaned against his knees
for support. Sliding his hand under her life vest, he
gingerly felt across her wet back. After several moments of examination, he said, "I think it's dislo-

cated." He could feel the blade separated from her shoulder. As gently as he could under the circumstances, he laid Aly down on her back. Grimly, he said, "Hold on, this is going to hurt like hell."

Aly didn't have time to prepare. She felt his strong hands upon her shoulder, front and back. In the next second, Clay jerked her entire body in one, single movement. A cry clawed up her throat, and the pain was so intense that blackness enveloped her.

It was dark when Aly regained consciousness. She was aware of the rolling motion of the raft, the constant pelt of rain against the roof and the roar of wind all around them. When she realized she was held in someone's arms, she stirred.

"Lie still," Clay ordered her, his voice low, "I've got you."

A dull ache throbbed through her left shoulder. Aly found herself huddled against Cantrell, his arm around her. Her right arm was wrapped tightly around his waist. Even in unconsciousness, her terror of being washed overboard had made her cling to him. Relief spread through her.

"We're alive," Clay reassured her in an unsteady voice. "How are you feeling?"

Slowly, Aly raised her head. It was so dark she could see nothing at first. Then she realized that there was a blinking red light on the bow of the raft. It would make them visible to rescue searchers. She looked up into Clay's harshly drawn face, barely visible. The rain had plastered his hair to his skull, and his eyes were dark with concern as he studied her. She noticed that he had positioned himself between the main two seats of the raft. He'd maneuvered Dan and herself on either side of him, one arm around each to keep them from getting tossed around and possibly increasing the severity of their injuries.

"Okay," she mumbled. Thirst. She was dying of thirst. "Dan?"

Clay's face softened slightly, some of the lines of tension easing around his mouth. "Concussion, I think. A bad one. We won't know anything more until daylight comes."

Aly nodded, her brain seeming spongy and disconnected. She felt so safe and secure under his arm. Trying to think coherently, she croaked, "The radio?"

Clay offered Aly a slight smile to buoy her spirits. She looked like a bedraggled kitten, her face reflecting the faint red glow from the bow. "Up and working. I'm sure the coast guard has received our Mayday signal. It's just a matter of time until they locate us with one of their Falcon jets. I don't think they'll attempt a rescue until this storm dies down, though. Maybe we'll see them at daybreak."

Trying to protect her face from the biting, never-ending wind whipping through the flaps, Aly strained to sit up more. She placed her head against Clay's broad shoulder, her lips near his ear so that he could hear her. "What about the *Titania*?"

With a snort, Clay said, "If she saw us go down, she didn't wait around to help rescue us. I think that Red sub scared her off. She's probably halfway up the Baja peninsula by now."

Real anger wound through Aly. Tiredly, she rested her head against Clay's neck and jaw. How good it felt being in his arms. "And you? Any injury?"

"None. Just some bruises from the crash. You had a separated shoulder. How's it feeling now?"

"Like hell. Where'd you learn to put one back into position like that?"

Chuckling, Clay said. "From my days in football at college. I suffered one myself. When the coach put it back in, I thought I was going to die."

"I thought I had," Aly answered. His voice was like balm. She was more afraid than she'd ever been in her life. They were alone on an ocean in the middle of a typhoon.

"Look, there's nothing else we can do right now. Try and go back to sleep."

"But what about you? What time is it?" She struggled to look at her watch on her left wrist. When she raised her arm, pain hit her hard, making her gasp.

"Easy with that arm, honey," he crooned, gently running his hand down her left arm. "You won't have mobility for a couple of weeks. As soon as I can, I'm going to fashion a sling so you don't keep aggravating it every time you move."

*Honey.* Aly stared up at Clay, her lips parting. His voice was incredibly gentle, his fingers even gentler as he skimmed her injured arm in a protective gesture. She saw him frown and suddenly look away from her. Despite their circumstances, that same old pain shook her heart. It had been a slip on his part—and now he was sorry he'd said it.

"I-it's almost midnight," she whispered lamely.

"Yeah. Go back to sleep, Aly. There's nothing else to be done. The raft's riding the waves fine. According to the compass, we're heading in a northeasterly direction, toward Baja."

Baja. She closed her eyes, snuggling deep beneath Clay's supportive arm. Savoring his closeness, the warming heat of his hard, masculine body, Aly closed her eyes. Tonight, Clay would hold her. It was more than she'd ever dreamed of. He embraced both her and Dan. There was a heroic side to Clay. He didn't have to hold either of them, but he must have realized that body heat was depleted in a cold rain like this. It didn't matter what his reasons were, Aly told herself. Shivering, she placed her hand against the vest he wore. The trauma of the crash, followed by her injury, had left her utterly exhausted. Despite the banshee cry of the wind surrounding them, the pitching of the raft and the unrelenting rain, Aly slept. She was safe.

Clay jerked awake at dawn, bathed in a cold sweat of fear. He'd been dreaming of the crash all over again, experiencing a gamut of violent emotions. He lay with his shoulders against the rubber raft amidships. Dan's head rested on his right shoulder, Aly's on his left. Sometime during the night, she had crowded close, her body contoured against his. It felt good and right. No longer was she shivering, and neither was he.

Clay needed to rub his burning eyes. He moved slowly, trying not to disturb either of his sleeping crew members. Every bone in his body ached. His muscles were stiff and sore. He heard Dan groan. Instantly, his attention focused on the engineer. Was he finally becoming conscious? God, he hoped so.

Aly heard Dan's groan and groggily awoke. As she stirred, she immediately felt Clay's arm tighten about her shoulder.

"Take it easy," he said, his voice rough from disuse. "It's Ballard. I think he's coming around. Can you help me, Aly?"

The rain had stopped. Aly rubbed her eyes, slowly sitting up. Her shoulder ached, but the pain was at a manageable level. Focusing her attention on Dan, she got to her hands and knees, moving awkwardly around Clay and to his side.

Trading a look with him, she wondered how badly hurt Dan was. "Dan?" she called, placing her hand against his shoulder. "Dan? Can you hear me? It's Aly."

The engineer groaned again, his lashes fluttering against his pale, drawn face. But he didn't become conscious.

Aly looked up at Clay. "I think he's got a serious concussion."

"Yeah," Clay agreed grimly. He twisted around, looking for the compartment that held three survival blankets. Glancing out the flaps, his eyes widened. "Look!"

The sudden surprise in Clay's voice made Aly look up. There, between the flaps, and no more than a mile away, was the Baja desert. Golden yellow hills of sand flowed in a north-south direction for as far as they could see. "Land!" Aly croaked, hope in her voice. That would be even better for rescue!

Moving stiffly, Clay got to his knees. "Aly, can you paddle? I don't know if this current or wind will hold this direction long enough for us to make land. Can you use your right arm to paddle with?''

Aly nodded, slipping her numbed fingers around the oar. The paddle was placed between the overhead roof and the raft. "I'll do it."

Clay grinned tiredly. "You're one hell of a woman."

His unexpected smile sent a shaft of warmth through her. She pushed the damp hair out of her eyes. "Come on, Cantrell, quit the sweet talk and put your money where your mouth is. Let's go for it."

Clay wanted to reach over and pull Aly into his arms. He loved her unflagging spirit, her courage under brutal circumstances. And the smile she gave him made him feel hot with longing. "Let's go for it," he challenged her huskily.

"Last one to the beach is a rotten egg, Cantrell!" And they began to paddle.

"Prepare to land!" Clay warned Aly nearly an hour later. His arm was numb, and his shoulder hurt from paddling for so long and hard. He knew that Aly must be close to exhaustion. If she was, she wasn't complaining. Maybe it was that famous Trayhern stamina coming through for them now. Whatever the reason, Clay knew they wouldn't have reached shore without her superhuman effort. Just as he'd suspected, the current had started moving northward half a mile away from shore. It would have swept them back out to sea. The last half mile had been hellish, but they'd forced the raft through the choppy waves, aiming it for a desert landfall.

The waves were huge from the typhoon. Clay stowed both paddles and then pulled Aly into the center of the raft with him. The darkness beneath her eyes gave away her true state. She was exhausted. "Stay down and hold on to Ballard," he shouted above the crashing of the waves. "We're liable to tip over if we don't stay low and in the center of this thing. Hang on!"

Aly slid her right arm under Dan's shoulders, holding him next to her body, trying to protect him in case they were approaching a rocky shore, or if the raft should flip over. Her eyes widened when Clay came around to sit behind her, his arms around both of them. He pressed her down until she was almost lying across Dan. When she realized that Clay was protecting both of them with his body, tears leaked into her eyes. Despite his hard facade, Clay was an incredible man. And Aly loved him fiercely for it.

## Chapter Seven

Miraculously, they landed upright, sliding along the smooth, grainy surface of the beach. Clay was the first out of the raft, pulling it high up on the shore with the aid of the nylon rope.

He watched as Aly shakily climbed out of the raft. She held her left arm against her torso, and he knew she was in plenty of pain from the dislocation. Tugging the raft completely out of the grasp of the heavy waves, Clay wrapped the nylon rope around a large black rock sticking up out of the sand, using it as an anchor point.

Clay looked up as she approached. "Aly?" He hadn't realized the full impact on her of their bid to paddle ashore until just then. Her eyes were dark with exhaustion, shadows beneath them. And that beauti-

ful mouth was compressed into a single line of suffering.

"Yes?"

He rose to his feet. Sliding his hand around her
good arm to steady her, Clay guided her toward a
large, sandy bluff that stood to the left of the landing
area. "First things first. I want you to sit down before you fall down. As soon as I can get Dan comfortable, I'll take care of you."

The sand was packed hard from the continuous
rain, but Aly stumbled, nevertheless. Clay's hand
tightened on her arm to prevent her from falling.
Tiredness was lapping at her, and she wasn't thinking
clearly. "I—I think I'm in shock, Clay."

He gave her a tight smile, motioning for her to sit
down. "I know you are."

Giving him a confused look, Aly rasped, "Why
aren't you?"

Her hair was in utter disarray around her face,
curled and stiffened by the saltwater. But to Clay, she
looked beautiful. Leaning down, he cupped her cheek.
"I had a crash before, remember? Maybe that experience prepared me this time. I don't know. Stay here."

As badly as she wanted to contribute to the team
effort, Aly was simply too fatigued. She sat watching
as Clay briskly went about the business of setting up
camp. The tarp over the large, oval raft would pro-
vide them with protection against all kinds of weather.
And each raft was equipped with an array of items,
from ten gallons of fresh water stored in quart plastic
bottles to enough dehydrated food for two weeks, a
radio, a first-aid kit and other essentials.

Aly studied the turbulent gray clouds, dark with threatening rain. The wind was warm, and her stiff, salty-smelling flight suit was nearly dry. This was Baja, and it was September. Aly wondered how hot it would get when the storm finally passed them.

Clay was satisfied with his hour's worth of effort. Dan was resting peacefully, although still unconscious, beneath the protective tarp on the raft. He'd placed two blankets over him, to keep him warm. Setting up the radio to send out the Mayday signal was his last major chore before he could attend to Aly.

Every once in a while, Clay would look up to check on her. She had lain down, curling on her side, using her right arm as a pillow for her head. Adjusting the radio control to the on position, he set it to broadcast their plea for help. He was certain that within twenty-four hours, they'd be discovered by the coast guard. His spirts were solid, and he felt good. They had survived the crash.

As he picked up the first-aid kit and climbed out of the raft, Clay didn't try to hide from his feelings. Seconds before the crash he'd realized that he loved Aly. Regardless of her background or her family name, he loved her. Confused about what to do with that knowledge, he now trudged slowly up the slope toward her. He was scared. More scared than he'd ever been in his life. How could they ever have a relationship when he was the one who had so effectively destroyed it in the first place? There was no hope, and he sadly dismissed the dream.

Aly roused when she saw Clay coming up the hill and gave him a game smile as he knelt in front of her.

His eyes were dark gray, filled with concern for her. It made her feel good, and she rallied.

"I must have dozed off."

Clay returned her brief smile of welcome and went about the business of unzipping her vest. "You'll need a couple more catnaps in order to shake off the shock. Let's get this vest, and part of the flight suit you're wearing, off you. I want to examine that shoulder."

Aly tried not to flinch as Clay stripped her of the vest and then pulled the Velcro of her flight suit open. She wore only a white cotton bra and panties beneath the suit. Heat stole into her face as she allowed him to gently work the sleeve from her stiff left arm. Every movement hurt.

"Take it easy," Clay soothed, gathering the last of the material off her hand. He realized Aly was embarrassed at having to partially strip in order for him to check the injury. Focusing on the task at hand, he tried to ignore the soft pliancy of her flesh. Allowing her to keep the flight suit on her right arm and shoulder, he maneuvered around her so that he could look at the injured area.

"You have a nice back," he told her huskily. It was a deeply indented back with a strong spine. Clay lightly ran his hand across the dislocation area.

"Is that good or bad?" Aly joked weakly, wildly aware as his hand grazed her shoulder. His touch was knowing without being hurtful as he gently pressed here and there to find the extent of damage.

Clay smiled distantly and placed his hand directly over the injury. The flesh was badly swollen and hot to his brief touch. "A compliment," he assured her, only inches separating them. "You're lucky you didn't get your arm ripped out of the shoulder socket."

"That bad, Clay?" It was so natural to call him by his first name, Aly thought, giving up on trying to keep the normal distance between them. She was too tired to erect those walls they both hid behind so well.

Frowning, he muttered, "Bad enough." He looked down at her. "I think the only thing we can do is put your left arm in a sling and keep the entire shoulder as immobilized as possible." His hand settled on her bare arm. "Are you in a lot of pain?"

His gentle attention was unraveling her. It was impossible to ignore Clay when he was like this. It wasn't an act—this was the real Clay Cantrell that she'd fallen helplessly in love with. The serious agony was in her heart, and there was no cure for that. Ever.

"Just a little."

He got up and came around to her left side, facing her. "You sure?" Easing her fingers and hand back through the sleeve opening, Clay helped her get the flight suit back in place. "Or are you hiding behind that tough Trayhern name?" He'd deliberately goaded her to get an honest response. From the set of her mouth, the way the corners pulled in, he knew she was in misery.

Aly flashed him an angry look. "There's nothing wrong in minimizing pain, Cantrell," she said, stung. With quick, sure movements, Aly pressed the Velcro closed, the flight suit once again in place.

Clay patiently held her blazing blue eyes. "There is when we've got medication to ease it." And then he looked down at her gloved hands, noticing a rusty color staining them. "What's this?" He picked up her left hand and turned it over.

"You little fool," he breathed, examining the glove that was shredded, exposing her badly burned palm that had bled freely. She must have gotten the wounds when the nylon line had nearly been ripped out of her hands. "Why the hell didn't you tell me—"

Aly could barely tolerate Clay's hand cradling hers. But she couldn't jerk out of his grasp—her shoulder hurt too badly. "It was just some rope burns," she muttered defensively.

Clay lifted his head, meeting and holding her defiant gaze. "Lady, you may think you're Superwoman, but this kind of damage invites infection."

"Stop haranguing me!"

There was a wobble in her voice. Clay saw the tears gather in her wavering stare. His mouth tightened, and he laid her hand across his knees. Reaching for the first-aid kit, he opened it, and took out a pair of scissors. The tension was palpable between them as he carefully cut away the rest of her glove. Part of the fibers had stuck to the oozing wound across her palm.

"This is going to hurt like hell," he warned her.

Aly couldn't stop the tears. But they weren't caused by the pain as Clay gently pulled fragments of the glove from the burns. No, they were welling into her eyes because she had no defense against his closeness or the little barbs he was throwing at her.

When Clay saw the tears drifting down the taut planes of her cheeks, he winced visibly. "These are nasty," he muttered, spreading salve across her palm. "You must have gotten them holding that raft against the hatch."

"Y-yes." She sniffed, taking her right gloved hand and wiping her eyes dry.

Cantrell risked a look at her as he gently wrapped gauze around her hand and palm. "You look pretty even when you cry. Makes those blue eyes of yours even larger, if that's possible."

Aly withdrew deep inside herself. One minute he was insulting her, the next, praising her. Frantically, she searched for some neutral topic. "At least we survived the crash," she whispered in a raspy voice.

Grimly, Clay nodded. He took some adhesive tape and finished bandaging the dressing. "Yeah."

"I was so scared."

"That made three of us. Okay, let me look at your other hand."

Reluctantly, Aly gave it to him, trying to prepare for his reaction. She knew her right hand was far worse than the left. She watched his eyebrows draw together as he examined her palm.

"Lady, you have one hell of a tolerance for pain, that's all I can say." He met and held her gaze. "Do you want medication?"

She shook her head. "No. Drugs make me groggy. At least pain keeps my head clear so I can think."

With a derisive laugh, Clay agreed. "Yeah, that's the truth." He began the same procedure of cutting the glove away from her hand. "After I crashed that F-14 into the deck of the carrier and ejected at the last second, I didn't feel anything at first, either. It was only after I woke up in sick bay that I felt the pain."

Starbuck had told her about Clay's crash. And knowing that he'd lied to her, Aly wanted to know the truth. There was a warmth between them right now, and she hesitantly asked, "What happened, Clay? Dan mentioned that at one time you were a fighter pilot. What changed that?"

The glove fell away and Clay carefully examined the palm of her hand. Aly had such exquisitely long fingers. He'd bet anything that she'd get permanent scars out of this.

Aly took his silence as a negative. "That's all right, you don't have to tell me about it. I'm sure it's a horrible memory."

"What? No, I don't mind telling you, Aly." Cantrell pointed to her palm. "I was just thinking it was a shame to have such beautiful skin scarred like this."

She flushed, unable to hold his sincere gaze. "Wh-what about the crash?"

He smiled briefly, and realized she was blushing. Any color coming back into her cheeks was better than nothing, in his opinion. Taking the salve, he daubed it across the burn. "It happened a year and a half ago while I was aboard the *Enterprise*. Starbuck was in my squadron." He looked up. "I suppose he's already told you that?"

Aly raised her head, anger in her voice. "Starbuck lied to me about a lot of things, but yes, he did mention the fact that you flew together."

Chuckling, Clay murmured, "Said I was on the verge of losing my nerve after the crash, too, no doubt."

"How did you know?"

"Because Starbuck is a jealous bastard at best, and a back stabber at his worst. He and I were in competition for the top-gun slot in our squadron. I was ahead of him in points, and he didn't like it." Clay sobered, his voice lowering. "My RIO, Lieutenant John Holding, was slated to rotate stateside. We had to fly one last mission on a rotten night. It was stormy, and winds were high and variable. The F-14 started developing an engine problem, so we came back to the carrier." Clay set the salve aside and began to wrap her palm with the gauze. One corner of his mouth twisted into a grimace. "I've never seen a night like that. I was calling the ball, holding the aircraft steady. Everything was lined up. The deck on that carrier was lifting and falling more than I'd ever seen it before.

"At the last second, the wind threw the plane off course, and I had a bolter, going around for a second try. I called the ball and lined up. Everything looked good. Then, just as I dropped the hook, pulled full flaps for the landing, the starboard engine that was giving me problems flamed out." Clay held her hand, staring off into space, the images still vivid. "The plane nosed down. I brought it up, but in doing so, we literally starting falling toward the deck. There was nothing I could do but yell a warning, hoping John would punch out."

Aly wanted to reach out and touch Clay's shoulder, to somehow assuage his agony. "Were you both able to eject?" she asked softly.

Clay shook his head, anguish in his tone. "John couldn't . . . didn't. I don't know why he didn't punch out. Maybe he wasn't fast enough. Maybe the ejection phase jammed. We'll never know."

"So, you survived and John didn't?" Aly guessed.

"That's right." Clay shook off the sorrow from the past, continuing to bandage her hand. Just the gentleness in Aly's husky voice made him want to confide in her. He'd never talked to anyone except the investigators about the accident. "I ejected and landed in the ocean. The rescue helicopter fished me out ten minutes later."

"How badly were you hurt?" Aly knew that ejecting could cause back and ankle injuries.

"I suffered a pretty serious concussion, some minor back trouble and the normal assortment of colorful bruises."

She studied his bent head. The urge to tunnel her fingers through his short, black hair was almost tangible. Risking everything, Aly slowly raised her left arm, resting it on his shoulder. The look of surprise in his eyes when she did it made her heart lift with joy. It had been the right thing to do.

"If I know you just a little, you probably suffered more because of John's death."

Clay met and drowned in her tender expression. In that instant, he simply wanted to take Aly into his arms and make slow, exploratory love with her. Her hand resting on his shoulder sent warmth throughout his cold, knotted gut. "Yeah, you're right. John was married to a great woman, Maggie. They have three of the brightest kids." He avoided her gaze. "They're like family to me, Aly. John and Maggie sort of took me under their wing." He managed a strained laugh, completing the bandaging. "I'm the kids' 'uncle.'" And then hesitantly he added, "I always will be. I never forget Christopher, Mark or Jenny's birthdays. I've got them circled on a calendar I carry in my wallet. It doesn't matter where I'm stationed, I always send them a card and a gift."

Aly closed her eyes. His pain and suffering was far greater than her current physical discomfort. "I'm sorry, Clay " His words about the loss of his brother serrated her: 'I lost all of mine.' Stephen Cantrell had died on that hill. "Surely, you're an uncle to your own family members?"

Clay allowed her to retrieve her hand. He remained kneeling there, hands resting on his thighs. Unexpectedly, tears stung his eyes. Tears! He hadn't cried in years. "What you don't know is that when the Marine Corps officer visited my mother with the telegram informing her of Stephen's death, she suffered a stroke two hours later that killed her."

"No!"

Clay heard the raw anguish in Aly's cry. He slowly turned his head, meeting and holding her shadowed blue eyes. "They were all I had. My brother and my mother. I never knew my father, because he died in a jet crash when I was barely a year old. My dad was an orphan who worked his way through college and then joined the Navy, attaining flight status. My mother was an orphan, too. All they had was each other." He gave Aly a twisted smile filled with sadness. "Maybe now you can understand why John's children are so important to me. They're my other family." Clay got stiffly to his feet, unable to stand the tortured look in Aly's eyes. At that moment, he didn't know who hurt worse.

The day passed slowly for Aly. Forced to huddle with Clay and the unconscious Dan Ballard in the tent when the rains came, she remained silent, replaying their prior conversation. Off and on, she slept—partly to escape the ordeal of feelings surrounding Clay's softly admitted story, partly to escape the widening pain in her heart for him.

Clay sat, Dan on his left and Aly curled up at the other end of the raft under a blanket. His arms were wrapped around his drawn-up knees. Moodily, he listened to the wind outside. The storm was slowly abating, the rain coming less often, the wind less powerful. That was good. He wanted the rescue to hurry up and happen.

Clay's gaze drifted back to Aly, as it always did. This was the first time he'd gotten a chance to observe her for any period of time without continual interruption. There was something healing about watching her, he decided. Maybe it was the way her lips parted, free of tension. Or just the way she curled up like a lost kitten, looking alone and vulnerable. He wanted to curl up beside her and pull her into his arms.

*Funny,* he told himself, *how a plane crash brings everything into sharp clarity.* Clay hadn't meant to tell Aly about his other crash, or the fact that Stephen's death had also taken his mother's life. Rubbing his face savagely, he felt dirty and small. The anguish in Aly's tone and eyes tore him apart. It was as if she personally took responsibility for the tragedy at that moment. Nine months ago, he'd have gleefully told her the awful consequences of Morgan's decision, just to strike out and hurt her as Morgan Trayhern had hurt him. But now he had the opposite feeling. Somehow, Cantrell wanted to take away the guilt he saw in her eyes. Aly shouldn't have to be burdened with Morgan's dirty laundry.

Clay quietly got up and went over to check on Dan, taking his pulse again, and feeling his skin to make sure he was being kept warm enough. Was the engineer in a coma? God, he hoped not. Dan had a blond hellion for a wife, whom he adored. Not to mention those four kids who were often a bright spot in the dark tapestry of Clay's life.

"Dan?" he called softly. "Listen, buddy, you've *got* to pull out of this. You hear me? You've got a great wife and kids waiting for you. Don't let it all go. Hang in there. We're going to be rescued any time now." Dan's lashes didn't move. Grimly, Clay kept his hand on the engineer's shoulder, as if to will him out of the netherland he drifted in.

Aly stirred, and Clay looked over at her. She was groggy, her eyes a bit puffy, but endearing. He gave her a slight smile of welcome, then tucked the blanket around Dan. If he stayed, he'd want to move those few feet and take Aly into his arms. She looked so damned lonely and hurting. He forced himself to get up and exit the raft.

Taking a deep breath, Clay studied the ocean's churning whitecaps. Where was the rescue plane? Why hadn't he even heard an airplane engine? He shoved his hands deep into his pockets, walking slowly down the beach, his head bowed in thought.

Aly took care of her personal necessities, then walked back toward the raft. The evening sky was fraught with swiftly moving clouds. The wind tugged at her loosely fitting flight suit, and she lifted her face toward the ocean. She remembered awakening, hearing Clay's lowered voice as he pleaded with Dan. And then her gaze moved to the right. She saw Clay a quarter of a mile away, a lonely, dark figure against the mighty expanse of sky and earth.

Alone . . . he was terribly alone in a way she'd never imagined. Her family was tightly knit and close. They'd stood together, deriving strength from one another, through every storm life had hurled at them. But Clay had no one. Rubbing her head, Aly fought back the tears. Clay wouldn't take her tears of compassion as anything less than pity. And she was sure he wouldn't tolerate that. Dejectedly, Aly walked back to the raft.

When Clay returned, he found her busy preparing two MREs—the dehydrated meals packaged in plastic bags. He nodded a greeting in her direction when he entered the raft. Tying the flaps shut, he carefully made his way down to where she sat.

"What's cooking?"

She managed a small smile, handing him the dried food packet. "Not much, believe me."

Clay sat cross-legged next to her, their knees almost touching. There wasn't much room in one of these things. "Bet your cooking's great in comparison to this stuff." He took the small bottle of water, putting a bit of liquid into the bag.

"Don't be so sure." Aly laughed softly. Her spirits rose unaccountably just being with Clay. His face was clear, and she saw less tension around his eyes and mouth.

"I'll bet you're one hell of a good cook."

"I don't poison myself, if that's what you mean," she answered dryly.

He grinned. "Spirited, aren't you?"

Aly flushed. "Not really. I just can't stand all this depression. When things get bad, I tend to get a black sense of humor in order to lift myself out of it."

"Yeah, I know what you mean." Clay picked up a plastic fork. The dried food had plumped up considerably with the addition of the water. He watched Aly pick at her meal.

"You need to eat."

"I know." And then Aly rallied. "What's your favorite meal, Clay?"

He leaned back, stretching his long legs across the width of the raft. "Ahh, food is one of my favorite topics." He grinned at her. "I guess it is for every bachelor who struggles with boiling water or burning soup in a pan. I'm a meat and potatoes man. Nothing fancy about me."

"Roast beef, mashed potatoes and gravy, right?" Aly ventured.

He gave her a look of praise. "Bingo. You're a pretty insightful lady, you know that?"

"Thanks," she murmured, responding to the warmth of his tone.

"How about you? What's your favorite meal?"

The MRE food was dreadful, Aly decided. She wrinkled her nose and held Clay's gray gaze, filled with amusement. His smile sent her tumbling on a rainbow of emotions. "Me? I like Greek food. Good, tart feta cheese, those nasty-tasting little black olives and some lemon soup with rice."

"God, that sounds good. What do you say we take a walk over the hill here, and visit the first Greek restaurant we see? I'll even spring for some retsina wine."

Aly laughed and held out her right hand toward him. "You've got a deal!"

Her laughter broke the pall Clay had felt around him. Gently taking her bandaged hand, Clay shook it and matched her smile. "First thing I'll do when we get back is take you to a real Greek restaurant over in Palo Alto."

The joy died in Aly. He was teasing her. Nothing was meant by his statement. If only they could forget their past! There was such a richness that lay between them to be explored and discovered together.

Clay saw the laughter die in Aly's eyes and on her lips. Why? Unable to ferret out an answer, he changed topics and released her hand. "I don't know about you, but I think waiting for this rescue to come is the pits."

The food tasted like cardboard, but Aly forced herself to eat it. "Are you sure the radio is working, Clay?"

"Yeah. I checked it a while ago."

"Is it possible that because of all the storm's activity the signal might be getting shorted out in the stratosphere?"

He nodded glumly. "That's a possibility."

Aly toyed with the rest of her meal, unable to finish it. "Clay?"

He looked over at her. "Yes?"

"What if rescue doesn't come?"

Silence hung in the raft, the sound of the wind buffeting them. He poked at the food with his fork, his brow wrinkling. "The map in the rescue packet says that there's a Huichol Indian village inland over the coastal mountain range. We may have to do some walking."

Aly digested the possibility. "Baja is hot this time of year from what I understand."

"Roger that. Hot and arid. No water anywhere."

"Would we have enough water and food for that kind of trek?"

Clay nodded. "If we're careful, we'd have five days' worth. That should be enough to reach that village and find help."

Baja was such a desolate place, though. Aly kept the thought to herself, mulling over the possibilities. "We've got to be rescued." She muttered it with such feeling that Clay looked up in surprise at her. "Dan's badly injured," she explained.

"Yeah, and if push comes to shove, we're going to have to leave him here with half the supplies and go inland to get help."

"What?" Aly's eyes rounded. "You can't be serious. He's hurt! You can't just leave him!"

Clay measured the sudden emotion in her voice. "We may have to, Aly."

Anger swept through her. "You don't just go waltzing off and desert someone in Dan's condition!"

He set aside the MRE, facing her. The word *desert* smarted. Morgan Trayhern had deserted Stephen and his men. Was that why Aly was suddenly so protective of Dan? "Look," he began quietly, trying to get her to calm down, "we've both been taught survival methods. If necessary, Dan will stay here, and we'll go for help. That way we increase our chances of being found. Dan can stay with the radio and monitor it. If he gets rescued first, he'll have our coordinates, and we'll be picked up anyway. If we get to a village, we can get help for him. Either way, it increases our chances of survival, Aly."

Her hands knotted, and she glared at him. "I won't leave a man to die out here alone when he could come with us."

"Aly, be reasonable—"

"No! You're the one who wants to leave Dan behind! I won't do it, Cantrell. I swear, I won't!"

Clay set his jaw, assessing her emotional response. Obviously he had struck a raw nerve in Aly. He'd suggested many times the threat of her deserting him and the crew in the face of danger. Now he was reaping the results of his misfired anger over Morgan Trayhern's activities. Dammit! Rubbing his jaw that was bristly with a day's growth of beard, Clay held her fiery blue gaze.

"Look, calm down, Aly. We aren't at that point yet. I'm sure that as this storm continues to weaken, our chances of being discovered increase."

Aly's nostrils flared with a caldron of tapped feelings. She scrambled to her feet, glaring at Clay as she moved by him. Right now, she needed some fresh air. Her voice was strained. "You'd better hope like hell we get a rescue, Cantrell, because I *won't* leave Dan behind." She jerked open the ties and slipped between the flaps, disappearing into the gray twilight.

"Son of a bitch!" Clay glared at the flaps. He was getting a taste of that famous Trayhern bulldog stubbornness he'd heard about. For everyone's sake, Clay hoped rescue would come by daylight tomorrow. It had to. It just had to. . . .

By dusk of the second day, Clay knew rescue wasn't coming. He stood alone on the beach, his hands in the pockets of his flight suit. The ocean was calm now, almost glassy in appearance as the sun slid toward the horizon. What few clouds were in the sky were high cirrus, a harbinger of good weather.

The day had been filled with ups and downs. The good news was that Dan Ballard had regained consciousness. The man was seriously felled by a concussion. There was no way, if they had to trek across the mountains in the distance, that Dan could make the trip. Releasing a sigh, Clay headed back toward the raft, girding himself for a coming battle with Aly.

When he lifted the flap, she jerked a look up in his direction. She was changing the dressing on Dan's massive head wound.

"Feeling better, Dan?" Clay asked, moving inside and sitting opposite where Aly knelt.

Dan managed a wan smile. "Yes, sir. Just a little bitty headache, is all."

Clay grinned down at him. "What is it about redheads?" he teased. "Do you all fib about the amount of pain you're in?" Glancing at Aly, he saw her scowl. All day she'd avoided him, barely saying two words. And one look into those blue eyes fraught with anger and emotion told Clay they were still at loggerheads.

"Maybe some aspirin?" Dan asked.

Clay reached for the first-aid kit. "Yeah, we can do that for you." He took two white tablets out of a bottle, and waited until Aly had completed the dressing. Slipping his arm beneath the engineer's shoulders, Clay lifted him enough that he could wash the aspirin down with some water.

"Thanks..." Dan uttered, relaxing back on the pallet that Aly had made for him earlier that day.

It was going to be dark soon. The light was fading rapidly inside the raft. Clay put the bottle back in the first-aid kit. "Listen, Dan, there are some things we need to talk over."

"We aren't going to be rescued," Dan guessed.

"Chances are looking pretty slim," Clay agreed quietly. He risked another look at Aly. She was kneeling, hands tense on her thighs, her eyes very large and very round.

"Do you think the combination of weather and ocean current has thrown them off our track?"

"Yeah, I do, Dan." Clay picked absently at his bootlace. "I'm sure the coast guard tried to figure out where our crash occurred and flew a search pattern. But we all know that in a typhoon, ocean currents change like the wind. They may be hundreds of miles west of us, still searching over the ocean."

"That's what I thought, sir."

"What about the radio?" Aly demanded, her voice tight, accusing.

Clay glanced at it. "It only has a certain radius. If those search planes are flying too far away, they won't pick up our signal."

Dan moved his head slightly, his eyes on Clay. "So what's in the cards, Skipper? What should we do?"

*Here it comes.* Clay braced himself and addressed both of his crew. "I think our only chance is for Lieutenant Trayhern and I to climb that mountain range and try to locate the Indian village we know exists on the other side."

"No!" Aly exploded. "You aren't going to desert Dan! He's a valuable member of our party, too. You can't just walk off and leave him!"

"We aren't deserting him, Aly," Cantrell said in a low voice. "Now, get a hold on yourself. Hysterics aren't going to help any of us."

Aly fought her anger. "Dammit, you're not leaving Dan here to—to possibly die by himself! What if he goes back into a coma? Who will feed or care for him? What if—"

"Don't worry, Miss Trayhern," Dan protested weakly, I'll be okay here. Really, I will."

She was shaking with rage and frustration. "You aren't well enough to decide anything, Dan! You've got a six-inch gash across your head! It could get infected, you could get a horrible fever and go wandering off in delirium!"

"He'll be fine," Clay growled, holding her tear-filled eyes. "Dan's as tough as they come. He's been taught survival techniques just as we have. He'll be able to tough it out here alone until help arrives."

The heat in the raft was stifling. Both men were looking at her. Didn't they understand? No Trayhern left anyone behind! Her father had crashed in Korea behind enemy lines while trying to rescue her mother who had been taken prisoner, and he hadn't given up. Nor had he surrendered. Instead he'd fought his way back to safety. Her family sense of honor would not allow her to leave a fallen comrade behind. Ever!

"Excuse me, I've got to get out of here," she rattled, climbing awkwardly to her feet. With her left arm in a sling, Aly didn't have the balance she wanted.

Struggling to control her anger, she wedged past Clay, escaping into the cool evening air.

Tears blinded Aly as she ran down the packed sand toward the ocean. They didn't understand! Dan could die without continued care! A sob tore from her, and she slowed, stumbling to a halt. Aly buried her face in her right hand, her weeping drowned out by the crash of waves along the beach.

Clay was on Aly's heels and closed the distance between them. He reached out, gripping her arm gently and turning her around. "Aly, listen to me—"

She reacted as if stung, jerking her arm out of his grasp. Stumbling back a step, she screamed, "Don't touch me!"

He froze. "Aly, for God's sake! I'm not *deserting* Dan. And neither are you!"

"Yes, you are!" she cried out between sobs. Her face contorted, glistening with tears. "I was taught never to leave someone who was injured. Our family doesn't leave people behind! Not now, not ever! You go take a hike over the mountains. I'll stay here and tend Dan."

Grimly, Clay advanced upon her. He took her firmly, but gently, by the shoulders "Now look," he grated, his face inches from hers, "You'll do as I order. I can't help it if you and your family have an exaggerated sense of honor toward others. This is one situation that demands that both of us leave Ballard." His fingers dug more firmly into her arms. Aly's eyes were wide with anguish. "Dammit, listen to me! You're not deserting Dan. Not in my eyes."

"That's all you've ever accused me of!" she shrieked. "How many times did you throw it in my

face that I might desert you or the crew at a crucial
time?'' Aly tried to break free of his grip, but it was
impossible. She saw his face contort with a series of
emotions. ''That's right! I've heard it long enough and
loud enough, Cantrell. Well, I'm not leaving Dan, and
that's final! I'm not going to go back to Moffett with
you telling everyone that *another* member of the
Trayhern family deserted someone at a critical point,
possibly causing loss of life! No way!''

He wanted to shake some sense into that red head of
hers, but Clay knew he had no one but himself to
blame for her reaction. ''Okay,'' he whispered harshly,
''this is my fault, Aly! I pushed you into a corner. I
was wrong as hell to keep goading you about deserting us. I'm wrong, do you hear me? The past nine
months you've proved yourself in my eyes. I don't
consider you a quitter or a deserter. Do you understand?''

With a cry, Aly jerked away. It cost her dearly in
terms of pain, her shoulder beginning to ache again.
Placing her right hand against the shoulder in the
sling, she sobbed, ''I don't believe you, Cantrell! Not
a word of what you say will make me change my
mind! I was this way before I ever met you and had the
miserable pleasure of being harassed daily by you
calling *me* a traitor!''

Running his fingers through his hair, Clay snarled,
''Your brother's a traitor—you're not!''

''It's one and the same with you, though, Cantrell.
Isn't it? When you look at me, you see Morgan. You
see your brother, Stephen, and your mother!'' She
jabbed a thumb into her chest, advancing upon him,
breathing hard. ''You've never seen *me*! The only

thing you live with daily is the damned past. You drag it around like a good friend." Her nostrils flared. "Well, now we're all going to pay for what you've insisted upon doing. I'm not leaving Ballard. You can court-martial me after we're rescued, and I won't give a damn. My honor, my personal integrity toward others is a hell of a lot more important to me than what you deem important!"

Clay stood frozen as she shouldered on by him, stalking up the slight hill and disappearing into the darkness. Dammit! He threw his hands on his hips, clenching his teeth. Glaring out into the dark ocean, he wanted to cry. Not for himself, but for what he'd done to Aly in his blind hatred toward her brother. His chest hurt, and his throat constricted. Tears jammed into Clay's eyes. He turned on his heel, walking blindly away from the raft. His hatred had turned Aly into the shrieking, wounded woman who had stood crying unashamedly in front of him. Taking a ragged breath, Clay staggered to a stop, hot tears rolling down his cheeks.

His hatred had turned Aly's vulnerability and honesty into something twisted and ugly. God, what had he done? Sinking to his knees, he realized that the coolness of the sand couldn't stop the heat of utter guilt from consuming him. He'd hurt Aly so badly that she was going to make a last-ditch stand to salvage what pride and integrity she had left. If he forced her to go with him, he'd end up destroying that. And the last thing he wanted was to hurt Aly any more.

## Chapter Eight

Half an hour before the sun rose above the rugged mountains of Baja California, Clay ended his lonely all-night vigil at the edge of the ceaseless ocean. He stripped out of his flight suit and dived into the warm water, scrubbing his skin clean with the abrasive sand. Afterward, he used a disposable razor against his dark beard, scraping his skin free of the whiskers. By the time he'd shrugged back into the uniform, he felt slightly better. But only slightly.

He spotted Aly just coming out of the raft, and waited. Waited and prayed. When he saw her returning from the bluff area, he slowly rose off his haunches and walked toward her, his eyes never leaving her drawn features.

Aly's heart started a slow pound as she watched Clay walk with purpose toward her. Her fingers slowly knotted into a fist at her side. He hadn't returned from the beach last night after their fight. She knew that, because once an hour she'd awakened to find him still missing from the spot in the raft where he normally slept.

Searching his face, Aly saw that his eyes were red-rimmed and bloodshot. There was a silver glimmer to the black gaze that he trained on her. A shiver ran up her spine, and she stood, torn between running and staying. She tensed when he reached out, capturing her right hand.

"We have to talk, Aly. Come with me?"

His voice was low and off-key, and it shook her badly. His mouth was compressed, but not in the hard line as before. Aly searched the rest of his face, and saw exhaustion present, not anger. Mutely, she nodded, trying to reclaim her icy fingers from his.

Clay refused to give up her hand, leading her away from the raft and toward the rock where he'd sat all night. A lump formed in his throat, and he tried to swallow it away, to no avail. Aly was coming hesitantly, dragging each step. Clay couldn't blame her.

Fighting a gamut of emotions on tap just below her surface calm, Aly halted at the large, flat rock in front of them. It was scarred smooth by countless aeons of time, worn down by the ocean and the wind. That was how she felt—worn down and unable to fight any longer. Clay slowly turned and faced her. She felt his fingers tighten gently around her hand. His face was tortured-looking.

"There's no way my apology is going to undo the things I've said and done to you, Aly," he began unsteadily, holding her shadowed blue eyes. "Last night—" Clay swallowed hard, forcing out the words. "I've damn near stripped you of yourself, Aly, by allowing my hatred of your brother to get in our way."

With a small cry, Aly tried to pull away.

"No," Clay pleaded, placing his other hand on her injured shoulder. "Stay, Aly. Stay and hear me out. Please?"

Tears blinded her. "I—I can't take any more, Clay," she whispered hoarsely. "I hurt too much...."

He groaned, his fingers tightening around her shoulder. Closing his eyes, he hung his head. "It's my fault. This is all my fault. Listen to me, please." He opened his eyes, holding her anguished gaze. "Ever since you came to Moffett, I've been gunning for you. Last night, I realized what I'd done. I was punishing you for your brother's act. I wanted to lash out and hurt someone...anyone, for my family's death." His tone grew raw as he held her wavering eyes. "You don't know how sorry I am, Aly. A-and I know there's no way to make it up to you. I'm not going to ask for your forgiveness, even if you could find it somewhere in your heart to give it to me. I don't deserve it. I promise, things are going to be different from here on out between you and me. God," he whispered, reaching out, smoothing strands of hair away from her damp cheek, "I'm sorry."

Dizziness washed over Aly. She stood frozen, the brief touch of Clay's fingers brushing across her cheek making her heart explode with grief, with loss.

"I want you to stay here with Dan. You don't have to go with me. Understand?" Clay's voice grew urgent, his gray eyes burning with a fierce light. "I'm not going to question your honor or integrity in this matter, Aly. I won't destroy what's left of you." Reluctantly, Clay released her and forced a bleak smile. She looked as if she were in shock.

"I'm going to pack enough provisions to last five days. As soon as I get them together, I'll take off. According to the map, the village is three days northeast of here." Clay raised his hand to reach out and caress her hair, but thought better of it. He allowed his hand to fall back to his side. "No more fighting, Aly. I'm calling a permanent truce between us. It should have been done a long time ago. A war doesn't determine who's right or wrong, only who's survived. I'm going to try and salvage what's left of our relationship. Instead of creating more wounds for you, maybe I can help heal up some of the ones I'm responsible for... I don't know...I'll try, if you'll let me..." He held her luminous gaze, which was filled with tears.

Aly backed away from him, her hand pressed against her lips. "I—I never expected this. Let me...let me get over the shock."

He dug the toe of his boot into the sand, bowing his head. "I wouldn't blame you if you never spoke to me again, Aly. But there's something between us—I can feel it. Maybe it's one last thread of trust." He lifted his chin, staring over at her. "Follow your heart in this matter. I know you have good instincts; I've seen you use them on the missions. Use that same gut feeling with me to see that I'm honest about my apology to you."

Dizziness washed through Aly and she closed her eyes; Clay's sudden change in attitude overwhelmed her. "All right," she whispered unsteadily. "I'll feel my way through this."

Clay nodded, hope burning in his charcoal-gray eyes. "It's more than I should ask of you, Aly, but I can't help myself anymore, where you're concerned." He walked on by her, heading back toward the raft, his shoulders slumped.

Dan looked up from where he was sitting in the raft when Aly returned an hour later. He looked worried. "Miss Trayhern?"

Wearily, Aly sat down, facing him. Dan looked better. He even had some color in his cheeks. "Yes?"

"Look, I don't mean to butt in where I don't belong, but I really think you ought to reconsider your decision to stay here."

She sat down. Clay had left fifteen minutes ago, hiking toward the lower desert hills. A part of her had wanted to go with him, but another, more stubborn part, wanted to remain here. "About what, Dan?" Aly felt gutted, her feelings numbed by Clay's halting apology.

"You really ought to go with Mr. Cantrell."

"He said that?"

"No, ma'am. He said you were staying, and he felt it was best that way."

"I see."

"I don't think you do, ma'am." Dan forced a weak smile. "Look, I know you two have had your problems with each other. And I know it wasn't your fault. Mr. Cantrell got carried away, there's no doubt. But he's trying to make amends, Miss Trayhern."

Bleakly, Aly studied the engineer. "Then you heard our fight last night?"

"Yes, ma'am." Dan held up his hand. "But I can promise you, I'm not Lieutenant Starbuck. What I hear stays with me."

"Thank you, Dan," she murmured, meaning it.

"That's why it's important you go with Mr. Cantrell."

Aly tried to busy herself by picking up the items in the raft and stowing them neatly here and there. "Oh?"

Dan leaned forward, gripping her arm to get her attention. "Listen to me, Miss Trayhern, no one ought to be trekking that desert for days on end alone. It's dangerous out there. What if Mr. Cantrell falls and twists an ankle? Worse, what if he slides off one of those rocky hills and breaks a leg? Where does that leave him? He'll die out there alone. He's only got enough water for five days. He has no way to signal for help. The radio's here, not with him."

Aly blinked, assimilating the feeling behind Dan's words. "My God," she whispered, "I never thought about those things."

"Of course you wouldn't," Dan agreed, "because you were upset. You had a right to be. But you have to look at the bigger picture. I'll be fine here by myself. I've got shelter, a radio, enough food for seven days and plenty of water." His hand tightened on her arm. "Please, go with Mr. Cantrell. Swallow your pride. You don't travel that kind of mountains without a teammate. You're his copilot, you're supposed to be with him. I know you're raw and hurting right now, but be strong enough to put personal feelings aside."

He was right. Aly felt shame flow through her, and she hung her head. "Okay, Dan, I'll go."

"Whew! Boy, am I glad! There's another pack. Take those extra five quarts of water and pack 'em in there. The MREs are in the corner. Hurry, and you can catch up with him."

The first hill was a killer, Clay decided, winded by the time he reached the top of the rocky summit. His boots and lower legs were coated with the yellow dust. Shifting the backpack across his shoulders, he sat down to rest. The sun was rising higher, and already he could feel the intense heat building around him. There were three series of hills, scalloped upward toward the jagged mountain range in the distance. Those peaks were close to eight thousand feet high. Somewhere on the other side was an Indian village.

Checking the compass once again, Clay got to his feet to start across the nose of the ridge and head for the downward slope.

"Clay!"

He halted, frowning. That was Aly's voice! Turning around in disbelief, he looked down. Aly was halfway up the hill, a small pack slung across her right shoulder, climbing toward him just as fast as she could. Scowling, Clay wondered what the hell she was up to. Twice, she slipped on the loose rocks and gravel because her arm was in the sling, throwing her off balance. She was going to injure herself more if she didn't slow down! Cursing roundly, he met her three-quarters of the way up the hill.

"What the hell are you doing?" he rasped, gripping her by her good arm to steady her. The flight suit she wore was coated with dust. Damp strands of red hair stuck to her brow and temples. And the sheer dark blue of her eyes, when she lifted her lashes to meet his, struck hard at his heart.

"I—" Aly gasped for breath "—I had to come. Dan was right—" She took in another couple of breaths before continuing. Despite her daily five-mile runs, this kind of climbing left her unprepared. She defiantly held Clay's dark scowl. "What if something happens to you? Who will take care of you? Dan's right—I was wrong, okay?"

Convinced she wasn't going to fall, Clay released her. "Nothing's going to happen to me, Aly. Now why don't you turn around and get your rear back down there?"

"You—you stubborn, mule headed idiot!" she shouted. "There's no pleasing you, is there?"

A grin leaked through his scowl. "Stubborn? Mule-headed? Me?"

"Cantrell, you are the most contrary man I've ever had the misfortune to meet! And I'm not going to turn around and go back. You need a partner. We're a team, remember? I'm your copilot. So just wipe that silly smile off your face and start walking. I'm not leaving!"

Scratching his head, Clay muttered, "Damned if I can figure you out."

Aly glared at him. "Don't bother trying."

"I always said women with red hair were complicated. I was right. Come on, get on up in front of me so I can catch you in case you decide to take a nose-dive into these rocks."

Blinking, Aly looked up at him. "Then, I can stay?"

"Do I have a choice?"

A tight grin crossed her mouth. "No, you don't." And she walked past him, taking the lead.

The climbing, sweating and deep breathing sloughed off Aly's pain, frustration and anxiety. By the end of the first hour, she'd relaxed. The rocky hills were dangerous to tread because of the loose stone and pebbles. She'd lost count of how many times she'd tripped or fallen. And every time Clay was there to help her back up. Once, he muttered, "You're the liability on this trip, not me. It's a damn good thing *I* came along." There'd been amusement in his eyes and tone, so she hadn't reacted except to give him a smile of thanks. His returning smile tore at her raw heart, sending joy through her.

"Aly, let's take a break," Clay called.

Gratefully, Aly sank to her knees. They were halfway up the second hill; the sun was scorchingly hot. Clay walked up and sat opposite her. Sweat was running freely down his face, dark splotches beneath each armpit of his flight suit.

"This is hard work," she confided, breathing raggedly.

"Yeah. I don't think we're in shape for it." He handed her a plastic bottle filled with water. "Drink just a little, and slosh it around in your mouth before swallowing."

"Right." The water was warm, but heavenly. "Thanks," she whispered and handed it back to him.

Clay took a swallow. Afterward, he pointed toward the Pacific Ocean. "Beautiful view, isn't it?"

Aly nodded, savoring Clay's closeness. She needed his gentleness after the storm that had broken between them last night. "Yes, very beautiful."

Quiet stole across the hill as they absorbed the spectacle of the dark blue ocean against bright yellow terrain. Clay had drawn up one knee, resting his chin on it. Peace flowed through Aly as she studied his profile beneath her half-closed eyes. There was almost a hint of a smile to the corner of his mouth, if she wasn't mistaken.

"What are you smiling about?"

Clay closed his eyes. "I was thinking about beauty, what it means to each of us. How many of the pilots back at Moffett could find beauty in this desolate place?"

"Probably not many," Aly returned softly. She hungered for his thoughts, his feelings. Every small thing Clay shared with her, healed her a little more.

"Right." And then Clay opened one eye, looking over at her. "Like right now: you're beautiful."

Aly gave him a startled look, and then she frowned. "Oh, get out of here, Clay!"

"No, really." He pointed lazily to her hair. "The sunlight makes your hair look like fire is dancing through the strands. That's beauty. You're beautiful...."

The words, spoken so softly, caressed Aly. She looked away, unable to deal with his honesty. "Right now, I don't feel very beautiful, Clay. Inside or out."

He nodded. "I did that to you."

She rubbed the perspiration from her face, feeling the grit beneath her fingertips. "I let you do it to me," she corrected.

"I don't understand."

Aly drew her legs up, resting her cheek on them. She hesitantly admitted, "My father had a long talk with me right after I got to Moffett. I told him how much you hated me because my name was Trayhern, and the fact we were going to have to work together." She closed her eyes, unable to stand the look of compassion in Clay's features. "He counseled me to treat you like a wounded wild animal, to keep you from biting me."

"And so you chose not to confront me every time I attacked you?"

"Sometimes retreat is the better part of valor." And then Aly whispered, "I never wanted to fight with you, Clay. I understood some of your pain. There was nothing I could do to take away or change the past. All I could hope for, pray for, was that someday, you'd get past your hate and see me, judge me for who I was—not for my name or my family's history."

Clay fought the urge to reach over and caress Aly. There was so much pain in her voice. "It took me a long time to realize that."

"It could have taken forever," she reminded him. "I mean, I have another year in the cockpit with you. Maybe the second year will be better than the first."

Clay held her gaze. His voice was resonant and husky. "You can count on it, honey." Rising to his feet, he held out his hands to her. "Come on, we've got another hill to climb—together."

Shaken by the intensity in his voice and eyes, Aly dumbly reached out, placing her hand in Clay's. As he pulled her to her feet, she was mesmerized by his mouth. No longer was it pulled in at the corners or compressed. There was an ease to it, and she breathed deeply in relief. "This is all a dream," Aly confessed unsteadily, standing inches from him.

"What is?" Clay asked, holding on to her hand.

"All of this. Do you know how many times I dreamed of us calling a truce?"

"Believe it. It's real, Aly. Ready?" If Clay didn't move, he was going to lean those spare inches and kiss those luscious lips that were begging to be worshiped.

"Y-yes. Let's go."

"You first."

At noon they found an overhanging ledge to hide beneath, out of the sun. The land had heated up like an oven with no thermostat to control it. Aly's suit clung damply to her, and her hair was plastered to her skull. She wished for a hat of some kind to protect her head from the brutal rays.

She sat down on one of the two rocks in the niche. Clay sat next to her, their bodies touching. He handed her the water, and she drank sparingly. Every swallow counted. Giving it back to him, she muttered, "What I'd do for a bath right now!"

"Same goes for me." Clay took a sip, capping the bottle. He looked over at Aly. "How are you doing?" Heat could be a killer if they weren't careful. Not only could they become dehydrated, but a heatstroke or sunstroke was possible.

"Okay." She wiped her face with the back of her hand, grimacing. "I've never sweated like this before."

"We've never been in Baja before, either," he pointed out dryly, opening two MREs for lunch. Mixing them with just a bit of water, he handed one plastic pouch to Aly along with a fork.

Aly thanked him for the MRE. In spite of their discomforts, the past few hours with Clay had been heaven. She looked forward to each rest stop because it gave her a few minutes to simply talk and share with him. This was the real Clay Cantrell she'd met on the Bayshore on that day so long ago.

They ate in silence, watching a buzzard flying around in lazy circles far above them.

"If that buzzard had a boom on his tail, he could be mistaken for a P3," Clay pointed out.

Aly's laughter echoed down through the series of hills. She saw Clay's eyes burn with some unknown emotion as he stared over at her.

"When you laugh," he said, "I feel light inside. The way you laugh is free and uninhibited."

She blossomed beneath his praise. "Thank you."

"Your laughter reminds me of the alto mission bells at San Juan Capistrano. Ever been down there? It's a little Spanish mission near San Diego."

"No, never been there." Aly liked his comparing her to a lovely mission bell. "Is it pretty?"

Clay leaned back against the rock, getting comfortable after finishing his lunch. "Yeah. It's right in the middle of a town, but when you walk into that courtyard, it's like walking back in time. It's peaceful... sort of like you."

Aly followed suit, relaxing against the wall, the overhang protecting them fully from the sun. She was pleasantly full and suddenly very tired. Closing her eyes she muttered, "I remind you of peace?"

Clay nodded. "I wasn't the only one to notice that quality about you. Dan and Sam did, too. We all agree you're like an island of peace when there's a storm raging around us. I think part of it is your husky voice. Another part of it is just you, the way you handle yourself during an emergency. I know it makes me feel more relaxed having you in that right seat.''

She luxuriated in his softly spoken compliment. "I haven't felt like an island or haven of peace since we met, Clay."

"That's going to change," he promised her.

"I'm glad," Aly whispered, barely opening her eyes. "And I've got to tell you, it feels good to know that."

His smile was gentle as he opened his eyes and met hers. "It feels good for both of us."

Aly couldn't agree more, the hot noontime air making her sleepy. "Clay... I'm beat. Can we catch a few minutes of sleep?"

"Yeah," he muttered, "go ahead. We shouldn't be walking in this kind of heat, anyway. Take a long nap, Aly. We're going to wait until 1600 before we tackle that hill again."

Tipping her head back, Aly strove to get as comfortable as possible, glad that Clay was sensible about the trek. "Great," she murmured, "I'll see you in a few hours...." Within minutes, she was sleeping deeply.

It wasn't hard for Clay to fall asleep, either. He'd been up all night, thinking and feeling his way through the mess he'd created for himself and Aly. Her smile wavered before his closed eyes. Her laughter had sent such a sharpened shaft of longing through him. She had laughed! With him! Ever since that first harrowing night at sea when she'd clung to him in her sleep, Clay had hungered to have her near him once again. He dreamed that Aly was in his arms once again.

* * *

Aly awoke slowly, drenched in sweat. The air was hot and dry, and as she inhaled, Clay's unmistakable scent entered her flaring nostrils. Her head lay on something softer than a rock. She rubbed her cheek, feeling the texture of cloth beneath it. Confused, she dragged her eyes open.

Sometime during the afternoon hours while she'd slept, Aly had turned to the right, using Clay's body as a pillow. Her head lay on his broad shoulder, her cheek tucked next to his jaw. Shocked, Aly lay very still. When had she turned and snuggled up against Clay? And then she realized that he was snoring softly, asleep, and unaware of what she'd done.

Relief fled through Aly, and she relaxed. Clay would never know that she craved his closeness, hungered to have his arms around her as she had the night in the raft. She gently pressed those feelings into her heart. Absorbing his scent, his quiet masculine strength, Aly lay still, more content than she had ever been.

Clay invited a sense of peace, too, she thought languidly. Little did he realize just how much he was an island, a haven in her tension-filled world of flying. Still, it was kind of him to confide that he and the crew liked her calming ability on the flights.

Unconsciously nuzzling beneath his jaw, Aly smiled softly. How could she tell Clay that she had never expected him to be able to see what he was doing to both of them, much less apologize to her? Aly knew that it took someone of incredible depth and honesty to search himself ruthlessly like that. And it said something vitally important about Clay Cantrell: although he had a strong ego, he didn't allow his pride to get in the way of making apologies. So few men had the ability to release their pride and allow themselves to be wrong, much less admit it!

Aly's interlude was interrupted when she felt something crawling across her hand that was in the sling. She frowned and raised her head, looking down. A scream escaped her. It was a scorpion crawling across her fingers!

She leaped to her feet, slapping at the poisonous creature, flinging it off her. As she did so, her booted feet slipped on the shalelike rock, and she fell backward.

Clay jerked up at Aly's first scream. Disoriented, he felt her leap away from him. He opened his eyes just in time to see her start to fall. Automatically, he threw out both his arms to catch her.

"Oh, Clay!" she cried, sagging against him.

"What? What's wrong?"

Aly trembled, finding safety within his arms as he turned her toward him. "It was a scorpion! Ugh! It was awful!" she wailed, pointing at the area where it had landed.

Worriedly, he looked down at her, sleep torn away from him. "Did it sting you?"

"N-no. I was just coming awake on your shoulder when—when that horrible little creature started crawling across my left hand. Ugh!" And Aly buried her face against his chest, closing her eyes.

"Damn," Cantrell muttered, holding her tightly to him, "that was close. Those little bastards are really poisonous down here in Baja." Automatically, Clay stroked her hair, finding it thick and warm beneath his fingers. "It's okay, Aly. It's gone, and I don't see any more of them around."

The terror began to recede and Aly was wildly aware of Clay's arms around her, her breasts pressed to his chest. She gulped in a breath, her right hand sliding across his flight suit, feeling his muscles leap and respond beneath her palm. She pushed the hair away from her eyes. "I—I'm okay now," she whispered. "You can let go of me." She wanted anything but that!

"Sure?" Clay held her at arm's length, keeping both hands on her shoulders. Aly was pale, her eyes dark with fear.

Nodding jerkily, she muttered, "Sure." When his hands fell away, she felt bereft. "I don't want to have to use that snake-venom kit we're carrying," she stammered.

"That makes both of us, sweetheart." He watched her for a long moment, to make sure she wasn't going to faint or something. Clay tried to forget their close contact, and how good her small breasts felt against him. She was so much woman that it made him ache.

"What else does that manual say about this area? What other kinds of poisonous creatures lurk around here?" Aly demanded.

Clay grinned, leading her back to their niche and helping her to sit. "We've got tarantulas."

"Ugh! I hate spiders even more." Aly shivered.

"They aren't poisonous, really," Clay tried to assure her.

"I'll bet there are snakes, too. Probably rattlers."

"Yeah, plenty of them."

"What else?"

He grinned at her. "What is this? Punish Aly with as many ugly little creatures as we can find? Are you a masochist?"

She gave him a nervous smile. "I may be Superwoman in the cockpit, but insects are my undoing."

"Where do snakes fit in on your priority list of horrors?" Cantrell teased.

"Insects are number one. Snakes are second."

"You'd better add coral snakes, too, then."

Aly groaned. "Clay, those are the most poisonous snakes on the North American continent! Are you telling me they make Baja their home?"

He suppressed his smile. "Yes." Aly was truly shaken. But he had to admit that he kind of enjoyed her little-girl reaction. It was nice to know that she wasn't perfect, and that this was an area where he could be strong for her. Crawling creatures didn't faze him in the least.

"What else is in your Little Shop of Horrors, Cantrell? You're gloating over my reaction. I can tell you are...."

His grin widened by inches. Reaching out, he gripped her right hand, giving it a tender squeeze. "I can't help it, Aly. Snakes and such don't bother me at all."

"Good for you, Cantrell. They do me."

She was beginning to smile. That was good. If he could tease her out of her terror, that made him feel of some use in this new and tentative partnership. "There's one more—"

"Ohh, I knew it! You're saving the worst for last, aren't you?"

Chuckling, he said, "Gila monsters."

"Oh, they're lizards."

"Not all that terrible, eh?"

Aly hedged. "Well, they have four legs and they look a little less threatening than a spider or a horrible scorpion."

"They're the most poisonous, next to a coral snake. You'd better set them first on your list," he warned.

"I used to have a pet horned toad," Aly assured him, her fear dissipating under his attention and care. She gave him a strained smile. "Lizards are okay in my book."

"Well," he growled, "the Gila monster isn't your friendly neighborhood lizard. He's got a set of choppers that dispense some of the worst poison known to man. That snakebite kit we carry will hardly counteract that bastard's venom."

"You sound like an expert on the little fella," she taunted good-naturedly, delighted that the shoe was on the other foot.

"While you were sleeping last night, I was reading our survival manual by moonlight. Seriously, Aly, if you see a black and red lizard, stay the hell away from it, you hear me? The manual said if the lizard bites, his fangs remain sunken in you until he can close them."

Aly had the good grace to lose her smile. "You mean his jaws lock?"

"Yeah, and it's not pretty."

"Okay," Aly breathed. "I swear, I'll stay away from Gila monsters."

Satisfied he'd convinced her of the danger, Clay nodded. "Smart lady." He looked at his watch. It was nearly 1600. The worst of the heat was over by now. "You ready for another stroll?"

More than ready to leave the area where the scorpion lived, Aly got to her feet. "Let's go. I don't like the critters in this neighborhood."

## Chapter Nine

The second set of hills were crossed by early evening. Occasionally, Clay would look over at Aly, who walked at his shoulder. Right now, they traversed a small, sandy valley, the hills surrounding them like rounded loaves of golden brown bread. He was happy, he realized, almost having forgotten what the feeling was like.

After the scorpion incident, Aly had withdrawn again, remaining silent for the most part during the past two hours. Was it because he'd held her? Sadness moved through Clay. He couldn't blame her for that kind of reaction. If someone had rebuffed him for nine months solid, he wouldn't trust them much, either.

Trust . . . The word moved gently through him as he thought about it in relation to Aly and himself. He needed to build a bridge of trust between them again. *Why?* With a snort, Clay knew the answer. He'd fallen in love with her. But he had to be out of his mind to think, even hope, that she might eventually love him. How could she, after what he'd done to her?

Still, Clay wanted to establish a beachhead of trust. He wanted to be friends with Aly, if nothing else. With his spirits buoyed, his step lightened.

"See that set of boulders?" he asked her, pointing straight ahead. Three oblong boulders rose thirty feet into the air, positioned next to one another in a semicircle.

Wiping the sweat from her brow, Aly nodded. "Yeah. We get to rest?"

"Dinner stop," Clay promised, flashing her an easy smile.

Frowning as they approached the boulders, Aly muttered, "I wonder if there are any spiders or scorpions around?" And she began to look in each nook and cranny.

"Let me look. You sit down and rest. You're beat."

"Thanks," Aly said, finding a spot relatively free of rocks, and sliding into a sitting position. The sun had sunk behind the first set of hills, the strong rays divided upward like spokes in a wheel. The sky was turning salmon pink.

"No, I don't think there are any creepy-crawlies," Clay told her, settling next to her. Bare inches separated them. "Hungry?"

"Starved."

Clay grinned at the fervor in her voice, settling the large backpack in front of him and digging out two MREs.

Aly leaned back, resting her hand against her left arm. Her shoulder ached from all the jostling and jerking it had received. Admittedly, if Clay hadn't caught her a couple of times, she'd have fallen, and possibly done more damage to it. She barely opened her eyes, watching Clay through her lashes. His face was incredibly relaxed, and there was a glint of silver in his eyes; something she'd seen only once before—and that was when he kissed her when he was drunk.

"I actually think you like this hike we're taking," she muttered.

"Yeah, I'm enjoying it."

"You must have grown up in the country," she accused.

Clay fixed up the MRE with a bit of water and handed it to Aly. "And you must have grown up in a city."

She took the plastic bag, scowling at him. "Is it that obvious?"

"It is when you shriek every time you see a little critter."

Aly had the good grace to laugh, realizing he was baiting her. Clay's answering smile tore at her senses, and she found herself wanting to move into his arms, just to be held. "You're a sadist, Cantrell. You're enjoying the discovery of my Achilles' heel a little too much." Aly wasn't able to stop the grin from crossing her mouth.

Settling back, Clay spooned into the MRE. "So tell me, what city raised you?"

She arched an eyebrow at him. "It was a number of cities, smart aleck. My father was a general in the Air

Force, and we literally got transferred all over the world."

"That should have gotten you used to a lot of different situations."

"Most of the houses we lived in didn't have spiders and scorpions in them, Cantrell."

"Just where did you develop this fear, Miss Trayhern?"

She loved the boyish look on Clay's face, and she welcomed his attention and teasing. "Well," she muttered, "If I tell you, do you promise not to be like Starbuck and blab it all over the station?"

"No one's like Starbuck," Clay growled. He brightened and held up his right hand. "Scout's honor."

"Were you ever a Boy Scout?" Aly probed mercilessly. "I know how you jet jocks are. You've got lines for any and all occasions. You guys lie for a living when it comes to women."

Chuckling, Clay nodded. "Man, you've got our type pinned down, don't you?"

"It comes from experience, Cantrell. Those student jet jocks hit on me too many times at Pensacola. I got pretty good at seeing a line coming from a mile away." Aly held his amused gaze. "I even had a couple raise their hand just like you did, and swear on Scout's honor, only to find out later that they'd never been Boy Scouts. Now you understand why I question *your* gesture."

This was the real Aly, he realized humbly. A wise-cracking lady who could land on her feet. His smile widened, and he fought a very real urge to slip his arm around her shoulders, draw her close and kiss those upturned corners of her provocative mouth. "First of all, I *was* a Boy Scout. Matter of fact, I made Eagle Scout."

"Impressive. You must have gotten your hand-em-a-line badge after you joined the Navy."

"Watch it, Trayhern."

Delighted, Aly hooted. "To fast for you, fly-boy?"

"No one's faster than me," he gloated, a threat in his tone.

Aly chuckled between bites, trading warm glances with Clay. What a wonderful sense of humor he'd been hiding from her all these months. Momentary sadness struck her, but Aly rallied. He was trying to change, she realized. Clay was trying to make up for all the pain and hurt he'd caused her. Her smile dissolved as she made that connection.

"Aly? Where'd you take off to?" Clay had seen the dancing gold highlights disappear from her wide, telling eyes. And her smile had disappeared, too.

"Huh? Oh, I'm sorry, Clay. I just got to thinking, was all. It's nothing."

He cocked his head, catching her gaze. "Nothing?" he mimicked, trying to cajole her into telling him what she was really thinking about.

Forcing a slight smile, Aly muttered, "Don't mind me. I nose-dive every once in a while."

Not convinced, but not knowing how to pull whatever was bothering her out into the open, Clay straightened. He took another tack.

"After my father died, my mother moved us back to Dubuque, Iowa. She loved the fields of corn and wanted to raise us in the country, away from the cities." He ate more slowly, allowing those memories to well up within him. "I guess they found my mom on somebody's doorstep around Christmas one year, and she was raised in a succession of foster families in New York City. She hated big cities, telling us that concrete, glass and steel weren't going to teach us a thing. We had to go to the country to find out what life was all about." He laughed softly and shared a warm look with Aly, who had stopped eating and was listening intently.

"So, after my father died in that jet crash—which I don't remember, because I was barely a year old—we moved to Iowa. My first memories are of sitting on top of this huge black and white Holstein cow. I must have been three years old at the time. My mother was holding me up there, and Stephen was taking a picture of the two of us. I was bawling my eyes out because the cow scared the hell out of me."

"Did your mother like animals?" Aly asked, touched that Clay would share such a personal moment of his life with her.

He finished off the rest of the MRE, stowing the bag and plastic spoon in the pack. "She *loved* animals. Horses, especially." Leaning back, his hands behind his head, Clay watched the changing colors of the sky as sunset neared. "I guess as close as she ever got to having a horse was that big old cow. We rented an old four-room house from this farmer who owned a dairy herd. And this one old cow, Bossy, was real tame. Actually, it was Stephen's idea to put me up on Bossy and pretend that she was a horse for me to ride. Mom went along with the idea. They had great fun, but I was scared to death."

A soft smile touched Aly's lips. "It sounds as if you had a wonderful time growing up in Iowa." Pain over Stephen's death made her ache for Clay. But he didn't appear unhappy right now. Instead, there was excitement in his voice, as if he were sharing these vignettes for the first time.

"Yeah, well, if you knew Stephen... He was five years older than me, and he was always plotting and planning something. Usually something that included me as the naive twit who got suckered into it."

"I know what you mean." Aly laughed. "My two older brothers, Morgan and Noah, used to blame me for whatever they got caught doing behind my parents' backs."

The mention of Morgan's name hit Clay hard. He wrestled with it, praying his face remained neutral. And when he saw the happiness in Aly's eyes over those memories, he wanted to push beyond his own painful barriers to find out more about her. "Sounds like those two were in cahoots, and you were the odd person out," he teased.

"Oh, believe me, I was! I remember one time when Morgan wanted to play Indian fort. He was always cooking up ideas, and of course, Noah and I just innocently toddled along." Aly sat up, animation in her voice. "He had the greatest ideas sometimes, Clay. That particular time, he dragged a whole bunch of cardboard boxes up from the basement, and we made this wonderful fort out of them. I mean, we had boxes strung all through the living room, one and two stories high."

"Where were your parents?"

"Dad was off flying a B-52 mission, gone for two weeks. Mom was over at the base exchange, getting groceries. Morgan was twelve, so he was baby-sitting the two of us while she was gone."

"Perfect recipe for trouble." Clay chuckled.

"You got it!" Aly set down the MRE and launched excitedly into the rest of her story. "Noah got this great idea to use sheets as a roof for our fort. So they told me to go up to the linen closet and get them. I must have come back with fifteen of them!"

Clay groaned. "Oh, God, what did your mother do when she saw this concoction?"

Laughing, Aly reached over, her hand resting on his shoulder. The action shocked both of them. She quickly removed her hand. "By the time Mom got home, the entire living room comprised our fort. With the sheets, we had a wonderful roof, and even had enough of them left over for curtains to hang over some of the boxes inside the fort. It was *really* a neat fort, Clay."

He grinned. "I'll bet it was. And I'll bet your mother had a canary, too."

Giggling, Aly said, "She about dropped the groceries at the entrance to the living room when she saw it. Noah and Morgan had heard her car pull up in the driveway, and they scooted into the fort to hide. They told me to go out and tell Mom all about it."

"Uh-oh . . . they were setting you up for the fall."

"You got it! I ran out to the kitchen to meet her, bubbling over about this fort we'd built." She slanted him a wry glance. "Now, keep in mind, I was only six years old at the time. Anyway, Mom came to the entrance of the living room, and her mouth fell open. I was rattling on in my little voice, my arms waving here and there about how we'd built it. When she finally spoke, there was this tone in her voice that meant we were in big trouble. Mom ordered Morgan and Noah front and center."

"Did they come crawling out of the fort and face the music?" Clay asked, grinning.

"Not at first," Aly hedged, fondly recalling the incident. "Mom demanded that Morgan and Noah show themselves or else."

"Did they give up?"

"Morgan had talked Noah into carrying a white flag of truce out with him, thinking Mom would find it funny and relent. She didn't. Both my brothers pointed the finger at me, telling Mom that I'd taken the sheets from the closet. They hoped to transfer the blame to me, because they knew a paddling was the next order of business."

Clay shook his head. "Your brothers were mean."

Chuckling, Aly said, "That's okay. Little sister grew up in a hurry under those conditions. I learned real fast never to be around when Morgan and Noah started cooking up another one of their grandiose plans."

"So, what happened to the fort?"

"You haven't heard the best of it." Aly laughed. "Mom grabbed Morgan by the ear and demanded to know where he'd gotten all those cardboard boxes. There must have been twenty-five or thirty of them in there. He confessed to Mom that he'd gotten them from the basement. She nearly laid an egg on that one."

"Why?"

Aly laughed for nearly a minute, holding her sides. Wiping the tears from her eyes, she finally managed to get out, "Morgan *unpacked* those boxes from our recent move to this new base. Twenty-eight boxes of stuff were now helter-skelter all over the basement floor. Mom almost died when she went down and looked." Her eyes sparkled, watching Clay grin. "The upshot of it was that Morgan and Noah spent the next week, every night after schoolwork was done, repacking each of those boxes. They hated it! Noah was really mad at Morgan, because Noah hadn't gotten the boxes out of the basement in the first place."

Shaking his head, Clay asked, "What about those fifteen sheets?"

"Morgan had to not only wash and dry every last one of them, but he had to iron them as well!"

"So, your Mom read between the lines and saw that you were the innocent in their diabolical plot?"

Twittering contentedly, Aly leaned back. "Yup. For once naive little sister got a reprieve. God, that whole thing was so funny, Clay." She traded a happy look with him. "I'm really glad you started talking about your family. I haven't remembered the fort incident in years." Reaching out, she briefly touched his arm. "Thanks. It feels so good to laugh again."

They had managed to scale the third set of hills before darkness fell across Baja. Clay pulled Aly to a halt. She leaned slightly, her body brushing his.

"Let's call it a day," he said.

"Good, I'm beat to hell, Clay."

He squeezed her hand. "You're a trooper, though." Aly had never complained, but kept doggedly climbing hour after hour. "I'm amazed at your stamina," Clay admitted, allowing the heavy pack to slide off his shoulders.

Aly stood wearily, more tired than she'd ever thought possible. Clay was the one who carried the pack, but he didn't appear to be nearly as exhausted as she felt. "Must be the family genes," she offered. "What do you want me to do?"

"Nothing, just sit down and rest."

"Thanks ... I owe you one."

Clay noted a slice of moon was coming up, providing just enough light to barely see her facial features. "And I intend to collect," he warned her huskily.

A tremble of anticipation moved through her. Aly sat facing him. He couldn't be serious. No. "Uh-oh," she baited, "my body or my life, is that it?"

Taking out the plastic ground cover, Clay laid it down after clearing a spot of rocks and pebbles. "Say, now that's not a bad trade."

She snorted. "Cantrell, you're such a male chauvinist."

He took the blanket, placing it over the plastic cover, smoothing it out. "I'd take your body in trade."

"You would."

He sat up, hands resting on his knees. Seeing that Aly wasn't sure whether he was teasing or not, Clay decided to test her, to find out just how far her disgust with him went. "Now, I'm very picky about the body I make love with."

Aly avoided his dark, probing eyes. She lowered her lashes. How many times had she dreamed of Clay loving her? Of their sharing laughter and joy together? "So am I," she parried.

"But if there was a choice between losing your life or giving yourself to me, which would it be?"

Aly licked her chapped lower lip. "Well..." she hedged.

"Is it my looks that turn you off?"

"No! Of course not." Aly risked a glance at him, realizing he was watching her intently. "What I mean is, you're not ugly or anything."

"Whew, that was close!" Clay dramatically placed his hand against his heart.

She gave him a dirty look.

"Since I'm such a handsome devil, you wouldn't find it personally distasteful to fall into my arms?"

Aly dug the toe of her boot into the dirt, trapped. "Okay, so you're not bad-looking," she admitted, refusing to answer the rest of his question.

"I love the way compliments roll off your tongue. I practically have to drag them out of you."

"Oh, shut up, Cantrell!"

Chuckling, he got up and walked over to where she sat. He crouched down in front of her. Aly refused to look up. "What's this? Are you blushing, Aly Trayhern?" And he placed his finger beneath her chin, forcing her to meet his gaze. "Why, I believe you are."

Unable to speak, Aly held his smiling dark eyes. There was tenderness burning in them, and when she realized he wasn't laughing at her, she panicked. Clay was so close, so pulverizingly male that she ached to lean those scant inches and feel his mouth on hers again.

"My shy little violet," Clay said huskily, lightly caressing her cheek. He saw something in her huge blue eyes, and it wasn't fear. If he read her correctly, it was longing. Need. That shook him badly. Instead of disgust or anger aimed at him, he saw desire. In those shattering seconds strung between them, Clay realized that Aly didn't hate him at all. And then he remembered the passion of her returning kiss so many months ago. He gave her a little smile, hoping to reassure her that he wasn't going to take advantage of her.

"Come on, let's get ready for bed," he murmured, slowly rising to his feet. "I'd like to sleep until about 0500 when it starts getting light, and walk while it's still cool. What do you think?"

"That sounds fine," she whispered. It took Aly a good minute to gather her strewn feelings. Clay could have kissed her, and she would have welcomed it. Somehow, he'd sensed that she wanted him! His eyes had grown dark, and she'd seen that silver flame in their depths. Her heart was pounding erratically.

Clay shed the vest he was wearing and plumped it up for a pillow to lay his head on. He twisted around, looking over at Aly. She was shaken. Using humor, he growled, "Come on, Miss Trayhern, get your rear over here. If you don't lie down, you're going to fall off that rock and hurt yourself when you fall asleep on it."

Nervously, Aly rose. She looked at the small square of bedding, realizing that both of them would be sleeping on it. "Clay," she began in a strangled tone, "two people can't sleep on that!"

He started untying his bootlaces. "Sure, they can."

Lamely, Aly approached the foot of it. "But—it's only big enough for one person."

"You didn't bring your gear with you. We'll have to make do with mine."

Despair flooded her. Clay was right. She'd rushed off in such a hurry to catch up with him on the trek that she'd packed only the essentials of food and water, not sleeping gear. "I—uh, I think I'll just sleep on the ground. You go ahead and use that pallet."

"And let the creepy-crawlies get you?"

"Clay Cantrell!"

He struggled to give her his best innocent look. More than anything, Clay wanted Aly near him. Tonight, he wanted to salve more of her wounds by being close, letting her know that he didn't hate or dislike her. "Well, I mean scorpions are night creatures. And they're always looking for a warm body to snuggle up to...."

With a cry, Aly moved to the blanket. She gave him an angry look. "You're such a rat, Cantrell! You know I can't stand those things!"

He swallowed his smile and returned to unlacing his second boot. Pulling it off, he set it aside. Absently patting the blanket next to him, he said, "Come on, Aly sit down. I'll help you get those boots off."

She glared at Clay, more frightened of her reaction to him than anything else. "You take off anything more than my boots, and you're in big trouble, fella!"

"Threats, threats!" Clay laughed, reaching up and pulling her gently down beside him. "Really, Miss Trayhern, I'd hope I'm the lesser of two evils." He gloated as he untied her bootlaces. "I'd hope I'm more desirable to you than a scorpion. If you chose that fellow over me, that'd really hurt my feelings.''

"You're impossible, Cantrell! Utterly, certifiably impossible!''

He chuckled as he removed her boots. Aly had such small, delicate feet. There was concern and wariness in her features. Clay lay down, his back to her. "Come on, stop spitting and clawing like a cornered cat, and lie down.''

Grumbling under her breath, Aly lay on her right side, facing his broad, powerful back. She had no choice but to wedge next to him, the narrowness of the blanket forcing them together. She saw him rise on one elbow, pull the blanket over them and then lie back down. She clamped her eyes shut.

Clay grinned into the darkness, hotly aware that Aly was only inches away from him. "Good night, little hellcat. Sleep tight.''

Aly refused to respond to his husky voice. She tried to inch away from him, balanced precariously on the line where the blanket ended and the desert began. He was just too close, too overwhelming for her rattled senses.

Clay felt Aly move away. "Scorpions like to find the edges of blankets to crawl under,'' he told her.

With a little cry of fear, Aly scooted back to him. "Damn you, Cantrell!''

Clay stifled a laugh. "Better get a little closer, Aly. That way, no scorpions can wiggle their way between us.'' His grin widened as she hesitantly fitted her body against his back and legs. "Better,'' he groaned. "Much better.''

Aly knew her eyes must be blazing, even in the dark. "You're going to pay for this, Cantrell. You're enjoying this at my expense."

Clay shook with laughter. God, but Aly felt good contoured against him. He checked his desire to lift his arm and place it across her hip. "Yeah, I am. But you know something?"

"I don't want to hear another word out of you!"

Smiling, he murmured, "Well, I'm going to tell you anyway. I like the way you feel against me. You're warm, soft, and all woman. What a way to go...."

Aly refused to answer him. A minute later she muttered, "You're arrogant, Cantrell. You ought to be ashamed of yourself for using a situation like this on me. I can't help it if I'm scared of those horrible insects!"

Clay couldn't help himself. He slid his hand carefully beneath the blanket until it came in contact with her slender hip. Giving it a gentle pat, he murmured, "Good night, Aly. Sleep the sleep of the angels, because you are one."

The gray cape of dawn was just barely edging the horizon when Clay awoke. But that wasn't what awakened him. Sometime during the night, he'd turned over on his back. Aly had somehow found her way into his arms. Her head lay in the hollow of his left shoulder, her red hair smooth and springy against his jaw. Gently, he squeezed her, delighting in her feminine length against him.

The stars hung close in the night sky above him. A coyote yipped and then cried, his howl lonely across the quiet of the desert. There was no wind on top of

the hill. Everything was silent, as if holding its breath.
Contentment flowed through Clay. He savored each
precious second with Aly, feeling the rise and fall of
her breasts against him, her breath moist across his
neck. What pleased him most was the fact that her left
hand, despite the sling, lay against his torso.

She was sleeping deeply, and so Clay risked everything and pressed a kiss to her hair. He inhaled her
fragrance like a starved man. Wasn't he? Yes. He was
starved for her. And if he was able to read between the
lines of Aly's reluctance to lie here with him, she too
was aware of the possible chemistry that might flare to
life between them. His contentment increased, and he
closed his eyes, absorbing her into his eyes, absorbing
her into himself. If only... if only it could be like this
every day for the rest of his life.

"We belong together, little hellcat," he told her
softly. "You and me. We're a good team, and I think
you're just realizing that."

Aly stirred, her leg resting across Clay's. Unconsciously, she nuzzled upward, meeting the hard length
of his jaw. In her dreams, she heard him speaking to
her in a low voice. His arm held her safe and protected. She reveled in the feel of his masculine body
against hers. There was such strength in him, such
gentleness.

Clay groaned as Aly pressed languidly against him.
Sweet heaven... Just that one, innocent movement
brought him to hot, burning life. He wanted so badly
to kiss Aly, to feel her warm, willing mouth beneath
his once again. Carefully, so as not to awaken her,
Clay gently maneuvered Aly onto her back, his arm
beneath her head, cradling her shoulders.

He lay propped on his elbow, looking down at her in the predawn light. Her hair was tousled, and he longed to sift through those errant waves. As his gaze moved downward, Clay realized how long and thick her lashes were against the freckled planes of her cheeks. A beginning of a smile pulled at his mouth. Lifting his free hand, he lightly traced the length of her thin, aristocratic nose. She was a lady, through and through. His fingers trailed downward, and against all his better judgment, Clay barely touched her parted lips.

Aly's torrid dream state had her lying in Clay's arms. She felt his fingertips outlining the shape of her mouth, and a smile unconsciously curved them upward. With a sigh, she turned her cheek, feeling his palm cradle her face. The longing for Clay, for his touch, continued, and she nuzzled deeply into his hand, seeking, needing his warmth.

"Sweet Aly," Clay whispered, leaning over, his mouth resting against her cheek. Her skin was delicate, inviting, and he kissed her gently.

Aly felt his mouth against her cheek, and she turned her head, seeking him. Where did a dream end and reality begin? It was so real, her heart picking up in pounding beat as she felt his hand slide across her hip, bringing her against him. She wanted him so badly. A whimper broke from her as his mouth slid across the expanse of her cheek.

With a low groan, Clay covered Aly's waiting lips. She was incredibly soft, her mouth molding hotly to his. Fire shattered all his resolve, and he drank of her, tasting her, teasing her into wakefulness within his arms.

The instant Clay's mouth touched her own, Aly drew out of the folds of the twilight she lingered in. It wasn't a dream, it was wonderful reality. Dragging her lashes upward, she met and drowned in the hungry flame in his gray eyes. His mouth was cajoling, teasing, erasing her momentary panic and fear. He tasted so male, and with abandonment, Aly responded to his offering. His hand sliding across her rear, moving her against him, increased her sense of urgency. He was hard and ready and she melted within his embrace, swept away by the heat he shared with her.

Clay's mouth was hungry, searching against hers. He tasted strong and male, his scent mixed with sweat entering her nostrils. The rough texture of his beard scraped against her flesh, sending tingles riffling through her. A little cry escaped her, his name coming out in a pleading tone. She slid her fingers upward, her arm lifting, caressing Clay's hair. The strands were soft and thick. Her heart pounded urgently in her chest, and Aly pressed herself to him, feeling him groan. The reverberation thrummed through her, exciting her, putting a keen edge on her need of him.

"I need you," he muttered hoarsely against her wet, willing lips. Blindly, Clay closed his eyes, his hand sliding downward until he cupped her breast. She was so small and firm, so completely woman, her hip melting against his, creating a fire storm of hunger within him. Without thinking, Clay pulled open the Velcro of her flight suit, sliding his hand inside it, wanting to give her pleasure instead of pain for once.

Her breast was firm, the nipple taut, expectant. Gently laying her on her back, he pulled the fabric of the uniform away. Aly's breath was coming in short sobs, her fingers digging frantically into his shoulders as he leaned over, pushing the bra aside, and capturing the erect nipple.

A cry drove from deep within her as his lips covered the aching peak, and Aly arched against him, an intense heat spreading throughout her lower body. Sobs of pleasure whispered from her as Clay worshiped her as if she were some priceless, beautiful object that might break.

Clay struggled to get hold of himself. Too much was happening too fast. Aly wasn't ready for this. He fought himself, fought to try to ignore the sweet, moist texture of her lips, the passion that was making him tremble. It was enough, he screamed at himself as he reluctantly broke contact with her, that she had so willingly responded to him. One look into those sultry eyes staring up at him, and Clay knew that her feelings toward him were genuine. Joy raced beside his guilt. He didn't deserve this kind of reward for hurting her the way he had over the past nine months. Removing his hand from her flushed, rosy breast, he brought the bra back into place. Dutifully, he closed the Velcro on her flight suit, holding her confused stare.

Gently, Clay eased Aly to the pallet, his arm still beneath her head. An unsure smile tugged at his mouth as he smoothed several strands of red hair from her brow. "When I awoke, the stars were hanging over us like huge, white lanterns in the sky," he confided huskily, continuing to caress her cheek. "And I lay here a long time, thinking how lucky I was. Most importantly, you were in my arms." His voice grew gritty. "I couldn't help myself, honey. When you moved against me in your sleep, I lost all my good intentions and kissed you." Caressing her lips with his thumb, Clay whispered, "You're as hot as the color of that beautiful hair of yours. I was so cold inside and you warmed me with your fire...."

His words seemed to fall softly through Aly, into her heart. She absorbed his shaky admission and closed her eyes. She was equally at fault in this. The crash and being stranded had made her take risks that she'd never have entertained otherwise with Clay. But one look into the smoky depths of his eyes, and Aly had felt the simmering heat within her build to an explosive point again. Clay didn't even have to touch her; all he had to do was give her that smoldering look of need, and she responded. "Oh, Clay," she whispered. "I'm so afraid...."

"I know," he said, allowing his hand to rest on her shoulder, "so am I."

## Chapter Ten

Clay watched Aly withdraw deep into herself after he kissed her. She was silent, and he longed to know what was going on inside that head of hers. They were both scared. Maybe for the same reasons, maybe for different ones. He simply didn't know.

The climb across the mountains effectively drew their focus and attention. Cliffs of rock rose like sharp spires flung skyward. Taking the lead, Clay tried to find a route between them. The rocks were solid under their booted feet, and for that he was thankful. Both he and Aly were drenched with sweat, their flight suits clinging to them when they stopped to eat and rest at noon.

Aly tried to find a spot that wouldn't force them close together. Clay's kiss had unstrung her. It was everything and more than she had ever dreamed about. Her response to him had frightened her even more. Struggling to resolve the taut situation between them, Aly started a conversation after they had eaten their MREs.

"About last night . . . I mean, this morning, Clay."

Aly was two feet away from where Clay sat on the ground, leaning against a boulder. He saw her lick her lower lip nervously. "What about it?" he asked gently, afraid of what his kiss might have cost him in terms of Aly's trust. He wanted her on all levels and all ways, in and out of bed. The fear was very real in her blue eyes.

Aly picked up a small rock, turning it between her bandaged hands. "I'm not the type for a one-night stand, Clay. Never was. Never will be." She risked a glance at him. He was excruciatingly handsome, strands of his black hair dipping across his forehead, those gray eyes dark and fathomless. A quiver tremored through her as her gaze settled on the mobile mouth that could make her heart beat faster every time he smiled at her. He wasn't smiling now.

"A long time ago, I liked one-night stands," Clay admitted slowly, holding her unsure gaze. "Part of the fighter jock image, I suppose. But . . ."

Aly saw Clay smile slightly. "But?" Her heart was pounding again, and it wasn't from the brutal climb they'd made earlier.

"Well, the crash changed a lot of things for me," Clay admitted. "I almost died, and that's when I found living was a little more important than flouting death every day. The main reason I switched from fighters to land-based aircraft was because I wanted to take time to smell the flowers."

"I wondered why you got out of fighters. Most guys would die to fly a Tomcat."

He pursed his lips and nodded. "Yeah, you're right. But I'd had two and a half years racing around the skies like Parnelli Jones. And I can't say I miss those night landings on a heaving postage stamp of a deck out in the middle of an angry ocean."

Clay's voice was balm to her aching heart and, almost unwillingly, Aly began to relax. And with his quiet soothing, some of her fear of their future dissolved, too. "But you still chose an aircraft that does dangerous work."

"Sure." And then Clay awarded her one of those heart-stopping smiles. "I like danger. I was bred for it, I suppose. My father had been a Navy fighter pilot. It's in my genes—the way stubbornness runs in your family."

There was no accusation or anger in his voice when he referred to her family. Aly was still in shock over his decision to release the past and treat her as an individual. "I prefer to call it tenacity," she managed to parry.

"Yeah, pit bull style," he chortled. "So, what's this ultimatum about one-night stands all about?"

His softly spoken words caught Aly off guard. She eyed him for a long minute, the wind lifting strands of her hair as it wove in and around the crags surrounding them. "I like your sensitivity," she murmured, staring down at the rock in her hands.

"You invite it, Aly."

His voice was deep with promise. A promise she dared never hope for. "I—damn, this is so hard to say...."

"You want me to back off?"

Giving him a lame look, she nodded. "Yes."

Instead of wanting to make her feel guilty or bad, Clay wanted her to realize he would support her decision. "It's as good as done, little hellcat." And then he grinned, striving to lift her spirits. "I promise I won't keep using the creepy-crawlies as an excuse to get you into my arms, okay?"

"You're crazy, Cantrell."

He grinned with her, watching the shadows dissolve from her wonderful blue eyes. "Yeah, but you like me anyway."

Relief spread throughout Aly, and she was suddenly tired. Leaning back, her head tipped against the unyielding rock, she closed her eyes. "I'm taking the Fifth on that one."

"I would, too."

"Thanks for understanding, Clay."

"You deserve it. Take your siesta," he coaxed, "we aren't going to start hiking until 1600, anyway."

"And then we'll walk until it gets dark?"

"You got it, honey. Go to sleep."

Without the moon's thin wisp of light, Clay wouldn't have been able to make their bed. Aly sat on a rock, watching him in silence. The wind was howling through the mountains, the temperature dropping rapidly.

"Sweat during the day and freeze at night," he told her, placing the blanket over the plastic cover.

"Isn't that the truth," Aly said, and shivered. Clay had found a depression where they would be protected from most of the wind. "I wish we could make a fire."

"No wood. This is the most desolate place I've ever seen."

Miserably, Aly agreed. The climb today had brought them near the top of the mountains. "Do you think we'll reach that village by tomorrow evening?"

Clay took off his vest and made a pillow out of it. "Depends on how easy it is to climb down off this mountain." Getting to his feet, he walked over to her. "I want to change the dressings on your hands before we go to bed. I'm afraid you'll get dirt in those healing rope burns."

Aly looked at the dusty gauze that encased her palms and wrists. "They feel pretty good, Clay."

Crouching and opening the first-aid kit, he placed her right hand across the surface of his thigh. "Just let me play nursemaid, okay?"

She smiled tiredly. He was so close, and all she wanted to do was rest her head against his capable shoulder. Amazed as always at Clay's gentleness as he cut away the old bandage, she muttered, "You're a good doctor."

"Maybe it's the patient," he answered, catching her gaze. Examining her palm carefully, Clay could see that the wound was doing nicely. "Maybe I did miss my calling. Your palm is looking good."

"Maybe it's the guy doing the doctoring."

Clay grinned up at her. "What is this? A mutual admiration society we're starting?" Aly was so close, and those ripe lips of hers parted, needing to be kissed again. Stifling the urge, Clay expertly rewrapped her palm.

"There's plenty to admire about you," Aly parried, "and you know it."

"Naw. I'm just a brash ex-fighter jock. Cocky, self-assured—"

"Don't forget handsome."

"That, too. Brilliant mind, great sense of humor—"

"And nice," Aly added softly, meaning it. She saw him shrug as he gently eased her left hand out of the sling.

"Trying to be. With you, it's long overdue." Clay met and held her gaze, drowning in the gold fire. The need to slide his arms around her, draw Aly to him, was almost tangible. Fighting his raging desire, Clay croaked, "How's your shoulder feeling? I haven't heard one peep about it all day."

As she allowed her arm to ease from the bent position in the sling, Aly tested it carefully. "Pretty good."

"Does it hurt to rotate your arm in any direction? Try it, but be real slow about it."

Testing her arm, Aly found she had about fifty-percent mobility. To raise it above her breasts produced excruciating pain. "Maybe if I just let the arm hang and don't put it back in the sling, I'll get more mobility," she suggested.

"Yeah, try it. Keep the sling off tonight while you sleep. If you need it tomorrow, we can always put it back on."

He looped the sling around her neck. "There, it's nearby if you want it."

"Thanks, doc."

Clay got up reluctantly. "Anytime. Come on, let's hit the sack."

Aly chewed on her lower lip, watching as he walked back to the depression where their bedding and gear were waiting for them. To lie next to him was going to be sheer agony. Would he keep his word? Would he not touch her? Could she fight her own desire to reach out to him?

Already settled on the bed, his back to her, Clay felt Aly finally slip down beside him. He sensed her tension as she got closer. Wanting to defuse her anxiety, he murmured over his shoulder, "Just how did you get this phobia about creepie-crawlies? You never finished telling me."

Grateful for his teasing demeanor, Aly snuggled close, seeking his body heat. "My two brothers bought a bunch of small black rubber spiders at a dime store one day. They laid them all over my bed one morning while I was still sleeping. And then they stood there, waiting to see me wake up. When I did, I saw my blanket covered with the horrible things."

Clay began to laugh, trying to stifle it.

"See? You think it's funny, too."

His laughter rolled out into the darkness. "I'm sorry, honey, I can't help it. It sounds like something Stephen and I would have cooked up."

"All little boys are up to no good, if you ask me."

"Well," he asked between chuckles, "what happened?"

"I screamed and leaped out of bed. Noah had put a couple in my hair, which was long at that time, and I was trying to bat them away."

Clay started laughing again.

Aly hit him in the arm. "You're just like them, Cantrell. Good night."

He reached over, patting her hip again. "Good night. Sweet dreams for a sweet lady...."

All her worries dissipated, and Aly closed her eyes, sighing softly. "I hope you get nightmares, Cantrell, for laughing at me...."

The last of his laughter dissolved beneath her husky voice. What he'd give to hear her tone drop to a purr as he made love to her. "No way, lady. Tonight, I'm going to dream you're in my arms again."

"I'm going to dream of finding that village by to-morrow evening," she muttered in defense.

"I'll bet my dreams will be far more enjoyable than yours."

"Good night, Cantrell."

"Good night, little hellcat."

They stood near the bottom of the mountain slope, the sun low on the horizon. Aly glanced at her watch: it was 1800. They were right on schedule.

"Look—" Clay pointed "—I think that's the village. See it?"

Aly moved to his side, following the direction of his finger. She squinted her eyes. Heat rolled in waves across the arid wasteland, but she could make out a dark object in the distance. "Are you sure, Clay?"

He took out the map, double-checking it. "Yeah. The map says it's a major Huichol village."

"'Major'? Does that mean they'll have a pay phone so we can call for rescue?"

He wiped the sweat off his brow with the back of his hand. The heat was stifling. "Major in terms of population. There are all of fifty people living there."

Aly's left arm felt good after being out of the sling most of the day. She rested her hands on her hips, studying the miragelike village. "Where could fifty people possibly find enough food or water to survive out here?"

"Got me." Clay looked over at Aly. Her face was pink from sunburn, but she looked damned good to him. Last night, he'd barely slept because she'd been next to him. But Aly looked as if she'd slept like a proverbial rock, he observed wryly, her eyes clear, and no shadows beneath her lovely eyes. "Well, it's five miles away. Ready?"

She gave him a game smile. In another mile they'd be off the mountain and onto a plateau scattered with a few tenacious small plants that hugged the desert. "You bet. Let's go for it, jet jock."

The miles fell away. Aly felt a new sense of exhilaration, matching every step Clay took at her shoulder. Once he awarded her one of his devastating smiles. She wanted to stop, throw her arms around his shoulders and kiss him. And he must have read the desire in her eyes because he leaned down, placed a quick kiss on her hair, then resumed his striding walk without missing a beat. Aly didn't know whether to be pleased or disgruntled about it. Clay merely smiled that cocky smile of his, completely pleased with himself.

The village took form and shape as they drew closer. There was a huge pile of yellowed rock about a mile from the Indian hamlet. They'd been walking hard and fast, and Clay called a halt, wanting a drink of water.

Aly plopped down on a flat rock next to where he sat. "Whew!"

"Yeah," Clay muttered, tipping up the plastic bottle and taking a small swallow of water.

Shading her eyes, Aly said, "I don't believe it. There's a man on a burro coming toward us."

Clay handed her the water bottle and squinted in that direction. "Damned if it isn't. They must have spotted us coming off the mountain." He smiled. "Great, the Welcome Wagon is on the way. I hope you know some Spanish."

The water was heavenly, sliding down her sandpapery throat. Aly stoppered the bottle and gave it back to Clay. "I know enough Spanish to get by, but I don't know their Indian language."

"Doesn't matter. The survival info says most of them speak pidgin Spanish." He patted her thigh. "Well, what do you say we get this show on the road?"

Aly got to her feet, standing near him while he leaned down to stow the bottle back into the pack. Her smile disappeared. A scream lurched up her throat.

"Clay!" Her cry careened off the rocks that surrounded them.

To her horror, as Clay leaned down to pick up the pack that had been placed in a crevice between two huge boulders, Aly saw a red and black lizard leap out of the shadows toward his extended hand.

It happened so quickly, that she was unable to move to prevent it. The Gila monster attacked, its huge jaws open, hurtling toward Clay's fingers.

Clay had frozen at Aly's cry. Too late he saw the blur of the red and black Gila darting out of the crevice toward him. The next thing he felt was pain sizzling up the side of his left hand. With a croak of surprise, Clay jerked back. The Gila monster clung to his hand, its two-foot-long body swinging back and forth, its jaws locked firmly into Clay's flesh, releasing its virulent poison into his bloodstream.

With a grunt, Clay staggered forward. His eyes bulged as he tried to fling the lizard off his hand. Its jaws were locked! His mind worked like a steel trap, now. Aly's screams drifted into his narrowed focus as he whirled around on his heel. Clenching his teeth, Clay took the hand the lizard clung to, and with all his might, smashed it into the side of the rock face.

Aly shrieked as the Gila monster's jaws popped open, as it was killed on impact. Clay staggered and fell to his knees, holding his mangled left hand. She raced to his side. His flesh was already beginning to lose color. His eyes were large and dark. Sobbing his name, she knelt over him.

"The sling!" Cantrell rasped. "Get that sling on my upper arm. Make it into a tourniquet!"

Her hands shaking, Aly did as he ordered. The poison injected into Clay's hand would be moving rapidly up his arm. She took off the sling, wrapped it quickly around his arm, tightening it into position with a stick.

"Oh, God, Clay!" she cried. "What—"

"The venom kit," he whispered harshly, trying to force his hand to bleed. If he could make the four puncture holes bleed, some of the poison would drip out instead of being absorbed into his bloodstream. "Get it! Hurry!" The first wave of dizziness struck him. He could die! Clay tried to steady his ragged breathing. He had to stave off his panic. Aly's sobs heightened his fear. She fumbled through the pack, her hands shaking so badly that she dropped the kit once she'd located it.

"The shot," he told her, feeling his arm going numb because of the tourniquet on his limb. "Give me the shot as fast as you can, or I'm dead—"

Aly tore open the venom kit. Inside was an anti-venin shot. She jammed the needle portion into the tube containing the solution. "Where?" she cried.

Clay's breathing was becoming labored. He had to force each breath he took. God, but the poison was working fast! Sweat ran down into his eyes. He was so cold, and yet his entire body was wringing wet with sweat. "Anywhere!" he croaked. "My leg..."

She shoved the needle through the fabric of his flight suit and it sank deep into his left thigh. Pushing the plunger, Aly looked up at him. Clay was becoming semiconscious. Jerking the needle out, Aly tried to cushion his fall as he pitched forward. "Oh, God, Clay. Fight to stay awake! Fight!"

Aly's voice was like an echo in his head. Clay felt his hand slipping from his injured one. His mouth fell open and saliva drooled out the corner of it. He'd barely been aware of the needle entering his leg, or of Aly's hands settling on his shoulders to turn him onto his back.

"No!" Aly begged hoarsely, "Clay, don't die on me! Don't you dare! Fight back! You hear me? Fight!" She shook him hard.

Terror ate at Aly as she watched Clay struggle to stay conscious. His flesh was pasty, almost gray. His breath was coming in halting gasps, and he labored for every one he took. Aly released his shoulders, turning her attention to his injured hand. She retrieved the razor blade from the kit, slicing into two of the puncture wounds. There was a suction device, but her hands were shaking too badly to use it. Placing her lips over the now bleeding punctures, she sucked hard, spitting out the contents gathered, again and again. The poison would have pooled at the bottom of each hole the Gila monster had made. In moments, Aly had pulled as much out as possible from all four wounds.

She shakily got to her feet, looking around. The rider on the burro was much closer. Anguished, she knelt at Clay's side. His lashes fluttered, his breathing becoming shallow and fast.

"Clay? Clay, listen to me!" She gripped his shoulder, placing her mouth next to his ear. "I'm going for help, you hear me? I've got to get help! I'll be back. I promise I will!" She looked down at him. His flesh was beaded with sweat. "I'll be back—I won't desert you. I promise. Oh, God, Clay, hang on! I love you! You can't die on me!"

Sobbing, Aly staggered to her feet. She turned on her heel, and began running across the hard pebbled desert toward the man on the burro in the distance. Her throat burned with tears, her vision blurred. *I love you, Clay! Oh, God, please don't take him from me! We've just found each other!*

It was dark when Clay regained consciousness. His vision was blurred, and he was seeing double. The flicker of candles provided the only light in the darkened place. The first face he saw was that of a rotund Indian woman dressed in a blue cotton dress, with feathers and beads around her neck. She looked ageless, her black eyes glinting liked polished obsidian as she studied him in the thick silence.

"Clay?"

Aly! Her voice was terribly off-key, and he realized she was crying. Unable to move his head because he was simply too weak, he shifted his eyes to the right. Taking each breath was like inhaling fire into his lungs. It hurt to try to pull the air in or to force it out of his body. Aly's face was contoured with anxiety, her eyes large and filled with fear. Her cheeks were wet and glistening beneath the light of the candle.

"No, don't talk," she whispered, leaning forward, touching his damp brow with a cool cloth. "We're here at the Huichol village. Señora Madalena is their doctor, and she's going to help you."

He was so thirsty. Clay felt Aly's hand cradling his, holding on to it as if he would slip away. His throat was constricted, and he could no longer swallow. Blackness began to stalk him again, and he closed his eyes, focusing on Aly's cool hand, on her tremulous voice.

"I love you, Clay. You've got to fight back, you hear me? Please, don't leave me. I love you...."

Madalena nodded. "He returns to the Between. The Land of the Shadows beckons him," she grunted out in poor Spanish.

Aly looked over at her. Madalena's husband, José, was the one who had brought Clay to their village on the back of the burro. That was an hour ago. It had seemed like an eternity to Aly as she'd struggled to hold Clay on the animal's back. José had led the beast to the hamlet, bringing them to his wife. "Wh-what can be done to save his life? Surely, you must know. You live out in this godforsaken desert with those Gila monsters.''

''That is true, *señorita*. My ally told me of your coming. He warned me that a man would be bitten.'' Her eyes narrowed in her dark brown face, leathery from years in the brutal sun. ''That is why I sent my husband.'' She sighed heavily. ''The bite of a Gila monster is fatal.''

Fighting her anguish, Aly continued to grip Clay's listless hand. She didn't understand how Madalena could possibly have known of their arrival. Right now, it didn't matter. Madalena had met them at the door of her adobe home, a pallet already prepared for Clay. ''No! Please, can't you do something else for him?'' Already, Madalena had cleaned out Clay's gruesome-looking wound with a special medicine from one of the many jars on the shelves behind them, and bandaged it. The old woman had told Aly that she was the shaman for her people. Right now, help from anyone was better than nothing in Aly's mind and heart. Already, José was riding as quickly as possible toward a Mexican army outpost two and a half days from the village. Aly had given him written instructions to carry with him. The army would call the coast guard, and a way would be cleared for the rescue not only of Clay and Aly, but also of Dan Ballard. But any outside help would be too late to save Clay's life, and Aly knew it.

''You must fight to return his shadow to us.'' Madalena spoke slowly, wagging her finger at Aly.

''What do you mean?''

''I will perform a ceremony to call back his shadow from the Land of Death. You must be part of this, for your love of him is strong and unblemished." Madalena frowned, her gravelly voice dropping to a bare rumble. "Already he prepares to depart. His skin grows gray. Next, it will turn blue, and then he will be gone."

Aly hung her head, gripping Clay's hand. "He *can't* leave!" Tears welled in her eyes. "We've gone through so much with each other, Madalena! Through so much hell. A-and when we finally discovered we did care for each other, I—I got frightened."

"Humph," Madalena snorted, slowly rising to her thickly callused bare feet. Although the home was sparsely furnished and had a dirt floor, it was scrupulously clean and neat. She waddled ponderously to the rear wall of the small one-room adobe house, searching through the many fetishes that lay on shelves and hung from hooks. "Your love for him must outweigh your fear, *señorita*." She chose a gourd rattle covered with the feathers of a great horned owl, goddess of the night. The handle was beaded in a red and black design. Turning, she came back, her eyes slits. "Be prepared to see and hear and feel many unnerving things, *señorita*. The Shadow Song I will sing will call the spirit of the Gila monster, and I will ask his forgiveness, so that he will remove the poison from your man's body. And then you must close your eyes and see Señor Cantrell's shadow. When he comes to you, embrace him. No matter how much he struggles or resists you, hold on to him." She leaned down, staring deeply into Aly's large, frightened eyes. "You will want to run and scream. You must stay here, at his side, while I sing. Your courage and love must outweigh the Darkness I call."

Aly gave a jerky nod. "I don't understand what you're going to do, but if it'll help, I'll do anything you say, *señora*. Please, hurry, will you?" Under other circumstances, Aly would have pooh-poohed the ancient Indian ritual. But now, she welcomed any help that might improve Clay's chances of surviving. There was a wisdom and knowing in Madalena's eyes that outstripped present-day medical knowledge, and Aly's hope strengthened.

Madalena grunted, a satisfied glint coming to her eyes. Settling down slowly on her knees, she faced Aly and Clay. She raised the rattle, muttering in her own language, moving it clockwise over Clay four times. With a flick of her wrist, she snapped the gourd once, the stones rattling violently.

Aly jerked. It felt as if a sonic boom had smashed against her, and yet the shaman hadn't touched her with the gourd. Her eyes widened enormously as the shaman began a low, vibrating chant that rolled through the house like a reverberating drum. Aly's hands tightened around Clay's. The room felt as if it were tipping, losing its square shape. She blinked as the sonorous voice of Madalena rose and fell like waves crashing and beating against an unseen shore. Darkness and shadows began to dance around them. Aly blinked rapidly, thinking she was seeing things. She had heard of medicine men and women, of their powerful abilities, but she'd never been confronted with them before.

She tasted her fear as the song grew in volume and power. Each time Madalena made a circle around Clay's body and shook the gourd, Aly winced. It felt as if an invisible hand were slapping her hard each time, making her mind spin and tilt a little more out of control. Clinging to Clay's hand, wanting him to live more than anything else in her world, Aly accepted the distorted reality swirling around her that deepened and expanded every second, as the song thundered through the room.

Clay felt as if someone were pulling him back from the abyss he floated in. He felt light, a feather wafting on air. It no longer hurt to breathe or to struggle to get air into his lungs. The darkness gradually turned to light, and he saw Aly walking toward him, a serious expression on her face. He smiled, waving to her. He loved her so damn much that it made his heart ache with joy.

Why was Aly looking so solemn? He laughed and bounced like a deer toward her. Her walk was cadenced, sure. "Look!" he shouted, "I'm floating! Isn't this great?" And he circled around her as she came to a halt.

"Clay, you've got to come back with me."

He floated lightly to the ground, facing her. When he realized she wasn't smiling or feeling his happiness, he sobered. "But it's great here, Aly. I mean, I'm like a bird, flying free."

"You can't stay, Clay. I love you. I want you to come back with me."

The anguish was in her eyes and in her husky voice. Aly reached out, opening her arms to him. "Come to me, Clay. Come home with me. I need you, even if you don't need me. Please?"

"I need you, too, honey," he said, and he walked into her arms, sliding them around her small, strong shoulders. He kissed her hair. "God, I love you so much, Aly."

With a sob, she tightened her arms around him. "I know you do. Now, come on, let's go back...."

Aly sat at Clay's side, her head dropping to her chest. The movement awoke her. Madalena had left hours earlier after singing the Shadow Song. Aly roused herself, fatigue slowing each of her movements. Taking a cloth, she squeezed it out in the red pottery bowl at her side, and then wiped Clay's perspiring body as he lay naked and unmoving beneath a blanket.

Had a miracle occurred? Aly wasn't sure. At the height of Madalena's song, she felt totally disoriented, pulled out of her body. Aly remembered meeting Clay and their conversation. He'd come back willingly with her. When she'd awakened later, having no idea how much time had passed, she was lying on the floor next to him. Madalena had placed a pillow beneath her head and left them alone.

Tiredly, Aly sponged Clay's clean limbs, memories flooding her. Awakening after the song, Aly had scrambled to her knees, going immediately to Clay's side, wondering if he was alive or dead. To her surprise and joy, he had more color to his skin, and he was breathing a great deal more easily. Aly had removed his smelly flight suit and made him comfortable on the pallet. For the past hour or so, she had awakened off and on to bathe his sweaty body.

"You've got to live," she whispered, placing her hand on his shoulder. His flesh was warm again to her touch, not clammy as before. "I don't care if it was the antivenin shot taking hold or Madalena's song, Clay, you've got to pull through this. I love you...."

It was the middle of the next day when Clay became conscious. Incredibly weak, he felt as if it hurt even to barely lift his lashes. Light was filtering in from an unknown source behind him. Where was he?

"Clay?" Aly leaned over him, her voice hushed as she met and held his dark, hooded eyes. Anxiously, she touched his bearded cheek. "It's all right. We're here at the Indian village. Help's on the way. I—I think you're going to be okay."

He blinked, assimilating her trembling voice. She was no longer in her flight uniform. Instead, she was wearing a white knee-length shift belted at the waist with a multicolored sash. Her hair was clean and recently washed, too, framing her lovely but strained features. Nothing made sense. His mind refused to work.

"... where..." he croaked.

Slowly, Aly covered the events of the past day and a half. Clay was having difficulty absorbing her explanations. Slipping her arm beneath his shoulders, she gently maneuvered him upward, his head resting against her shoulder and breast. Madalena had prepared a special juice for him to drink, to help wash the poison from his body. Aly placed the cup against his cracked, dry lips.

"Drink," she urged him softly.

He was dying for water, slurping the drink noisily, some of the contents spilling from the corners of his mouth.

She smiled and pressed a kiss to his hair. "Madalena said you'd be thirsty when you woke up. More?" Aly removed the cup and blotted his mouth and chin with a cloth. Her heart swelled with so much love that she thought it might burst.

"Y-yeah...."

Dipping the cup back into the bowl, she allowed Clay to drink as much as he wanted. Four cups later, he was sated. Aly laid him back down. He looked more alert, taking in his surroundings. His gaze moved back to her.

"The dress..." Clay began with an effort. "You look pretty...."

Sliding her hand down his arm, she laced her fingers into his. "And you're a sight for sore eyes. Madalena is washing out my flight suit. Her daughter, Nina, loaned me something to wear in the meantime."

Exhaustion stalked him. Clay clung to Aly's husky voice and the coolness of her hand in his hot, sweaty one. Closing his eyes, he whispered hoarsely, "I love you...."

Aly knelt there, hearing the words and watching Clay sink back into a deep, healing slumber. The words she'd thought would never be spoken by him hung gently suspended in the house. Clay was barely conscious when he'd said them, perhaps still a bit delirious. But it no longer mattered to Aly. Nearly losing him had torn away any last barriers erected during their nine-month war. Their future was uncertain, but fear of losing Clay outweighed her fear of never having had a chance to tell him that she loved him. What he would do with that information, she didn't know.

Sighing, Aly released his hand and lay down next to him, her arm across his chest to comfort him, even in sleep. She knew how much Clay loved to have her next to him. Tiredness overtook Aly, and in minutes, she was sound asleep, her head nestled next to his shoulder.

## Chapter Eleven

Aly's clean scent entered Clay's nostrils. He stirred, inhaling her fragrance deep into his lungs. This time he was able to breathe easily. Lifting his lashes without much effort, he saw a sputtering candle sitting on a shelf opposite where he lay. Shadowy light danced and wavered throughout the quiet room. The wind could be heard, but the house was warm and protected from the desert elements.

His senses were sluggish and disconnected as he worked hard to remember where he was. Clay's attention focused on the warmth against his right side. Barely turning his head, he felt a slight smile pull at the corners of his mouth.

"Aly?" His voice was rough from disuse. She was lying beside him, her arm across his chest.

At first just stirring, Aly snapped awake when she heard Clay call her a second time. Getting to her knees, she tried to shake off her sleepiness. Automatically her hand went to his shoulder. His flesh was warm, not fevered as before.

Clay watched her from beneath half-closed eyes. She was wearing a thin cotton gown that fell to her knees. He could see her body outlined by the candlelight through the shift. "I didn't mean to wake you," he croaked, clearing his throat.

"It's all right," Aly reassured him in a hushed tone, reaching for the cup. "Are you thirsty?"

"Very."

With a slight smile, Aly brushed several strands of hair from her eyes and dipped the cup into the bowl.

Clay savored each of her ministrations, his head sinking against her shoulder and breast as she cradled him upward enough so that he could drink without spilling the water from the mug. After three cups, he nodded.

"Thanks, honey."

Quiet settled around them. Aly looked at her watch. It was nearly 0500. Soon dawn would break, and another day would begin in the village. "You're welcome," she whispered, laying him back down on the pallet. Maneuvering herself around so that she sat facing him, Aly felt Clay's forehead.

"Your fever's gone."

"I had one?" Clay hungrily absorbed her beauty into his heart. She looked incredibly frail and exhausted.

"Yes, for about twelve hours. Madalena, the shaman, assured me that it wouldn't last long." Aly reached over, sliding her fingers down the length of his forearm, holding his hand. "As usual, she was right."

Clay weakly squeezed her fingers. "But as usual, you worried?"

Aly rested her cheek against one knee that she'd drawn up against her body. Looking at him through her lashes, she admitted, "You know me too well."

His fingers tightened around hers. "I want to know you a lot better."

Aly's eyes widened, her heart racing momentarily.

He smiled gently. "When that Gila monster bit me and I started slipping into unconsciousness, I thought I was going to die, honey. And then I heard your voice, far away, telling me that you loved me." His smile dissolved, and Clay held her vulnerable blue gaze. "Was I making it up, or did you say it?"

She shut her eyes, afraid as never before. "No...I said it."

"Did you mean it?"

"Yes."

"Come here," Clay whispered huskily, pulling on her hand. "Lie next to me. I want you close."

She opened her eyes, staring down at him. The tenderness burning in his gaze told her so much. Aly slipped to his side, propping herself on one elbow, her face very near his.

Clay slid his bandaged left hand down her arm, coming to rest on her hip. He gazed at her, memorizing her shadowy features. "I've never met anyone with the courage you've had," he began quietly. "I nearly destroyed you in nine months, and yet you took every beating, every insult and dig I could throw at you, and kept your head up. Looking back on it, I think I fig-ured out why you were able to do that.''

"How can you hate someone you've loved from the moment you met him?'' she asked, her voice strained with tears.

"I fell for you the day we met, too, Aly.''

She nodded, her throat constricted.

"It was your love for me that allowed you to take my hatred, wasn't it?''

"Yes.''

Clay sighed deeply, feeling the pain that she'd car-ried so long in her heart. "I don't deserve you, but I'm not going to throw this chance away.'' He raised his hand, outlining the contour of her cheeks, watching her tears drift silently down them. "It took my al-most dying for me to realize that my biggest fear was of losing you after I admitted how much you meant to me.''

Aly sniffed, and held his burning gray gaze. "It was my biggest fear, too.''

He snorted derisively. "Figure it out—we both didn't want to admit we loved each other because we were afraid the other would say 'no.'''

"Will you?'' Aly quavered, fear at its height in her. She'd admitted her love to Clay, but he'd whispered his love to her as he'd fallen unconscious a day ago. Did he remember saying it?

Murmuring her name as if it were a reverent prayer, Clay slipped his hand across her shoulders, asking her to lean down so that he could kiss her. Aly came, a willow bending to his desire, her breath moist as she shyly touched his mouth. Although he was incredibly weak, Clay framed her face with his hands, molding his mouth to hers, showing her just how much she meant to him. Aly was willing and vulnerable to his campaign to convince her, his mouth claiming hers in a fiery kiss that consumed both of them in those explosive seconds.

"There," he growled thickly, holding her captive inches from his face, "does that answer your question?"

Aly managed a bare nod, dazed in the aftermath of his hungry desire.

His eyes glinted with an unknown emotion. "After we get rescued, and after I get back on my feet, you and I are going to do some serious talking, Aly." A weak semblance of a boyish grin split his serious features. "I'm so damn weak, I can't even undress you with my eyes. But that's going to change once we get home. You can count on it."

"Doc, if you don't release me today, I'm going to climb these damned walls." Clay stared at the Navy doctor who stood at the end of the bed, studying his chart. After being rescued by the coast guard a day after he'd confessed his love to Aly, Clay's world had changed drastically. Another rescue team had flown across the mountains and picked up Dan Ballard. They had all been flown to Oaknoll Naval Hospital, situated in San Francisco, for treatment.

Dan was recovering quickly from his serious concussion in another wing of the huge hospital. And Clay was being monitored closely for the first week after his arrival. The doctors were unable to understand how he'd survived the Gila monster bite. Clay tried to explain Madalena's care of him, but they didn't want to believe that an Indian shaman might have been responsible for saving his skin.

Clay had a deep belief in the power of the unknown, and readily accepted that Madalena's ancient skills had helped to some degree. Aly didn't care who had saved him, just as long as he survived the experience. After one day in the hospital, Aly had been released for two weeks' recovery time. She had flown back to Florida to be with her family.

"According to all reports from the nurses, Lieutenant Cantrell, you've been peeling paint off these walls for at least a week already in your efforts to get out of here," Dr. Kenneth Black answered dryly, looking over his spectacles at Clay.

"Aw, come on, doc. Give me a break, will you? I've been in this place for two lousy weeks. My lady's due back from Florida three hours from now."

Black smiled slightly, penning his initials on several sheets of paper he'd brought with him and had attached to the clipboard. He hung the board back on the hook at the end of the bed. "I hear Lieutenant Trayhern has been spending her recuperation time with her parents down in Florida."

Clay got up, pacing the small white naval hospital room. He was dressed in a pair of light blue pajamas and a blue robe. "That's right." He shot Black a dark look. "And if you guys had released me a week ago, I could have spent a week with her in some Florida sunshine recovering there instead of being locked up in this box they call a room."

"You badger the nurses like this every day, Lieutenant?"

Cantrell stopped pacing and grinned. "A hundred times worse. I'll stop badgering them if you'll release me, doc."

"That's blackmail."

"But your people would breathe a big sigh of relief if I was gone."

Black rolled his eyes. "Normally, someone who's been poisoned as you were doesn't bounce back this rapidly."

Clay looked out the window that overlooked the colorful autumn gardens surrounding the huge hospital. "I had a big reason to get well in a hurry! Look, if you release me right now, I can just make it to the San Francisco Airport in time to meet her plane." He shot a look over his shoulder. "Get rid of me, Black. I'm a pain in the ass to everyone here. You know it, and so do I. I'm fine. I'm in the pink of health. That medicine woman gave me a hell of a start back on the road to recovery."

Chuckling, Black headed toward the door. "Get out of here, Lieutenant. You've tongue-lashed my people to death for the past week. Go meet that woman of yours."

Rubbing his hands together, Clay grinned. "Thanks, doc. You're a prince."

"I'm doing this to protect my nurses and orderlies from you, Cantrell."

Clay didn't take the doctor's dry teasing to heart. He headed for the closet where a set of civilian clothes hung. Late last week, Lieutenant Miles Cartwright had brought over clothes, and parked Clay's Corvette in the visitors' lot. Clay grinned over at the physician. "You're doing the right thing, believe me."

Black opened the door and smiled. "I've also approved your thirty days' leave."

Clay pulled the door open, grabbing his slacks. "How about Lieutenant Trayhern's leave? Were you able to swing it with that sourpuss officer over at Moffett Personnel? Did you convince him that Aly needed another month of recovery time before she sits back in the cockpit of a P3?"

Black shook his head. "Both sets of orders are approved, signed and on the clipboard, Cantrell." Black stood a second, watching Clay throw off the robe, draping it across the bed. "Tell me something, Cantrell."

"What?" Off came the pajama top. Clay slipped a fresh white T-shirt over his head, and then shrugged into a plaid shirt, rolling up the sleeves on his forearms. Only a small bandage remained around his left hand to remind him of his brush with death.

"Do you always get what you want? This past week, I've seen you pull strings and manipulate people like nothing I've ever witnessed before."

Smiling wolfishly, Clay climbed into his dark brown slacks, zipping them up. "Doc, when you want something bad enough, you'll do anything to get it. I'm in love with a beautiful lady, and I've got big things in store for us. I spent two weeks lying in this bed with nothing do but think, scheme and dream." Clay glanced up after slipping his belt through the loops on his trousers. "I owe you one. Thanks for all your help."

With a wave of his hand, Black disappeared out the door, laughing. "Any time, Clay, any time."

Hurry! Clay glanced at his watch, his mind racing ahead. It would take thirty minutes via the Bayshore to get to the airport. Great! That meant he had just enough time to get the rest of his plans set into motion. Whistling happily, Clay sat down, pulling on his dark brown socks, then pushing his feet into his favorite loafers. In quick movements, he reached into the closet, pulled out the corduroy sport coat, threw it over his shoulder and grabbed the clipboard. Wait until Aly saw him at the bottom of the ramp, waiting for her as she disembarked from that commercial flight! She thought he was still a prisoner in a hospital bed.

Aly's exhaustion over the six-hour flight was torn away when she saw Clay standing at the bottom of the ramp with two dozen purple, yellow and white irises in one hand, and the biggest welcoming smile on his face that she'd ever seen.

A day after their rescue, Dr. Black had told her that her family was worried sick about her. Clay had cajoled her into leaving him to fly back and visit with her parents while he was in the hospital. After all, he'd argued reasonably with her, he couldn't fool around with her under those circumstances, being so weak and all....

"Clay!" she cried now, throwing her arms around his broad shoulders.

"Mmm," he whispered, picking Aly up and holding her so tightly that the air was forced out of her lungs, "I missed the hell out of you, lady!"

Laughing, Aly kissed him repeatedly, not caring who was watching them.

He lowered her back to the floor, molding her close to him, his mouth hotly claiming hers. For that moment, nothing else existed in Clay's world but her ripe, sweet mouth moving in hungry abandon against his. Finally he broke free, breathing hard, laughing with her.

"Here," he said, bringing the bouquet between them, "these are for you."

Aly blushed and gently held the flowers. "They're beautiful, Clay. This is September. Iris doesn't bloom now. How did you—"

"Never mind," he gloated, pleased that she was enthralled with his gift. Actually, it had taken several long-distance phone calls to Mexico City to have the flowers flown up. Clay threw an arm around her, and they walked leisurely through the dissipating crowd. "I like it when you blush."

Aly inhaled the flowers' fragrance, leaning against Clay. "And you make me blush constantly. Clay, thank you for the irises. They're so beautiful!"

"You're welcome. And you," he said, kissing her hair, "love every second of my teasing."

"I can't deny it." Aly looked up, studying him in confusion. "Clay, you weren't supposed to get out of the hospital until tomorrow! What happened? Did you browbeat those poor people on your floor until they released you?"

He shrugged bashfully, walking on air because Aly was in his arms, where she belonged. "Something like that," he answered vaguely. God, she was beautiful in that long-sleeved gold silk dress. It brought out the gold highlights in her hair and in her sparkling eyes.

The black leather belt only emphasized her gorgeous legs. She was all elegance.

"Are you feeling okay?" Aly asked, concerned.

Clay tried to cover his leer, not succeeding.

"You're fine," she muttered, trying to hide a smile.

Clay squeezed her, bringing her close and kissing the top of her head. "You're gorgeous—" he looked down "—and what a pair of legs! Lady, you'd put a thoroughbred to shame."

"Now you're calling me a horse, Clay!"

"You're right!" He swept Aly off her feet, irises and all, and swung her around and around. Her laughter was sweet music to his ears as he finally set her back on her feet. They were both so dizzy that they had to lean against each other to stay upright. Clay barely gave any attention to the people who made a wide circle around them. But those he saw were all smiling.

Breathless, Aly leaned against him. "What am I going to do with you?"

"Well, for starters—"

She laughed. "I knew I shouldn't have given you an opening."

Clay ignored her, digging out two sets of orders, waving them under her nose. "As I was saying, the good doctor who handled my case managed to wangle thirty days' leave for both of us." He placed the orders in her hand, watching the shock set in.

Aly read the orders in disbelief. "This—this is incredible, Clay!" She looked up at him. "How did you manage this? I called Moffett Personnel to talk to Donnelly, but he turned me down flat."

"Guess it's just my silver tongue," Clay congratulated himself, watching the joy come to her eyes. "Thirty days of vacation, honey." He took the orders, neatly folded them and put them in the breast pocket of his sport coat.

Dazed by all the good news, Aly shook her head. "It's all like a dream, Clay...."

Placing his arms around her shoulders, he rested his brow against Aly's hair. "And that's not all. I've got my 'vette out front in a No Parking zone. Provided they aren't towing it away yet, we'll grab your luggage and head south, along the coast. There's a nice little bed-and-breakfast inn overlooking Monterey Bay. It's quiet, beautiful and private. How's that sound for starters?"

Tears filled Aly's eyes. Since their rescue, they'd never had the time they'd wanted together, always driven apart by orders or needs of others. She reached out, caressing his recently-shaved cheek. "I think it sounds wonderful," she quavered.

Clay lost his smile, pressing his lips to her temple, cheek, and finally finding her mouth. He tasted the salty tears on her lips, kissing them away. "And I love the hell out of you. Come on, we're going to Monterey Bay. Just you and I, little hellcat."

Hampton Inn stood beneath the twisted Monterey pines, a hundred feet away from a sheer cliff that dropped off to a beach below. The inn overlooked one of the most scenic bays on the West Coast. Aly stood beneath Clay's arm, watching the red sunset, the ocean glassy and calm. The wind was gentle and warm, filled with the fragrance of the sea.

"It's lovely," Aly breathed.

"No," Clay corrected, looking down at her, "you're lovely. That bay hasn't got a thing on you, lady."

Standing on tiptoe, Aly pressed a shy kiss to his wonderfully mobile mouth. "Mmm," she murmured moments later, "you taste so good."

He rocked her gently back and forth in his arms. "Must be all the champagne we drank earlier, huh?"

She giggled. "Yeah, on an empty stomach, Cantrell. That wasn't such a wise idea. I'm feeling giddy and silly."

"So am I." And he kissed the tip of her nose, content as never before. "You make me happy, Alyssa Trayhern, you know that?"

Closing her eyes, Aly leaned against his strong body, her mouth resting against his cheek. "No one can be happier than me."

"Wanna bet?"

She giggled and held Clay at arm's length. "You're such a rogue."

"No, Rogue would say that about himself," he teased, referring to her Border Collie. He saw the sudden concern in her eyes. "And don't worry, Dan Ballard and his wife *promised* to take loving care of Rogue for you while we're on vacation. You know his kids will love the collie."

That was true. Aly gave him a mischievous look. "You thought of everything, didn't you?"

Clay sobered slightly, running his fingers slowly through her short, silky hair. "I hope I have...."

"What's next?"

"Dinner with my best lady down at a very fashionable restaurant, and then dancing at a very trendy place a bit farther down that same road. Game?"

"Am I ever!"

"Well, let's go. We're going to do some heavy celebrating tonight!"

Aly made a face, dancing close to Clay. "Do I look like a turkey?" she asked.

He chuckled and studied her. She wore an incredibly beautiful pink silk dress that had a scoop neck, showing off her perfect collarbone and slender neck. The dolman sleeves moved like ripples in the breeze each time he swung her around to the slow beat of the music. Arching an eyebrow he said, "Definitely not a turkey. Why?"

"I feel like one. I ate too much, Clay."

"That was a good dinner," he agreed. The lobster in drawn butter had been superb, but her company was his dessert.

Aly settled against him, head resting on his shoulder, and closed her eyes. "I'm so happy, Clay."

He caressed the length of her spine, so supple yet so strong. "No regrets?"

She shook her head. "How can you have regrets when your dreams are coming true?" she whispered, looking up into his warm gray eyes. Aly ached to make love with him, each movement of his body inciting her, teasing her.

Getting serious, Clay said in a low voice, "You talked to your parents about this roller-coaster relationship of ours?"

"Yes. I told them everything, Clay."

"Our stormy beginning and middle?"

"They understood," she told him softly. "Both my parents are sorry that Stephen lost his life. And I am, too."

He sighed and nodded.

"My parents are very understanding people, Clay. They're sensitive, and they have an ability to see *why* people act or react the way they do. They don't blame you."

"They sound special," he admitted almost wistfully.

"My mother is a nurse," Aly explained. "She saved my father's life behind enemy lines in the Korean War. My father says he learned a lot from her about sensitivity."

"What's her name?" Clay asked.

"Rachel."

"Pretty name, but not half as pretty as you."

Aly tried to ferret out why Clay was retreating. "Clay? What's wrong? Are you upset because of the past?"

He leaned over, kissing her cheek. "No, I'm worried about the future. Come on, let's get out of here. I need a place where I can do some serious talking with you."

Aly felt Clay's tension on the drive up the coast toward Hampton Inn. The moon was full, casting its radiance across the desolate beauty of the Monterey Bay. Aly sensed Clay's worry and reached out, sliding her hand into his to reassure him. He squeezed her fingers, offering her a forced smile.

\* \* \*

Nervously, Aly smoothed the light flannel floor-length granny gown she wore. It was all she had—the only sleepwear she'd taken with her to Florida. Deep inside, she fretted over Clay's unexpected somber mood. Taking a deep breath, she opened the door from the bathroom and stepped into their spacious bedroom suite. She saw Clay standing at the sliding glass doors that overlooked the ocean. He had taken off his sport coat and tie. As she rounded the bed and walked to his side, she saw that his shoes had been tossed to one side, too.

Clay heard Aly approach, pulled his hands out of his pockets and turned around. Some of his terror abated as she halted and stood shyly before him.

"I know this isn't very sexy—"

"It's perfect," he whispered, moving to her, placing his hands on her shoulders. "With your tousled red hair and freckles, it suits you." She looked vulnerable in the simple gown, and so very, very beautiful.

Clay's tender smile drove some of the nervousness out of her. She slid her hands around his waist, pulling him to her. His groan of pleasure was music. "This is all I want," Aly whispered.

He embraced her tightly for a long moment, resting his jaw against her hair. "Sure?"

"Very sure."

"For how long?"

Aly nuzzled beneath his jaw, savoring Clay's closeness, his ability to share his complex emotions with her. "As long as you want." She sighed softly, feeling his mouth moving temptingly along the length of her jaw.

"I warned you once before, I only like long-term commitments," he growled, inhaling her spicy fragrance.

A small moan came from her throat as he sought and found her mouth, cherishing it with small nips and kisses. "Fine," Aly agreed breathlessly.

Clay said a prayer, his mouth hovering against her smiling lips. "Forever?"

Aly opened her eyes, looking dazedly up at him. "Forever?" she whispered, perplexed.

Clay's hands tightened around her, molding her form against him. "I want to marry you, Aly." There, the words, the need, were finally out in the open. Clay watched her blue eyes widen enormously, and she struggled briefly in his arms, but he wouldn't let her go.

"Marry me?" Aly repeated dumbly.

"I told you I liked long-term commitments, honey." Clay didn't know how to read the confusion he saw registered in her eyes. Aly's cheeks had gone bright red in reaction.

Faintness swept through Aly, and she leaned against Clay for support. "Oh, Clay... I never expected this...."

"What? Ever getting married, or me asking you?"

If she hadn't been so shocked by his proposal, Aly would have found that funny. But she was breathless as she sought his turbulent gray eyes, which were fraught with anxiety. "I had hoped someday to marry," she began lamely.

She wasn't going to say yes! Clay froze, fighting the terrible cold filling him. ''Then it's my name? My past, that you object to?'' The words came out in icy monosyllables of pain.

The awful clarity of their conversation struck Aly directly. ''No, Clay. God, no!'' She framed his face between her hands, drowning in the pain she saw in his features. ''Is that what you were afraid of? I loved you, but not enough to marry you because of your name? My name? Our complicated past?''

He nodded, words unable to come out because they were stuck in his throat.

Aly placed a warm, inviting kiss on his mouth, feeling him tremble in the wake of her sweet assault upon him. ''I love you, you crazy jet jockey,'' she breathed, nipping at his lower lip, cajoling him to join her. ''And I wouldn't care if your name was Humpty-Dumpty. None of that matters! You do, darling. Do you hear me? There's nothing more I want than you as my husband.'' She crushed her mouth against his, breathing life, breathing fire into the coldness that had inhabited him.

Gently, Clay lifted Aly into his arms, his mouth ravishing her moist, giving lips. She was going to marry him! As he carried her to the bed, he murmured, ''You're going to be my wife, Aly. I can't live without you. I need you—your sweet fire.''

As he laid her on the bed, Aly sat up and pulled Clay down beside her. Her fingers trembled as she unbuttoned his shirt to reveal his massive, powerful chest covered with black hair. His fingers fumbled with the buttons on her granny gown.

Looking up into his eyes, Aly found them burning with desire for her alone. "Ever since I met you, I've never wanted anyone else, darling. I need you, too." His shirt fell open, and she slid her hands beneath it, pulling it off his magnificent shoulders. Taking in a breath, Aly confided, "You're so beautiful."

Joy surged through Clay as he removed the gown from her shoulders, allowing it to pool around her hips. "And you," he said thickly, cupping her exquisite small breasts, "are even more beautiful...."

She drew in a quick gasp of air as he leaned over, his mouth seeking, finding a soft pink nipple. A little cry escaped her as Clay pulled her into his arms, their flesh meeting hotly for the first time. A thrilling arc of lightning danced through Aly as he sucked upon each nipple in turn, drawing them to budding life with his slow, cajoling movements. She lost sense of time, of direction.

Dazed, Aly watched through lowered lashes as Clay divested himself of his trousers. He was a consummate male animal, the darkness of his hair emphasizing his power, his promise of meeting and matching her hungry femininity. Reaching out, Aly welcomed him back into her arms, arching to graze his taut body with her own.

"Love me," she tremored close to his ear. "I need you, want you so badly, Clay..." She pressed her hip against his hardness resting between them. Each touch of his mouth upon her was explosive. As he teethed one nipple, his hand slid down the damp length of her long torso, slipping gently between her thighs, asking her to give him entrance.

Her breathing became erratic as his hand sought and found her moist womanhood, the center of her longing. Gripping his shoulder, feeling his powerful muscles flex and tighten, she cried out, twisting toward him, begging him with her eyes to enter her.

Clay smiled tenderly, sensing her every desire. She was so wet, so hot. Her lips upon his neck, spreading a sheet of fire across his chest, caused him to groan out in pleasure. He started his silken assault upon her, her thighs taut and trembling as he began to wreak pleasure from her.

"Let me show you how much I love you," he whispered against her cheek, kissing her hungrily. "Give yourself to me, sweet woman of mine...."

The shattering fire exploded to life as he teased her core, and she could do nothing but cry out, pulled tautly against his hard male body.

Clay laughed shakily. "You're so hot, so vibrant with life," he murmured as he eased across her glistening form, finding her, sliding into her liquid depths.

A gasp escaped Aly as she welcomed Clay into her. This was so right, so perfect, she thought as she rose and fell with the rhythm he'd established for them. His eyes shone with love as she looked up into them, nearly drowning in his lambent gaze. Her lips parting as she felt their mutual need quicken, Aly slid her hands around his corded neck, kissing him, taking his groan of pleasure as he released his life deep within her. A heartbeat later, a rainbow explosion tremored through her as she sought and found release within his strong, powerful arms. Her cry was drowned within his mouth as he kissed her long and fiercely.

Clay kissed her cheek, her closed eyes and that aristocratic nose of hers. Sweat glistened off the planes of his face as he lay within her, savoring her in every way. "Open your eyes," he breathed raggedly. Aly opened them, and he could see moonlight in their dazed, sated depths. He shifted some of his weight, smiling down at her.

"I've never seen you so happy."

Languidly, Aly reached up, her fingers trailing through those damp, errant strands of hair across his brow. "It's your fault, darling. All of it."

He kissed her swollen lips gently, soothing them with his tongue in the aftermath. "This is one time I'll take the blame for everything."

A softened laugh escaped her in a breathy rush. Aly sifted her fingers through his hair, memorizing the joyous flame in his gray eyes, that arrogant, self-confident smile on his male mouth. "I love you, Clay Cantrell. Even that inflated ego of yours."

Clay sobered, caressing her copper-colored hair. "And I love you, Aly Trayhern. *All* of you. Past, present and future." His voice grew hoarse. "I want you to know that, honey—that the past doesn't bother me the way it did. You helped me understand you're the way you are because of your family." He gave her a little smile, wiping the perspiration from her brow with his fingers. "You couldn't be this giving, unselfish and unconditionally loving unless you'd been raised in that kind of environment."

Tears gathered in Aly's eyes as she heard and felt Clay's admission. With a cry, she threw her arms around him. "Thank you," she whispered. "I was so afraid the past would get in our way again."

He gently left the sweet confines of her body and turned over on his back. "Come here," Clay called her softly, pulling Aly on top of him. Once she was comfortable, he cupped her face between his hands, looking deeply into her sultry eyes, sparkling with tears. "We are what we are because of our families. You've taught me that each person is an individual within that unit."

"We've worked through and understood our past. Now, we have the present and future to build on, Clay." She sighed, realizing they were both freed. "I like the idea of being Mrs. Alyssa Cantrell," she told him huskily.

His smile was very male and very tender. "Tomorrow morning, let's call your parents and tell them the good news."

Aly sniffed and nodded. "I think they already know we're in love with each other."

He kissed the two tears away, bringing her against him, her head on his shoulder. "Good, then they won't mind us dropping in on them a few days from now. Think they'll balk if we want to get married, say, two weeks from now, down at their home?"

Aly sighed, sliding her hand across his chest. She could hear the solid beat of his heart beneath hers. "No. The more you know of my family, the more you'll realize that we're flexible on a moment's notice."

Clay closed his eyes, content as never before. "And strong, and enduring, and so very, very loving," he murmured, kissing her brow.

Aly smiled wistfully, nuzzling beneath Clay's chin. "I can hardly wait until tomorrow, darling...."

"I can't, either, little hellcat." Clay brought up the sheet, covering them both, his arms settling around Aly. Embracing her, he murmured again, "I can't, either...."

\*   \*   \*   \*   \*

## *Silhouette Special Edition*

presents

### LOVE AND GLORY

from
Lindsay McKenna

Introducing a gripping new series celebrating our men—and women—in uniform. Meet the Trayherns, a military family as proud and colorful as the American flag, a family fighting the shadow of dishonor, a family determined to triumph—with **LOVE AND GLORY!**

June: **A QUESTION OF HONOR** (SE #529) leads the fast-paced excitement. When Coast Guard officer Noah Trayhern offers Kit Anderson a safe house, he unwittingly endangers his own guarded emotions.

July: **NO SURRENDER** (SE #535) Navy pilot Alyssa Trayhern's assignment with arrogant jet jockey Clay Cantrell threatens her career—and her heart—with a crash landing!

August: **RETURN OF A HERO** (SE #541) Strike up the band to welcome home a man whose top-secret reappearance will make headline news . . . with a delicate, daring woman by his side.

# Silhouette Intimate Moments®

## AWARD OF EXCELLENCE

**NORA ROBERTS**
brings you the first
Award of Excellence title
**Gabriel's Angel**
coming in August from
Silhouette Intimate Moments

*They were on a collision course with love....*

*Laura Malone was alone, scared—and pregnant. She was running
for the sake of her child. Gabriel Bradley had his own problems.
He had neither the need nor the inclination to get involved in
someone else's.*

*But Laura was like no other woman . . . and she needed him. Soon
Gabe was willing to risk all for the heaven of her arms.*

The Award of Excellence is given to one specially selected title per
month. Look for the second Award of Excellence title, coming out in
September from Silhouette Romance—SUTTON'S WAY
by Diana Palmer

Im 300-1

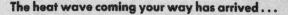